The Man Who Found Treasure

The Man Who F*o*und Treasure

Alan Williams

By the same Author:

The Daylight Thief (2015)

Published by Alan Williams

www.theredwriteralanwilliams.com

Twitter: @Redwriter64

Copyright © 2019 by Alan Williams

ISBN-13: 9781691622788

Cover photograph: 'Shadow of Hand on Beach' by Örjan Lindén, 2009.

All rights reserved. This book or any portion thereof may not be reproduced or used in any manner whatsoever without the express written permission of the publisher, except for the use of brief quotations in a book review.

Although inspired by real events, and reference is made on occasion to real individuals and places, this is a work of fiction. Names, characters, incidents, dialogues and the places where they took place are products of the author's imagination or are used purely fictitiously. Otherwise any resemblance to actual people, living or dead, events or specific locales is purely coincidental.

Every effort has been made to trace copyright holders for Marian Allen's poem, 'The Wind on the Downs', and to obtain permission for use of copyright material. The author apologises for any errors or omissions and would be grateful if notified of any corrections.

For Mum and Dad, for everything.

And in remembrance of Jack Oscroft 1881-1915

"I like to think of you as brown and tall,
As strong and living as you used to be,
In khaki tunic, Sam Brown belt and all,
And standing there and laughing down at me.
Because they tell me, dear, that you are dead,
Because I can no longer see your face,
You have not died, it is not true, instead,
You seek adventure some other place.
That you are round about me, I believe;
I hear you laughing as you used to,
Yet loving all the things I think of you;
And knowing you are happy, should I grieve?
You follow and are watchful where I go;
How should you leave me, having loved me so?"

From *"The wind on the downs"* by Marion Allen (1892-1953)

"Those heroes who shed their blood and lost their loves…
You are now lying in the soil of a friendly country so rest in peace.
There is no difference between the Johnnies and the Mehmets to us
where they lie side by side here in this country of ours…
You the mothers who sent their sons from far away countries wipe
away your tears. Your sons are now lying in our bosom and are at
peace. After having lost their lives on this land they are our sons
as well".

Words attributed to Mustafa Kemal Atatürk (1881-1938)

Chapter 1.

Turkey: 1998.

Stooped over a sink-full of soapy grey water, the occupant of room forty-three dipped his razor, before dragging it carefully across the flaccid and uncompliant skin of his face. Even despite his care there was a nick, and he winced. A delicate stinging hairline of red spread hesitantly across his jaw, before joining forces with the water that dripped from his chin. He pulled a blood-specked towel from his shoulder and quickly wiped the wound.

Although it was a morning ritual he'd observed almost every day for nearly seventy years, it didn't get any easier. Not for the first time, as he gazed into the distorted image in the steam-covered glass, he sensed that something else - something unseen, beyond the wide-open door of the bathroom - was being reflected there alongside him. He felt it in the cool prickling of his skin and in the sudden quickening of his heart. Using the palm of his hand he cleared away some of the condensation from the surface of the mirror, and his eyes fixed on the dimly lit hotel bedroom just visible behind his shoulder.

"It'll be soon... don't you worry," he heard himself announce.

The barest trace of a smile flickered briefly across his lips. He lowered his head and returned his attention to the sink.

In a building nearby, a man stationed alone upon a fifth-floor balcony made short work of a breakfast of menemem and strong black coffee. A meagre ribbon of watery daylight had improbably forged a way through the closed ranks of uniform sand-coloured towers, each with identical white balconies, that huddled around the block in which the man now sat. Under this pale spotlight Bariş Uzun checked a page in his scuffed Filofax.

4th April 1998: Mr. Kingdom. Party of one. Pick-up 9am at Çanakkale - Cağın Motel.

Bariş rocked back in his chair, cheered by the promise of an easy day. After all, he rationalised, today's party of one was an elderly English gentleman. He knew this because the two men had spoken a couple of days earlier, over a badly crackling telephone line to Istanbul. The short call only afforded the opportunity to confirm the pick-up details, but it had left Bariş with a lingering image of thinness and frailty, and of a white suit topped with a panama hat, all propped up with a wooden walking stick. He'd met the type before, although he acknowledged that it was now rare that men of such an age travelled alone; and rarer still that they were veterans of the *Çanakkale Savaşı*. Visits from those men – each of them bent with the weight of history – had dried up long ago. Bariş did the calculation in his head. No, it would have been impossible. The man certainly sounded ancient, but he was certainly not that old!

Whatever the reason for the Englishman's unaccompanied visit Bariş was confident that there would be no need to roam off the beaten track today. They probably wouldn't even need to get out of the car very much... maybe just for the odd memorial and, of course, a museum visit. His company motto - *'Bringing the Past to Life'*- would certainly not be under any threat. He could simply roll out the routine tour, the one that he could do in his sleep. "Easy peasy", isn't that what the English say? There was even a chance that he could be back home in time to catch the Black Eagles game against the Green Crocodiles of Bursaspor later that afternoon.

With his battleplan settled, Bariş began to pick at the cold remains of a green pepper. He washed them down with a satisfying slurp of the coffee.

Three and a half hours later Bariş, along with his party of one, were sheltering under the porch at Deniz's café in Alçıtepe. It was a regular pit stop. The old man was disgorging the highlights of his stay in Istanbul. The Grand Bazaar, the Blue Mosque, Hagia Sofia, the Basilica Cistern… a Bosphorus cruise. Bariş had heard it all before. The words hadn't registered, but he was sure they were all there, regurgitated, as they had been a million times in this same café. As he watched the silently moving mouth on the other side of the red Formica-topped table, he was thinking that he could have written the speech himself.

Instead of listening, Bariş studied the face of the old man. One adorned with a thin blueish mouth, so wet with saliva that a handkerchief was called upon periodically to stem the flow. It had a prominent but scholarly nose and heavy-lidded eyes. The face reminded him of someone. It came to him quickly: Thomas Jefferson. The Thomas Jefferson, that is, who was carved into Mount Rushmore and pictured on a postcard pinned to a board back at the office. It had been sent to him by an American client, a South Dakotan, and scrawled on its reverse was a spidery note of thanks for a tour that was now well beyond recollection.

It was an intelligent face, Bariş conceded… a kind face… the face of someone who had probably lived a worthy life. He backed himself as a reasonable judge of character. After all, people were his business and it was important to know who you were dealing with in this game. Despite his earlier inclinations, he now decided that this man was worthy of something less cursory than the set tour. The Black Eagles might have to wait. Even so, Bariş wasn't sure that he could dispel the image of Jefferson from his mind.

The frailty that Bariş had expected in his client was certainly evident, but mostly only when he was on the move. Despite the silver-whiteness of his hair, which had only receded a little, if at all; there were very few lines of age adorning his sturdy, gently tanned, face. He smiled a lot and liked to laugh, although there were times that Bariş hadn't really understood the joke.

Bariş had also noticed that the man's pale blue-grey eyes tended to occasionally lose their sparkle. It happened sporadically and without warning. When it occurred, those same kindly eyes suddenly projected something harder to fathom, and they distinctly turned a shade darker.

Bariş was intrigued by these sudden shifts in the man's disposition. He was a sucker for a back-story. Maybe there was something locked away in the annals of the old man's life that would translate into an anecdote; one that he could make use of. He was always on the lookout for new ones. He considered the matter further. The old man's general demeanour didn't suggest any unhappiness, that was clear to see. He speculated, that he might simply have witnessed the passing cloud of a sad memory, or even the outward manifestation of the pains of old age. Or might it be, instead, the sign of a defiant sense of purpose, despite that great age? Eyes, Bariş had learned from years of analysis, are arch deceivers, so it was difficult to be precise. Nevertheless, he declared himself satisfied with his latter assessment and he set his mind to wondering what the 'purpose' might be.

"Memories are like unruly children, aren't they?" smiled the old man. He spoke with a slightly raised voice, determined to make himself heard despite his companion's apparent aloofness. "They pop up out of the blue as if they are always trying to trip you up."

Bariş fell back into the present with a start, shaken from his rumination by a long silence and an attention-demanding salvo of glares shot from across the table.

"I'm sorry... what exactly do you mean?"

"Well, for instance, there are things that I did only yesterday that, just now, feel like they could have happened a hundred years ago. They are fuzzy... indistinct, you know? Or at other times I just forget things altogether. In fact, I'm getting to the point where I find it necessary to write important things down these days. Then a memory of the most trivial thing from fifty years ago might be as fresh and clear in my mind as the very second it happened."

Bariş nodded and offered the smile that he'd perfected for the benefit of his clients, for use on those occasions when he hadn't really understood what they were telling him.

"Of course, the fuzziness in my recollection of things is happening more often these days. Too often. Take this morning... when I woke up, it took me a good while to realise where the hell I was. I was in a panic for a moment or two. And then that picture came into my head out of nowhere. The one that comes so often these days... from my time in the Arakan. And then I remembered where I was, and in a funny way those images of Burma seemed, somehow, appropriate."

Bariş felt a glow of satisfaction. Once again, his instinct about a client had been proved right. There *was* a story here.

"Burma? You mean during the war?"

"Yes... they called us the 'forgotten army' you know... some people still do as a matter of fact."

The old man cleared his throat and leaned forward across the table. His words were delivered carefully and almost in a hush, as if about to reveal a prized secret.

"You know, of all the mornings I have ever opened my eyes to behold, that one in the Mayu valley is etched into my memory more clearly than any other."

A waitress appeared and disturbed the impending revelation. She wore a bright pink headscarf and a disarming smile. She placed a small cup of dark brown watery liquid in front of her elderly customer and he relaxed back into his seat. He nodded his thanks and she reciprocated with a curtsy, before scurrying back to the rear of the bar, an empty tray dangling by her side. The man's pale eyes watched her retreat. As his gaze lingered, another shadow fleetingly darkened his gentle smile.

"She's an attractive girl," he announced, before lifting the cup and sniffing at its contents.

"She's the daughter of the owner, he's a friend of mine. Her name is Emine."

Bariş grinned as he spoke. It amused him that, even at such an advanced age, there was still a glint of devilment in the old timer's eye.

"Do you like Turkish tea?" he asked.

"I'm not sure yet... but it is tea after all and I'm an Englishman, so it can't be that bad, can it? Anyway, when in Rome and all that..."

He took a sip and screwed his face up as he did so.

"It's an acquired taste."

Bariş tried to sound sympathetic, but he was eager to resume the previous conversation. He liked a mystery.

"So, tell me, why was that particular morning so memorable?"

"I've often asked myself why that should be. Why that same pesky little memory continually enters my head uninvited. It comes when I least expect it, in full and glorious Technicolor. It's a cliché I know, but it all still feels so real. I mean, I saw plenty of other things when I was out in Burma... things that you'd think were much worthier of remembering in the grand scheme of things... good, bad and bloody downright detestable."

He took another sip of the tea with an unsteady hand.

"I can imagine... I guess you saw some horrible things out there," said Bariş, softly.

"No, you can't possibly imagine," the old man retorted immediately, his voice rising and his body tensing.

Bariş nodded and broke eye contact momentarily. He had met many veterans, from many countries, mostly old soldiers of the great war; the conflict that had so greatly scarred the landscape in which they now sat. He knew when it was best to let them have the last word. He offered his client a cigarette from a packet of Camel filters which lay on the table.

"No, thank you. I gave that up a long time ago."

"Do you mind if I..."

"No, please go ahead. It's your country after all."

The old man waited until his guide had lit up before continuing.

"You know, even when I was a newspaperman after the war... well, I saw some horrors then too. Road accidents, suicides, that sort of thing. Perhaps my brain is trained just to lock the bad stuff away, you know... out of reach. I probably inherited that from my mam."

"You were a journalist?"

"More of a hack really... local stuff... on the whole."

"So, this memory from Burma. Perhaps it has now become a dream and that's why it keeps coming back?"

It was the old man's turn to chuckle.

"Who knows Bariş? Maybe it is a dream. What's the difference between a memory and a dream anyway? I often wonder if our ageing brains just invent them or at least embellish them. Still... they are often all that we are left with."

He beamed a smile until his eyes darkened once more.

"That morning in the jungle certainly began in an unusual way. I have always thought that's why it has stuck in my head for so long. But

I wonder if it's actually because *they* are all there with me in that one memory, all of them... or rather all of us... together, like a cherished family snapshot."

"They?"

"The section... my comrades, my friends," he wrestled to find the right words. "No, that's not right... calling them simply 'friends' doesn't really do them justice, does it? They *were* my family, out there at least."

He finished his tea and pushed away the empty cup, "...but even so, I don't think that's the actual reason why a picture of that morning keeps coming back to me."

Bariş's eyes widened.

"You see, I think it's because that was the day I met Johnson for the first time."

The old man leaned forward again, crossing his arms as he fixed serious and undimmed eyes on his companion.

"And, although I didn't know it at the time, it was the day when my eyes were finally opened to everything."

His expression froze in deep thought, his now frowning eyes turning away from Bariş and out into the dusty street. An empty plastic bag caught his attention. Powered by the humidity and a stiffening breeze, it floated and spiralled lazily up into the air. It hovered for a moment in front of a group of people, presumably tourists, who had emerged from a recently parked car and were now walking across to the white-fronted, red-roofed museum. Before they could enter, they each had to step cautiously over an ageing Labrador which was sprawled out, possessive and unmoving, in front of an entrance door that was bedecked with the Turkish flag. The frown slipped away from the old man's face.

"Tell me. Why are *you* here Bariş... why do you do this?"

"Me? It is my job, my friend!" the reply came with an impatient shrug of the shoulders.

"But why *this* job?"

Bariş contemplated this for a moment.

"I suppose it is because of my love of what is now in the past. I couldn't do it otherwise. You know, I remember when I was a kid, maybe eight years old, I was on vacation... not far from here actually. I was messing around with some other boys when something sharp stung my foot. I was so excited for a moment, because I thought it might be an old bullet or something from the war, maybe even one that had been fired by a Turk and had killed an Englishman! I picked up a lump of metal, but I was only to be disappointed; after I cleaned away the sand, I could see that it was something like an old brass brooch or a badge. It was, how do you say it... tarnished? But it had an intricate pattern on the outside. Then I looked more closely at it and I could see that it contained a photograph, an ancient, tiny, faded, photograph... but there was enough detail left for me to make out the outline of a woman's face. Suddenly, I felt a kind of connection with this thing. It was like electricity surging through me... the feeling that I was maybe the first person to see it, and touch it, since it had fallen here all those years ago. It was treasure to me."

"What did you do with it?"

"Oh, my papa made me take it to the museum... the one we've just visited over there actually," Bariş gestured towards the building across the road. "The curator told me that what I'd found was what they called a sweetheart broach and that it might have belonged to a Brit or Frenchman at the time of the war. No doubt it was just thrown into a storeroom with a thousand other similar objects, but I was hooked. I guess I've stayed here ever since... you might say I'm still looking for treasure."

The old man pressed a hand against the breast pocket of the white short-sleeved shirt he wore, letting it linger there for a moment as if he were feeling for his own heartbeat.

"You see Bariş, what happened to me on that morning in Burma is the reason why I'm here now, in your beautiful country."

"So, that is why you said it was an 'appropriate' memory?"

"Indeed."

"Would you like some more tea?" asked Bariş, seeing the empty glass cup, and anticipating that the story to come would be worth listening to.

"You know, I think I will have another one. It's not so bad after all, is it?"

Bariş waved his cigarette towards the waitress, pointing back to the table where the two men sat,

"Emine, iki bardak çay lütfen."

"Tamam," the waitress called back.

"Tell me all about it Mr. Kingdom. I would very much like to know."

"Please Barış, call me Walter… or just Walt, if you'd prefer."

Chapter 2.

Burma: 1943.

The new day showed itself hesitantly at first; hiding its light behind the mist that rose from the treetops around me. No doubt this was because it was as afraid as we were; fearful of what it might find as it opened its eyes to the morning. As if to emphasise the point, at that moment I was awoken by the most frightful of screams. Its sharpness razored through my protective barrier of sleep and into my head, opening my eyes and running its cold steel down the length of my body, until it became an unpleasant churn in my guts.

It's more than possible, I grant you, that the scream may become more ear-splitting each time I retell the story, but back then even the unflappable trees seemed startled by it, and their branches trembled with alarm. The birds that had spent the night resting there took flight, hundreds of them, revealing all the colours of the rainbow as they ascended into the sky. Noisy buggers they were too, flapping their wings and squawking so wildly that the harshness of the sound vibrated even those tiny bones deep inside my ears. The overall effect was like an echo, which in turn seemed to make the scream linger even longer in the air, numbing my hearing for a long time afterwards... although I expect the frigid air of the dawn had a part to play in that too.

Our company was dug in somewhere not far from a place called Buthidaung, close to the banks of the wide brown Mayu River. That old river rippled and bubbled along; minding its own business, out of sight beyond the trees, as it always had done. We slept unusually well, no doubt this was because most of us were exhausted from supporting the recent fighting around an unprepossessing piece of earth known as Donbaik, and our nerves were just about shot. To tell the truth, our unit didn't really do any fighting, and we were thankful about that; but witnessing the terrifying confusion of smoke and noise unfolding before us, we were permanently on edge, all of us thinking that it might be our turn next.

On that particular morning I must have been in a very deep sleep, probably the first proper nap I'd had for days, but I found myself sitting up inside my slit trench in an instant as soon as I heard that horrible scream. Instinct must have taken over, you see, even in my subconscious. As it comes back to me now, I can feel my chest pumping and that strange sense of not knowing where the hell I was. The echo of that feeling, carried on a million memories of my time in Burma, still makes my heart race, like all of it only happened yesterday.

The spell was broken, in the end, by a familiar voice from behind me. It asked in an affronted tone, as only soldiers can, as if it had been disturbed in mid-sup of a pint down the local pub,

"What the fuckin' 'ell was that"?

I had clicked alertly into fighting mode by then and my rifle was already in my hand. The trouble was that I still had my small strip of mosquito netting stuck to my face and I couldn't fight it off, so if Jap had been around I probably wouldn't be here telling this story to you now. A fat lot of use I would have been. It must have looked like I was re-enacting a scene from a Laurel and Hardy two-reeler. I can see why the lads ribbed me about it for weeks afterwards.

The voice belonged to Eric, of course.

Apart from my Lee Enfield rifle, Eric Newton was my best mate in the section. In today's language I suppose you'd say we were 'close', but it was a strange and intimate closeness that can only exist between fighting men. I instinctively knew that Eric was looking after my back and he could be sure that I was covering his too. You developed a certain telepathy between mates. Whilst I was flapping about in a panic trying to pull the netting from my face, Eric was as calm as you like.

"Don't bother Wally," he said in his gentle northern voice and with wild amusement written across his face. "I'm bettin' that it's one of the new lads... took his boots off in the night, or summat like that."

He had already begun the daily chore of cleaning and oiling his rifle. I heaved a huge sigh of relief. Eric gesticulated over to the edge of the clearing and I turned to see a pale youth from one of the other sections cursing loudly whilst furiously bashing his boot against the dusty ground.

"Scorpion you reckon?"

"That's my bet. But let's face it, there are plenty of things crawling about out here that are enough to put the willies up the hairiest Havildar-Major, let alone a kid fresh out the womb."

"It's those big bastard centipedes that get me."

"Nah... it's them bloody snakes that take the biscuit, or them fat red ants."

"Someone should have told him to keep his boots on, poor bugger."

Keeping your boots on at night was a non-negotiable rule, in Burma.

At that time of year, the air was cool at night, but it began to heat up pretty damn fast once the sun came up. It brought extra life to the mist. It twisted and spiralled as if it were made of supernatural creatures, unwittingly revealed to us by the watery rods of light that beamed through the trees. The trees, in turn, loomed like dark apparitions gathered behind a grey veil. It was hauntingly sinister and mesmerisingly beautiful at the same time.

As the air came alive, then so did the men of my section... Seven Section to be precise. This is the picture I can see now, clear as day, framed forever in my mind like one of those family groups that are captured walking up the ramp to the beach at Mablethorpe, the ones that everybody in my hometown seems to have in their old photograph albums. We were, every one of us, there together on that morning. Each of us full of life and bursting with purpose, unknowingly immortal in our jungle home.

Over there, that's Smitty, our Corporal, who you generally hear before your see him, he was that loud, even for a stick of a man. My memory has him standing in animated discussion with Platoon Sergeant Dickinson. His voice comes from the unintelligible lands somewhere north of Newcastle; it is so penetrating that it must carry right into the jungle and beyond. God knows how Jap don't use it to track us. Mind you, they probably can't understand a bloody word he says.

Sitting up right in front of me is Podge, our Bren Gunner. He's always cleaning that bloody gun, but it is the most precious thing we have I suppose; our lives depend on it working like clockwork when called into action. It occurs to me that whoever gave Jim Podger the nickname 'Podge' must have done it with a smile on his face. I reckon it was probably the same bloke who decided that Podge should be a Bren Gunner in the first place. He is the most unlikely Bren Gunner you could ever wish to meet, eight-stone wet-through and you can play the xylophone on his ribs even when he is well fed.

Coles, Podge's number two, is at his side, sprawled out on his belly. He's inseparable from Podge. I remember calling across to him,

"Good mornin' Errol."

He showers ash from his cigarette as he nods back to me. As always, he is studying his reflection in the tiny mirror that he carries with him as part of his kit, carefully arranging his heavily greased hair. Coles answers to the name of 'Errol', not because it is his given name, but because of a vague barrel-chested resemblance to Errol Flynn. It's an image he likes to live up to.

Something hard hits me in the forehead. It's an empty, crumpled cigarette packet, launched by the Lance Corporal, Fred Bailey.

"You lookin' after the brew Wally?"

"Give me chance to get out of bed, Fred," I reply, throwing the packet back in his direction, "and anyway I thought it was Soldier's turn?"

The section had two Freds: Bailey and Ince. To distinguish between them, Ince was simply known as 'Soldier'. Back when I first joined the section, I'd asked Smitty why it was that Ince carried such a patently obvious nickname. Smitty had launched into a well-practised speech,

"Ince 'as been in the army since he worra wee boy, laddie. He knows everythin' there is to know aboot this lark... every tactic, every drill, every weapon... and every trick and wrinkle in the boo-k. On top o' that he knows the Burmans, the Indians, the Gurkhas, the Japs and even them bloody African drivers better than they do... and he knows when the NAAFI wagon'll be here, even before it does. He's been there an' done it many times o'er lad... 'Soldier' says it all really... nothing else seemed to fit."

After a dramatic pause to let that sink in, Smitty continued with a hint of mystery in his voice,

"Rumour has it that Soldier was promoted to Corporal once, but he were busted back to Private... for misdemeanours unknown."

He tapped the side of his nose enigmatically.

I looked up to Soldier like no other after that, to the extent that I was slightly in awe of him. The respect in which Soldier was held by the other members of the section was immeasurable. For his part Soldier wore his nickname as comfortably as he did his uniform. By now our sweat-sodden jungle-green rags hung off us like rotten sails flapping on a mast, and we rattled around inside them like the skeletons that we were. Soldier's kit still fitted him as snugly as if he was sneaking off for regular adjustments from a Burmese tailor in a local village. You know what? It wouldn't have surprised me if that's exactly what he did do.

"Heck, if you're gonna trust anybody out 'ere lad... mek sure it's Soldier," I can remember Smitty imploring me.

"No mate... it's Wednesday," Soldier replies coolly, "I never brew char on a Wednesday."

If that's what Soldier says, then it must be true.

"Look 'ere, I'll bloody do it," Jimmy Munt offers with a resigned sigh, "We'll never gerr any bloody char at this rate if I don't... you bunch of shirkers."

He reaches out in front of Soldier and grabs hold of the tin we use for our brews.

"Well gerra move on then, Slowcoach," orders Fred Bailey, holding out his enamelled mug, "I'm ready for you."

Munt enjoyed the privilege of having two nicknames. 'Slowcoach' recognised his facility for always finding himself at the back of a march or a patrol, often several paces behind the others, whilst 'the Grantham Growler' was an epithet earned as a result his constant complaining... mostly from the rear of the line of course. To some these might sound like unkind names however, they didn't reflect on his popularity one bit. He was the toughest, bravest and most sinewy man in the section. In a fight of any description you could do worse than have him at your side.

"Come on lad, I'll show you 'ow it's done."

Munt is now addressing young Jack Coggins. The section had been slightly under strength, even before Donbaik, and Coggins is our latest recruit. Pale, nervous and covered in acne, he looked about as far away from a soldier as you can suppose. He's been with us only for a few days, after shipping down from Chittagong. Soldier had volunteered to keep an eye on him.

So that was them... my jungle family, a cosy picture of the closest thing I had to what you might call 'domestic bliss' through those strange old years.

The result of Smitty's conversation with the Sergeant was that he turned and jogged over in my direction. He had a large grin across his freckled and sun-reddened face, which generally meant trouble.

"Watch it Wally... Smit's gorr 'is eye on us. Could be bad news," Eric whispered to me.

"There's always summat... and it usually comes in our direction," I sighed.

"Tek it as a complement."

"Right lads... Wally, Eric... I've gorra nice wee number for you," Smitty announced. "You can tek young Coggins along as part of his education... that's if Soldier dun't mind bein' parted from him for a few hours?"

Soldier shrugged,

"Anything that gets me off nappy duty is fine by me Corp."

Coggins giggled nervously.

"By the look of evil pleasure on your face Corp, I reckon you've got us digging latrines or summat," I speculated.

"No lad, not this time. I said it was a nice wee number... and for once it is. There's an officer of engineers building a bridge across that big dry chaung just outside the wire, over behind that temple we scrambled through on the way in. You know... the funny lookin' one with the heads peekin' out of it? He needs a couple of big strong lads to keep the enemy at bay. So, thinks I to meself, who better than Privates Kingdom and Newton, the biggest, strongest, lads in the section."

"Why don't they send the Bren Gunner?" I suggested, I thought helpfully, whilst looking over at Podge who in turn was slowly shaking his head from side to side, his eyes turned to the sky.

"Nah… I thought I'd give you two layabouts a bit of exercise instead."

"Is Jap close then Corp?" questioned Eric.

"Jap's always close in these parts Private Newton. You just don't know when that sneaky little bogger is goin' to pop up again do you? You might think he's not around 'cos you can't see 'im or hear 'im… but he's just as likely to be waiting behind that tree over yonder, or you might find 'im right under your next footstep with a big grin on his face and a nice pointy bit o' steel aimed up your arsehole."

The smile disappeared from Smitty's face and some of the men nodded solemnly.

"Now then, none of this pointless speculatin' lads…Grab your chaggles and bugger off."

"Building bridges Corp? Sounds like something's brewing?" Soldier fixed Smitty with a firm stare. The rest of the section stopped in their tracks and turned to observe the Corporal's response.

"There in't even char brewin' around 'ere s'far as I can see," Smitty grinned back instantly.

"I mean why would they go to trouble of building a bridge for the likes of us? I reckon they'd only do it for the heavy stuff… tanks mebbe?" continued Soldier, attempting to push the Corporal further into revealing anything he was holding back.

Smitty shook his head,

"It's only a wee bridge lads."

Soldier smiled wryly.

So, the three of us - me, Eric and Coggins – set off to follow the beaten-down tracks which criss-crossed the increasingly sparse forest of trees, gripping our rifles tightly and scanning our surroundings with maximum attention.

Like most of the boys, I had a love/hate relationship with the jungle. I willed it to be on my side, wary of what would happen if it turned against me. I longed for it to be a green cocoon that I could wrap myself in; a nurturing spirit offering me its unconditional protection. But I was also aware that it could quickly become a Dante-esque hell. That is a label I apply retrospectively of course… I knew nothing of Dante then.

I often had the unsettling feeling that it was watching me as I moved warily through it. Who knows how many pairs of eyes were hidden behind its deep green foliage? If I stood still, then its quietness and vastness overwhelmed me. The trees seemed to speak to me, in secret, goading, whispers, like they knew my fate but wouldn't let on. It was able to hold its breath at will and, when it did, my chest tightened in sympathy with it. When it eventually exhaled it was generally in the company of a squealing commotion of feathers and fur high up in its fluttering branches, and a beat of panic in my heart. If I was ever drawn to gaze nonchalantly up to its summit then - when *it* knew I was off-guard - the ground shifted beneath my feet, making me feel dizzy, and I lost my bearings completely.

Many years later I visited the Palm House at Kew Gardens and all of those feelings came flooding back like a Tsunami. I couldn't bear it and had to run back out into the open air after a few minutes.

The jungle played other tricks on us too. Sometimes you couldn't really be sure that you were following the proper track. The vegetation shifted its position and the paths became overgrown in the blink of an eye. Like a scene from one of those surrealist paintings you were never quite sure of what you were seeing, and it was easy to get lost in its green maze. There were rumours that Jap used to create false tracks which led only to booby traps. Anyway, your nerves were always on edge and your eyes sought out the tiniest hint of shadows moving in between the gaps in the trees. Sometimes you saw them, even when they weren't there.

We slowed down almost to a halt with every crack of a twig or animal call, fingers raised to our lips for the benefit of Coggins. Every now and again the boom of distant artillery and the faint rattle of gunfire cut through the quiet of the woodland.

"How far away is that?" asked Coggins after a particularly feverish burst.

"Far enough," replied Eric. "Somewhere up in the mountains I'd say."

As soon as we arrived at the abandoned temple, Coggins veered off the track to have a closer look. The shrine was forlorn and overgrown. It was fronted by two rows of arches, one above the other; there had been a pagoda, but that had long since crumbled to the floor. It was guarded by several badly eroded figures of warriors or gods, I'm not sure which. The temple had been there so long that columns of bamboo had grown through it. One of the statues had been broken in half and then enveloped by the growing jungle. The piercing cold stone eyes of a plump little disembodied head stared out from it, eerily pressed between the base of two, thick, woody stems.

As soon as he noticed that Coggins had left us, Eric retraced his steps swiftly and yanked the young lad back hard by his pouches, spinning him round so that they faced each other.

"It's like dolls heads... stuck in the trees," Coggins squeaked, terror in his eyes.

"Leave it lad... tek it from me, you don't want to be admirin' the scenery round 'ere," Eric whispered tetchily. "You can come back after the war for that."

He let Coggins go with a sharp push, so that the youth staggered back a few paces. Eric stormed off ahead with a face like thunder. Coggins looked over to me for some support, but I could only offer a desultory shake of the head. I let him catch up with me and I walked alongside him for a moment, putting my hand on his shoulder to offer some brief reassurance. Coggins was still shaking.

"Eric's brother was out here too," I told him.

"Was?"

"... With Burma Corps through the retreat. They holed up in an old temple one night... a big rambling place it was, not like that piddling little thing back there. Bob found a pile of statues stashed in an alcove and thought he'd grab a souvenir."

"And?"

"And he's now back in Blighty without any bloody hands."

Coggins face reddened,

"I'm sorry. I didn't know did I?"

"There's a lot to learn out here Coggins. Just be grateful that you're learning it the easy way... for now."

I may have sounded like the sage voice of experience, but I knew that I was little more than a novice myself and I'd barely seen any action. Donbaik was the closest I'd come, but I was talking like a veteran already. Then again, experience is always relative when it comes to war.

"Why the hell are we here?" Coggins asked with more than a hint of exasperation in his voice. It was question that was never far away from any of our minds in truth. Mostly you just uttered it silently, to yourself.

"We're here to save the free world Coggins. Not everybody gets the chance to do that… do they? So, your luck's in lad," I replied.

He said nothing.

"You know, I'm going to pluck up the courage to ask Soldier that question one day. If I don't get a clip round the ear, then the answer might be worth listening to."

This time Coggins smiled and shrugged his shoulders.

The trees soon petered out into scrubland which was criss-crossed by chaungs of various depths. 'Chaungs' was the local name for streams or small riverbeds. Sometimes they were full of water or mud, sometimes they weren't. The chaungs were shallow enough and dry enough at that time of year for us to scramble across with a little bit of effort.

Even though it was a relief getting out of the jungle, you felt exposed out in the open, so your vigilance remained high. Eric pulled up to a standstill. He nodded towards the figure of a tall but slightly portly man, was who wearing the insignia of a lieutenant and standing on his own ahead of us in the open scrub.

"An officer of the fuckin' engineers if ever I saw one," he proclaimed in a whisper.

"A very sweaty fuckin' officer of the engineers," I added under my breath.

It didn't occur to any of us at the time, but what I saw on that morning was your archetypal cartoon caricature of a British army officer. He held a swagger-stick at his side, and he dabbed a handkerchief at his large moustache and uncomfortably red forehead with his other hand. Dark sweat patches covered his aertex bush shirt. We also noticed that he had a rather nasty red scar running down one side of his face.

"Caught one from a dervish at Khartoum, what?" Eric joked.

The officer spotted the three of us and walked across in our direction, limping a little uncomfortably, but sporting a wide and welcoming grin.

"Ah! You must be my soldiers? Jolly good stuff!"

We stood to attention, but he waved his handkerchief to dismiss us, "There's no need for that, far too hot... save that for when there's a superior around."

He stuffed the cloth into his pocket and held out a hand.

"Johnson... Second Lieutenant, Royal Engineers... on secondment, 506th Field Company."

He shook hands enthusiastically with each of us.

"Don't look so worried, we're not alone!"

He pointed his stick towards two sappers and an engineer corporal who were apparently examining the chaung in front of them. It was much wider than the other dry stream beds.

"Luckily we've got some busy bees as well... over there!"

He waved his stick again, this time towards the treeline where we spotted a group of twenty or so Gurkhas busily chopping branches and stripping bark from the trunks.

"How they do that so quietly I'll never know. Those chaps never cease to amaze," enthused Johnson, pulling out the handkerchief once more from his pocket to dab at his forehead. "Come with me men."

We positioned ourselves around the perimeter of the clearing. I lay belly down in the dry grass and watched the Gurkhas and engineers labour. They were an impressive ensemble, somehow managing to manoeuvre two pylons they'd cut from the trees into the bed of the chaung, so that they stood upright. It was the jungle version of precision engineering. The pylons formed a 'Y' shape at the top, with smaller logs laid across the poles to make a frame of sorts. It was all tied in place with stripped bark, and smaller chunks of wood were wedged against it for support. It reminded me of the sort of choreography we saw in those Busby Berkeley Hollywood musicals at that time; each one of those Gurkhas knew their place and each step was honed to perfection.

More Gurkhas emerged into the clearing, each dragging a bunch of Bamboo stems to lay across the frame. They secured them at each end to form the chassis of the bridge. Their tempo intensified as they began to tie down smaller branches of wood at right angles across the Bamboo.

I got to my feet to allow the blood to flow back into my legs and walked over to where Coggins lay, his rifle resting on a felled tree-trunk.

"Do you think they've done this before?"

"I dunno…but they aren't half mesmerising?" Coggins' face was as animated as I had seen it since he joined us.

As we glugged water from our chaggles, Johnson appeared at our side. He opened his mouth to speak, but his words were silenced by a sharp cracking sound, which came from somewhere beyond the bridge building party. The Gurkhas stopped work and instantly fell to their knees. Johnson crumpled awkwardly to the floor beside me and freed his .38 Enfield revolver from its holster. I set my rifle on top of the fallen trunk. Nobody said a word. The temperature seemed to rise in tune with the intensity of the nervous silence which pervaded the clearing around us. In those moments, you can hear nothing but the beating and pulsing intimate mechanics of your own body… which sound like they're being amplified and broadcast to the world.

Something rustled. It was out towards the trees at the fringe of the glade. Sweat poured from Coggins bright red face, dripping onto his rifle, his breathing became louder and more laboured and his hand trembled. Each drip of sweat seemed to echo around us as it landed on the gun metal. I reached over and gently moved Coggins finger clear of the trigger, then gave him a reassuring squeeze of the arm. You learn to hide fear, even if you can't stop feeling it.

There was another murmur of movement in the trees. Then the shrillest of cries, echoing like manic laughter, tore a hole through the uneasy hush… *ee-oow, ee-oow.*

I felt my eyes widen and my breathing stop, but to my amazement the Gurkhas visibly relaxed and some of them started to get back to work. One or two of them even appeared to be smiling and sharing a joke. I looked over to Johnson who was wiping his forehead and stroking the chain around his neck. His scar seemed to have become a deeper shade of scarlet. He shrugged his shoulders. There was another *'ee-oow'* noise and then a Peacock strutted out, nonchalantly, into the clearing.

"This bloody country," I cursed, through the exhaling of stockpiled breath. "It's the only place I know where you can pee your pants because of a bloody bird."

"Remember, it's all relative men," said Johnson re-holstering his gun. "Now, when I was your age, I was packed off to the Dardanelles... and I can tell you that *was* hell on Earth. Burma is a walk in the park in comparison, complete with Peacocks. Now we definitely didn't have any of those roaming about the place when we fought the Turks."

I shuddered inside for a moment at the words 'Dardanelles' and 'Turks'. Their emotional resonance never failed to stir me, but six thousand miles away from home - in Burma - encountering them again took me by surprise. I turned to look him in the eye.

"You were at the Battle of Gallipoli?" I asked.

"Yes... yes, I was there."

Johnson cleared his throat. His acknowledgement was delivered in a way that was half-way between pride and embarrassment.

"So was my dad."

To hear those words coming from my mouth was a surprise too. I turned back to face the bridge, where the Gurkhas were now weaving a kind of matting over the top using stripped bark and long twigs. Johnson was evidently relieved and he visibly relaxed.

"And did your father make it back home?" he asked tentatively.

I shook my head.

"I'm sorry about that Private. There were many a good man who didn't return home from that living nightmare."

"His name was Albert... but they called him Bert... Bert Kingdom."

My sight was still trained on the bridge, but it did feel good to talk about Dad for once. Johnson coughed and dabbed his face. He appeared to be a little unsettled again, perhaps by dark memories that were beginning to resurface.

"Our General Slim was out there too," he said, finally, after another cough.

"Really?"

I was impressed.

"He must have been a kid back then."

Johnson nodded and raised himself to his feet.

"We were all kids...," he flashed a restrained smiled and rested a hand on my shoulder, "but clearly only the best men got fight over there, didn't they?"

He gave me a firm slap on the back, before striding over towards the bridge. The Gurkhas finished their work and collected their kit, sitting down in a group, as the trio of engineers inspected their efforts. They appeared satisfied, and the sapper and corporal disappeared into the trees.

Half an hour had elapsed before the sound of an engine was heard to the south and, soon after, a line of armoured vehicles emerged from the scrub at the far end of the clearing. They were followed by a truck pulling a large gun. The convoy crossed the bridge and sped away.

"They're driving the wrong fuckin' way, aren't they? Are we retreating again?" asked Eric.

"Damned if I know," I said.

But I wasn't in a mind to think about our war at that moment. For the remainder of our time in that clearing I sensed that Johnson was staring at me, from a distance and out of the corner of his eye. I tried to convince myself that I had imagined it, but before we left to go back to our camp, the lieutenant shook our hands. He seemed to hold onto mine more tightly and for longer than the others. Close up, his eyes, which squinted beneath his sweating brow, barely maintained contact. Yet when he moved away, I could feel them examining me with an intensity that left me more than a little bit unnerved.

"Maybe he's one of them funny buggers?" offered Eric, after I mentioned it to him, once we'd made it back to the section. He confessed that he hadn't noticed any staring at the time.

"Funny buggers"?

"You know," he hushed his words, "...you've heard what they get up to in them public schools?" He leaned forward and whispered into my ear, "I bet he's got designs on you!"

I pushed him away and my discomfort must have been apparent because he changed the subject.

"Anyway Wal, you've said nowt about your dad copping it at Gallipoli before... not to me anyway," there was a hint of disappointment in his voice as if he'd been the last to find out.

"I've never had a reason to mention it, have I?"

"Maybe not. What was he like then... your dad?"

"I don't know... and that's the truth. I was only a baby. I've never even seen a picture."

"You must be joking! No photos?"

I shook my head.

"No, not that I know of. Anyway, Mam still won't talk about him, even now."

"I guess it must've been a tough life for them war widders... especially if they had nippers to look after. Why don't you try and ask her again? With you out 'ere an' all that, she might... you know."

"I'll think about it."

But I'd done nothing but think about it, and I'd already made up my mind anyway. The strange encounter with Johnson and the fact that I was fighting a war; all of this had stirred up a dormant but increasingly insistent desire to know more.

I was too young to remember the moment when I learned that Dad was dead; but his presence - his echo - had always been there somewhere. I guess it was built firmly into the sense I had of myself. Whenever I tried to conjure up a physical image though, all I could produce was this vague facsimile of a man without a face. He was both real and ethereal at the same time. Even then, I still needed to know that he was there next to me, sharing the moments that would make him proud... after all, that was what joining the army was partly about in the first place, wasn't it?

It was easy to picture my dad as the carefree and loving little brother that my Aunty Edie had told me about; but even the few words she had been able to share could only be done out of earshot of Mam. In Mam's presence he was a place I shouldn't go, a taboo; a forbidden room; one built by her selfish grief. Joining the army meant that I could escape its dark oppressive walls. I hoped too that it would free me from the pressure of *wanting to know*; and besides, all I really needed was to feel the sense that he was there, looking down on me, feeling pride at the way I was forging my own place in the world.

The thing about forbidden rooms though, is that they insist on tempting you. They call out to you in the darkest moments of the night, until you can only draw blood by scratching at their impenetrable walls. Despite what I might have hoped, it was clear that my forbidden room had followed me into my exile in South East Asia, and the temptation to break down its doors was now stronger than ever. With my resolve newly stirred by the encounter with Johnson, I told myself determinedly that I would not stop until I found the answers I needed. Even in this alien place, thousands of miles away from home, I now realised that running away just doesn't work.

We soon discovered that the bridge was not built for our retreat after all. Maybe that was wishful thinking on our part. Instead we were readied for an attack on Jap positions to our south near Taungmaw; although Soldier said he'd heard that it was only a diversionary attack to enable Six Brigade to get the hell out of Donbaik. I wondered briefly how many men die as mere diversions during war; but I could hear Soldier's voice telling me that I should resist such thoughts.

Our objective was to be reached by a night march. I just loved a night march, as if it wasn't hard enough when you could see where you were putting your feet! In this case the terrain was too difficult for the mules, and so we had to carry as much of our kit as possible. To make matters worse, it had rained heavily beforehand for several hours. You haven't known rain unless you've witnessed what can be unleashed in Burma, and the monsoon hadn't even properly started by then. Our canvas capes were no match for it, I could barely see a thing and my soaked skin and limbs became uselessly numb.

The rain had turned the chaungs into muddy pits, and I sunk in knee deep. It took every ounce of strength I had, to drag and heave my dead-weight of a body and pack through it all. Miraculously, when we arrived at the river, barely able to gasp for breath, assault boats appeared out of nowhere to ferry us across. Perhaps Johnson was responsible for the boats? He was out there… somewhere… I sensed it in my bones. I looked for him, but if he was there, he was just one of many shadowy puppet-masters directing this chaos in the rain. They were alien figures submerged in the night; their presence revealed only by the briefest pulse of torchlight reflected on a Mackintosh skin. All that us puppets could do was submit to their will, collapse into the boats and wonder where we would next enter the stage.

Chapter 3.

Burma: 1943.

The veteran Lieutenant knew that this moment would arrive. He'd felt it in his water for the past twenty years, although the thought of it invoked no feelings of guilt or self-reproach. Nevertheless, a creeping sense of imminent jeopardy had become stronger with each passing year. It was expected; he knew it would come. He just didn't know when.

When it did come, it was such a gut-wrenching shock that it completely muddled his mind… for a few frightening moments at least. He surmised, proudly, that it could only have been down to his soldierly instincts, finely honed over thirty odd years of service, that he managed to recover some composure. It was enough for him to successfully face-off that first contact with the enemy. Now, with the initial skirmish safely negotiated, he turned his mind to the long-term strategy; one of ultimate victory.

It would be necessary, of course, to jot down a plan of action in the red notebook that he always carried in his jacket pocket. He would write it in code, just as he had done with all his secret things, using a cipher based on his native language that he'd developed back in Monmouth School as a boy. Back then it enabled him to write down his private thoughts, safe in the knowledge that those brigands Alwyn Moss-Price and David Lewis wouldn't be able to steal them as they had stolen everything else of his. He had never given away the key to his secret language, even when that monster Arthur Cadell had him suspended by his ankles above the toilet bowl for so long that he couldn't walk for nearly a week.

"It's no use crying like a girl Johnson. Unless you tell me the secret code, I'm going to leave you here until you piss yourself, that'll wipe away those baby tears!"

Cadell could have hung him there until the end of term and he still wouldn't have spilled the beans. The remembrance of his youthful steadfastness stiffened his resolve even now, so many years later.

Johnson decided to name his new master plan 'Operation Affable', and he would mark the first page 'Brig Cyfrinachol' in red ink. Key to his strategy was the requirement to throw his adversary off the scent by embarking on a campaign of misinformation. The initial step must be designed to find out exactly how much the pretender knows. In this task he would bring his own brand of chummy geniality into play. He knew full well how the other men regarded him. To them he was no more than a washed-out dinosaur who had been passed over for promotion more times than anyone could remember. He was old. He was boring. He was a joke. He was also, to a large extent, the epitome of 'affability'. It was a disguise he could put to good use.

He decided that his first course of action must be to manufacture another meeting. He found himself enjoying the thought of this imminent subterfuge immensely. He would be the leading man in his own play. It was all he could do to fight back a grin. He was confident that this charade would go on to confirm what he'd suspected since that first meeting, that the enemy possessed almost no intelligence about the matter at hand; although he needed to be certain of that, of course. He knew too that there was only one other person on the planet who could ride to his opponent's rescue, but the chances of the two of them joining forces in common cause were, he was happily sure, less than zero.

Once that essential reconnaissance had been completed, the next phase of the strategy would be to commence a campaign of hiding… or rather watching… in plain sight, at least until they were each packed off to different theatres of battle. Even if that eventuality came to pass, he would make a note in his book to still expect contact... at every turn. He would write it in capital letters and underline it three times.

Wet through and cold, he was watching his nemesis right now. Even the torrential rain and the pitch dark couldn't prevent him from picking out his pursuer amongst the crowds of slithering bodies waiting for boats on the opposite bank of the river. It was as if his senses were now able to home in instinctively onto the danger. He wondered momentarily if the object of his attention had also spotted him in turn. But what did it matter if he had? Tonight, *he* was no more than an ant crawling about the jungle with hundreds of other ants. He considered the convenient possibility that *he* might not even return from whatever forlorn escapade the boats were launching him on. The Lieutenant felt the urge to raise his hand and wave, in regal fashion, across the water. Instead, he raised it to squinted eyes, curling his fingers around the ants in the distance, before slowly tightening his fist.

"Is all well Lieutenant?"

Johnson didn't need to turn his head to know that he was being addressed by that old bore Captain McIntosh.

"Oh yes, it's all going very well indeed."

"Good show. By the way, I've had it reported from some of the chaps here that you haven't moved from this spot for some considerable time."

"A good vantage point is worth is weight in gold, Mac. To ensure that the plan is being enacted with the requisite precision."

The Captain shuffled forward to stand in front of his subordinate, studying his scarred and bloated face as the rain beat out arpeggios on his cape. He raised his eyebrows.

"Are you actually smiling, Johnson?"

"Not at all. I think it might just look that way sometimes. My old war wound... it has a certain affect... especially in the rain. That doesn't mean that I'm not enjoying every minute of this though, Mac."

"No need to be flippant Lieutenant."

"No Sir."

Chapter 4.

Burma: 1943.

The boats delivered us to our assault position in time for dawn. Whether I managed a few minutes sleep I don't recall, but just the very fact that we'd made it to our destination seemed to restore me to life. I never really worked out how that miracle occurred, and I've never experienced it again since I left the army… not in such stark terms anyway. Maybe it was the restorative powers of the tea that did it? Magically, we managed to brew it anywhere; or maybe it was one of those deliciously sweet oatmeal bars from the jungle rations which were meant to be turned into porridge, though they tasted just perfect as they were?

When it eventually came, the attack was brief and loud. I recall it now as no more than a jungle-green blur of grenades and bullets. None of the gory detail has stayed with me, like it has with other skirmishes; no doubt the brain can only retain so much horror. I don't know how many Japs we killed, if any, but I wasn't looking to count bodies. The important thing was that I was still alive and we hadn't lost a single soldier. Though it was my first close encounter with a Jap, living or dead, there was no time to linger. The firefight had alerted their comrades elsewhere in the jungle and we regrouped and hunkered down on the forest floor, waiting for the protection that darkness would bring.

We lay there the whole of the following day in our foxholes, hoping that we'd mastered the magic art of invisibility. We knew anything that twitched even slightly would be a target for a Jap snipers' bullet, and that familiar 'crack', whoosh and soft thud was our constant soundtrack. The expected full-on attack, though, never came.

As dusk finally fell, the word came through that it was time to withdraw. For reasons I will never understand, Jap just let us go. Quite what we'd achieved, diversionary or otherwise, I never fathomed, but the most important thing was that we had survived... *I had survived.* What's more Coggins had seen his first action, and so he could count himself truly as one of us.

Then, at last, the monsoon came, and we withdrew from the line. We marched over the mountains at night, before catching a steamer across the River Naaf to a village called Dakshin. This was to be the place from where we were to ride out the rains, rest our weary minds and patch up our broken bodies.

By then the regiment had started to lose men in large numbers, hundreds every week, not from Jap bullets, but because of a much better camouflaged foe... mosquitoes. They were everywhere in the damp heat that came with the rains and they attacked without mercy, spreading Malaria, Yellow and Dengue Fever until it had become a mini epidemic. Men were literally falling to the floor around us, before they were packed off to a forward treatment station. We reckoned the Mepacrine tablets they gave us must be duds. For now, though, stuck in the middle of this carnage, seven section remained untouched and we toasted our luck with our mess tins. By the time we arrived in Dakshin we were exhausted, soaked, filthy and hungry, but from our point of view, the timing of the monsoon couldn't have been better.

It was whilst we were at Dakshin that something unexpected happened. The rest of the lads had been packed off to help dig some new latrines. For some reason, I was excused the pleasure. Rather than celebrating my good fortune, I sat down on the floor and stared at the two blank Air Letters draped over my knees. One was intended for Mam and my head thumped madly from struggling to conjure the long-overdue words I needed. The second letter was for Dinah, my girl back in Nottingham. The vast blankness of that page was just as troubling to me, but I couldn't bring myself to think about that one just yet.

The monsoon rain was doing its worst, pounding down on the tarpaulin like rapid gunfire and, right in the corner of our basha, it had broken through our defences. Eric had somehow managed to cadge a large tin bucket to catch the water. At first the sound of the rain hitting the tin was unbearable, but as it filled up, the rhythmic plop of the dripping became quite hypnotic, abetting my mood of contemplation. I was thinking that I would probably have to muster up the energy to empty the bucket soon, when I became aware of someone calling my name. It was a youthful native voice. I looked outside and saw that it belonged to Private Clive.

Clive was a young Burmese boy who had attached himself to the regiment, although nobody could be sure exactly when that happened. One day he was just there. He said nothing for weeks and just watched us. Some said he was a Jap spy. Then he just picked up a broom and started sweeping up, and before too long we were paying him to do errands around the camp. His English improved no end and in quick time, then some wag named him 'Clive of India', even though we were in Burma. Because he soon became an integral part of the regiment, it was only fair to honour him with the rank of private.

I peered out of the basha to see him standing barefoot, up to his ankles, in the river of brown water coursing through the camp. He wore his native red lungi topped with somebody's old service tunic, which was several sizes too big for him.

"Over here Private Clive... What is it?"

He splashed over to me and stepped under the cover of the tent.

"Private Kingdom sir. There is a gentleman who would like to speak with you at Lincoln Cathedral."

"Now?"

"Yes, Private Kingdom sir. Now sir."

"Did he tell you his name?"

"Mr. Jonser, Sir."

Jonser?

Johnson? Could it be?

But what would Johnson want with me now? No doubt with Eric's diagnosis still clouding my judgement, I was almost of a mind to send

Clive back with some excuse for me not to go, but a niggling sort of intrigue got the better of me.

"Is he an Engineer officer"?

Clive nodded.

"Then tell him I'll be over shortly."

I handed over a coin from my pocket. Clive bowed his head and pressed his palms together in the way of the Namaste before running back out into the brown-green watery landscape. After a few minutes I grabbed my cape and followed him over to the church, also barefoot, through the still raging torrent. A duckboard path had been laid to form a main thoroughfare, but even that was submerged here and there along its length.

The church itself was nothing more than a hut thrown together with sheets of corrugated iron and bamboo. A large tarpaulin had been pulled over it and a cross made of two strips of bamboo lashed together had been hammered into the ground beside it. Someone, maybe the same wag who had bestowed the name on Clive, had hung a painted sign on the outside which read, 'Lincoln Cathedral'.

I could see the unmistakeable bulk of Lieutenant Johnson lurking in the shadow of its doorway. He raised his cap to greet me.

"Private Kingdom! Good morning... stand easy... come in and take a pew. I wasn't sure that you were still here."

I followed him uncertainly into the church and we sat on two of the rickety wooden chairs occupying the dim space within.

"Well, neither Jap nor the mosquitoes have done for me yet Lieutenant."

I forced a nervous smile.

"Good, good... I'm very pleased to hear it."

"What can I do for you Lieutenant?"

Johnson looked a little flustered, but eventually he said,

"I think it's more a case of what I can do for you."

I must have looked worried and, if anything, this seemed to relax him a little.

"I'm sorry, I'm not explaining myself very well, am I? Look, I've had time to reflect upon our conversation, you know the one we had when we last met."

His eyes widened in my direction, clearly expecting a response.

"Sorry sir... I don't follow?"

"We talked about the Dardenelles if you recall... and more specifically your father?"

I nodded warily.

"I must admit the name Kingdom did ring some bell or other. It's very distinctive, isn't it? So, I've wracked my memory and I wanted to tell you that I'm sure that I did make the acquaintance of your father... the very same Bert Kingdom."

My heart began to pound heavily, and I could feel the heat rising to my face. I didn't know what to say. Johnson picked up on my discomfort.

"My dear chap, I didn't want to cause you upset. Your father was a Royal Naval Division man, wasn't he? He helped us out with transport and the mules as far as I recall."

"What was he like?" I eventually blurted out.

"From what I recall he was a jolly good fellow," he smiled brightly.

"Were you there when he... you know?"

"Oh no... not at all," Johnson responded instantly, shaking his head vigorously from side to side. "Ours was only a working acquaintance you understand, I only actually met him a couple of times. But, knowing the sort of straightforward fellow he was, I can only imagine that he met his end bravely."

"What did he look like?"

Johnson appeared to be completely taken aback by my question.

"My dear boy, you don't know that?"

I shook my head. I felt tears well behind my eyes and fought them back.

"Well... what can I say? It was a very long time ago. From what I remember he was a strong handsome chap, of good stock no doubt."

After a brief but awkward silence, when it was clear that I had no further questions, or rather I was too dumbstruck to think of any, he rose from his chair and slapped his large hand once again on my shoulder.

"Just like you are my dear boy."

He replaced his cap and tucked his swagger stick under his arm.

"Well, there it is then," he concluded, seemingly satisfied with the outcome of our tête-à-tête.

"Thank you, Lieutenant," I said quietly, still not sure exactly what 'it' was.

He lingered a few moments longer, opening his mouth slightly as if hesitating to say something else before turning abruptly and marching out into the rain.

By the time I returned, Eric was back in the basha and lying down on his well-worn palliasse.

"The wanderer returns," he declared laconically as I splashed through the open flaps and threw the cape in the direction of my bed.

I didn't reply. Eric sat up and fixed me with a look of concern.

"Are you coming down wi' summat? You don't look well lad."

I kept the details of my latest encounter with Johnson to myself.

"What do you expect with all this bloody rain and a bloomin' great war raging all around me? Look, I've got to write some letters."

"Well don't look so bleedin' happy about it."

After that, Johnson occupied my mind a lot. In fact, I thought about the latest encounter so much that it made my headache. At first, I tried to convince myself that it was good of him to go to the effort of seeking me out for a chat, but the whole thing just didn't sit right with me. I had learned barely anything else from the conversation that I didn't already know. There was nothing revealed that he couldn't have told me when we first met in that jungle clearing. It struck me that the whole set up at the cathedral seemed to be strictly for his benefit and not mine; but to what purpose? I could only conclude that he must still be holding something back; maybe some piece of information that he thought might distress me or else show him up in a bad light. My mind was racing away with me, but if I was right, then just what did he know? There was only one thing to do and surely, after encountering him twice already, he couldn't be too difficult to find again.

I scoured the camp, speaking to as many soldiers as possible, asking them about Johnson and the 506th Field Company. I went back to the cathedral and interrogated the chaplain, I even made Clive tell me all about his encounter with 'Jonser' in precise detail. It was all fruitless. Johnson was nowhere to be seen. None of the people I spoke to, other than Clive, could recall seeing him. I knew how easy it would have been for him to drift unseen in and out of the camp, just one faceless officer amongst many. Nor was there any indication, even amongst the engineers I spoke to, that any of the 506th had ever been billeted with us. I finally told Eric of my second encounter with the sweaty officer of engineers.

"He could be a ghost. You know, like the ones in that Christmas story... Dickens wasn't it?"

"You saw him. Ghosts don't sweat like that."

"Well I still reckon he's a funny bugger."

The whole episode with Johnson was a further distraction, but at least it gave me the kick I needed to write the long overdue letter to Mam, and the words had already started to form in my head. With that logjam broken, I first decided to make a start with Dinah.

Dinah had always been my girl, ever since we were kids. We lived on the same street, went to the same school and, over time, we had become inseparable. As the years passed by, our childish games of dobby or hopscotch in the street eventually became long walks or picnics by the river at Wilford and then, much later, into breathless but still innocent red-faced fumbles in the woods beyond. It was round about then that I told her I was joining the army; four years before the war started. She had promised me then, between floods of tears, that she would wait for me... no matter how long the wait was destined to be. In those days Dinah was an organic part of me in some way, I felt that very strongly... but I wasn't certain that I loved her.

As I sit here, many years later, I realise that my confusion was simply because I'd not seen her for two years. She was as distant and intangible as the white cliffs of Dover. In fact, I think I felt more of a connection with Vera Lynn... and at least I'd seen her... and heard her voice... whilst I was out in Burma.

The photograph of Dinah that I carried with me at the start of my service had never done justice to her brunette hair and piercing green eyes. Neither did it offer me the chance to touch again her soft skin, painted as it was with the faintest of freckles. There was a time when I treasured each one of those freckles, but that image had now long since been lost to the jungle. My letters to her had become rare and perfunctory and, deep down, part of me was desperate to release her from her promise. I couldn't bring myself to do it though. I'd convinced myself that that the vow she'd made somehow carried with it a guarantee that I would be going home one day, a bit like the thread that guided Theseus back to Ariadne in one of those Greek myths. It's funny that I never used to be superstitious before the war began.

Instead, I willed myself to find the inspiration to write something poetic and romantic, words that told of undying love and of the pain of missing my girl; but how could I do that when I could barely conjure up her image? I tried hard again to picture her face. It was a beautiful face, so why was it so difficult? It was as if the monsoon had washed her from my mind completely. She had become a ghost from a past that felt like it never existed at all.

Eventually, I motivated myself enough to begin scratching away at the paper, but without any enthusiasm. After what felt like hours of anguish though, I was quite pleased with my efforts.

My Darling Dinah,

Firstly, I must apologise, my dear, that it has taken so long for me to send you these few words from afar. The war and the weather in this inhospitable country offers me very little chance for writing letters to you all back home. Also, I have not received any news from Blighty for about a month, so I wasn't sure the postal service was reaching us this deep in the jungle.

As I write to you the monsoon rain is doing its worst, but I am safe and well and quite comfortable for the most part. In the pink as the other lads might say. One thing's for sure, I'll never complain again about those piddling little showers we get back home. You haven't seen rain until you've seen the stuff they get here. Despite everything we are keeping our spirits up, although there is not much happening now due to the weather.

I expect that the sun is shining down on you all at home. I bet you are eating ice cream by the Trent, looking every inch a starlet from those Hollywood pictures. I dearly wish I could be with you, walking in the arboretum or picnicking up in Derbyshire, but that all seems a long way off now - like a dream, not a memory. I don't want to think about those things too much, because I'm sure it will only make me sad.

As always, I hope that the next time we share our thoughts together the war will be over. Until then, I hope that this letter finds you well. I send you my love and best wishes to your family.

Your Walter
As long as my heart will beat XX

The final words were taken from a song that was playing on the radio the last time we met and which we always appended to our letters. It felt meaningless now. I folded the sheet over and addressed the front of it. On the back I wrote my name, rank and service number, together with the words 'written in English'. Then I carefully engraved the letters 'H.I.M.A.L.A.Y.A' to the back of the envelope. The acronym was a game we played with the censor. In this case the letters stood for 'Here is my ardent love and yours always', Dinah knew how to work it out based on what we agreed when we last saw each other. Some of the other lads added similar secret codes in letters to their wives and sweethearts, but most of them were a little more suggestive than the ones I was prepared to write on my letters to Dinah. She just wasn't that sort of girl... or at least she wasn't the last time I saw her.

Next, I started on the letter the that I was increasingly dreading to write, but which I knew now I had put off for far too long:

Dear Mam,

I hope this letter finds you in good health and not worrying too much about me. Our work here has prevented me from writing for a while, so I must apologise for that. Rest assured though that I am safe and well and away from danger as I write this. I do have some news though and this, in turn, leads me to make a request of you.

I have met an officer out here who served with Dad in the Dardanelles. He remembers him and has only good things to relate. This has stirred up my curiosity again.

I know this is difficult for you, but now that I am a man and a soldier and, what's more, serving in a war just like him, I think that it is time for you to tell me everything about my dad and about you and him. If you did keep any photographs hidden from me, then I would like to see them too. Who knows what is round the corner for me here? I am sure you would rather that I know these things now, before I meet him for the first time on the other side – if that is my fate. I am sorry if this letter makes you sad, but I know that you will do the right thing by me.

PS - Send my love to Aunty Edie and Uncle Tom.
Your ever-loving son.
Walter.

As I finished addressing the letter a scattering of ash floated down onto the paper. I looked up to see Errol entering the basha, his hair still immaculately groomed, even despite the rain.

"Look at you! Why so serious?"

He dragged on the cigarette which hung precariously from the corner of his mouth.

"He's been writing a letter to Dinah," said Eric tapping his nose as if he knew a secret.

"Ah! Lover boy getting all frustrated is he? You're not the only one around 'ere I reckon."

"Come on them Wally," added Eric, "what did you stick on the back of the envelope?... L.O.W.E.S.T.O.F.T? ... or was it E.G.Y.P.T?"

Taking me by surprise, Errol whipped both letters from my hands and quickly found what he wanted to see.

"H.I.M.A.L.A.Y.A! Bugger me... that's a tough 'un. What about 'Hard is my...'"

Eric must have seen the look on my face, because he leapt up and pulled the letters back out of Errol's hands before he could carry on. He handed them back to me.

"That's enough of that Coles."

Errol held up his tobacco-stained hands apologetically.

"Calm down ladies! It's not that bad is it? I'm only havin' a bit of a laugh wi' me mates."

I grabbed my cape with an exaggerated sulk and stormed off into the rain in search of the Royal Engineers postman.

Chapter 5.

England: 1943.

The warm weather that had bathed the faces of the people of Nottingham for much of August had begun to wane. Its benevolent heat had brought with it a cautious sense of optimism; a feeling which infiltrated beyond slab square and into the narrow rows and gates of the city beyond. This renewed confidence lingered, even as rainstorms lashed the streets of The Meadows, leaving them covered in a thick carpet of dust.

The ever-house-proud Alice Kingdom had had enough. In this war dust was her enemy. Her frontline was the doorstep. She knelt on a rolled-up towel and started to scrub the red stone threshold of her terraced house using a flat brush, dipping it occasionally into the grey suds that lapped the interior of the steel bucket at her side. She worked herself up into an energetic but steady rhythm, her hands pushing the scrubbing brush in a kind of rowing motion. The magnitude of the effort she expended was measured by her reddening cheeks and in the sweat bubbling up on her brow and upper lip.

"You scrub that anymore, Mrs. Kingdom, and you'll wear the ruddy thing away."

Alice's heart skipped a beat. She knew the voice belonged to Fred Clarke, the postman. Without looking at him, she pushed herself slowly and painfully to her feet and ran a hand across her damp forehead. Fred sensed her apprehension.

"Don't worry love... it's good news I think."

He held out an Air Letter of the type used for army mail from abroad and she took it.

"Thank you, Fred," she said, outwardly concealing the relief she felt gushing through her chest. "It's about time mind you, I can't remember how long it's been since last un."

"A few months that's for sure, but I reckon he'll 'ave plenty of other things to worry about out there."

"You might be right about that. It's good to get some news though. Got time for a cuppa?"

"If only I had, duck. I'm rushed off me feet at the minute. Bloody wars."

Fred doffed his cap and went on his way.

Alice returned to the house, bucket and letter in hand, and headed straight for the kitchen. After emptying the grey suds into the sink, she picked up the kettle. As she filled it from the single tap, she wasn't surprised to hear a knock on the front door. Neither was it unexpected that, before it could be answered, the door burst open and footsteps were to be heard stomping purposefully over the creaking floorboards of the front parlour, across the space at the foot of the stairs, and into the living room at the back of the house.

"Alice! Where are you, duck?"

Edie, Alice's sister-in-law, aimed her words into the air. There was an edge of deep concern to her voice.

"I saw Fred Clarke outside... the letter... is it ..."

Alice appeared in front of her.

"Edie Morton, I swear you can see through brick walls!"

Alice moved quickly to firmly shut the door behind Edie, locking them both into the dim space. The flurry of movement and vibrating wood had disturbed dust into the air so that it swirled in the watery light of the room's single netted sash window.

"You and your bloody doors", tutted Edie.

"I suppose you've got a reason for being here?" asked Alice, ignoring the tutting.

"I was just putting me nets back up and I happened to see you talking to Fred, that's all."

Alice held up the unopened letter for Edie to see.

"Air mail… from Burma."

"Oh, thank the Lord!"

There was no concealing the relief in Edie's voice either.

"That all depends on what it says dun't it? Anyway, tea's mashing, so sit yourself down and I'll fetch us a brew."

"Have you heard about Arthur," Edie called through the closed door to the kitchen as she sat down at a folded table at the edge of the room.

"Arthur who?" Alice shouted back.

"Little Arthur Atkins… Florrie's lad."

"What about him?"

"He's gone an' got 'is-sen killed… in the desert in North Africa. Harry at the shop towd me this morning."

Alice emerged back into the parlour carrying a tray and expertly negotiated closing the door behind her without using her hands. She set the teapot and china cups out on the table and parked herself on a chair opposite Edie.

"Then God rest his soul. I'm glad Florrie in't alive to hear that news… the poor lad."

There was no outward emotion in Alice's voice. Neither did she betray the sweet feeling of inner thankfulness she felt, that it was somebody else's son who had been lost and not her own. She stirred the pot and poured the tea, then the two sisters-in-law sat in contemplative quiet as they sipped from their cups.

"Why's this happenin' again, Alice?" Edie sighed. "Din't we learn nowt from the last bloody war? I never thought there'd be another un… not after all that death and dyin' back then."

Alice remained silent.

"I reckon it's because we chose to put it out of our minds." Edie postulated, after thinking about her own question for a few moments.

A shadow crossed Alice's face, and they fell into silence again.

"Well then… let's have it," prompted Edie eventually, unable to skirt around the important business any longer and impatient enough to disregard her sister-in-law's reticence.

"Well what?"

"The letter, duck!"

"Well... It's addressed to me for a start, not to you."

Alice took the letter from her apron pocket and inspected both front and back carefully before opening it. As she read it, her stony features cracked just enough for her to wipe away a single trickle of saltwater from her cheek. Saying nothing, she read it through once again before lowering it to the table and then looking pleadingly across to Edie with ever reddening eyes. Edie took the paper from Alice's hands and scanned its contents, before telling her sister-in-law, gently,

"You knew this day would come, love... and it's long overdue in't it? The lad's been so good about it. I've had to bite my lip so many times tryin' to respect your wishes that it's a wonder I've gorr' any lips left. I was so proud of my brother, like you were... I really want to mek Walter proud too."

"I know, I know. It's just... it's just hard... even after all these years have passed."

Alice struggled to get her words out through a tightening throat. Edie rose from her seat and beckoned Alice to get to feet.

"Come 'ere girl."

The two women embraced as Alice let sobs wrack her body for the first time in nearly thirty years.

"What are you goin' to do?" Edie asked.

"Do I have a choice?" Alice replied.

Edie shook her head firmly.

"No... you bloody don't."

"Little Arthur Atkins, eh? Poor, poor lad." Alice choked out the words. "Poor, poor Florrie. It only seems like two minutes since..."

Edie reached into her apron pocket and pulled out a tiny key.

"I know girl... I know. Look, I think it's time to find out if this still works."

Alice wiped her eyes and took it from her, nodding her head.

***

Alice sat up in bed with pen and notepad poised on her lap. She'd read the letter from her son several times over and now she turned her mind to the task of writing its reply. Before she could begin, the air raid siren began to howl out a warning of an imminent enemy strike.

She sighed and laboured to get out of bed so that she could look out of the window, steeling herself until she felt able to peer through the glass. A chill ran through her body. The ghosts from the last war were still present. They were there in the trembling shadows cast through the window by the waning crescent moon, even despite the blackout, and in the reflected memories of the window glass. Windows saw everything... and they remembered.

She saw only a few people stirring on the pavement outside; there was no urgency in their movements. It was clear that most of her neighbours had stayed indoors. Neither could she see the fussy local ARP warden, who was usually to be seen directing the traffic of bodies and admonishing those who weren't carrying their gas masks with a look of pensive agitation on his face.

Her memories flashed back to the cool early summer just two years before, when high explosives screeched down from the sky and the streets were a chaos of panicked bodies wrapped in overcoats and blankets. It was still new then, she thought to herself, for most people at least. She remembered Tom Morton banging hard on the door, imploring her to join him and Edie in their cellar, their pre-arranged plan for the expected Jerry onslaught. She could hear the screams of the falling bombs and the deep boom of explosions, but she sensed that they were not close-by enough to cause her any anxiety and, anyway, she felt safe inside the house. She didn't answer the door and Tom had quickly given up.

That night, she remembered, was the worst of it for Nottingham this time around. Sneinton and the city centre suffered most of all, but her street, and those just like it at the red-bricked fringe of the city, had escaped lightly. Edie reckoned, with a selfish disregard for anything beyond her neighbourhood, that it wasn't as bad as the Zep attack they'd been on the receiving end of back in 1916, but Alice could barely remember anything about those days during the so-called Great War; or rather she chose not to.

Back in 1941 she could see the fear etched in people's eyes for months on end. It wasn't just fear either. They were tired - tired of a war that seemed to be marching them inexorably towards defeat, and a future that would forever dismantle the comfortable certainties of their pre-war lives. They were exhausted from the dread of closing their eyes at night, until sleep finally made the decision for them. It was different now; the tide of the war had turned. Alice wasn't sure when things changed, but those people in the street believed they were winning. It was like the changing of the seasons, back in the days when she lived on the farm, only this time round 1941 was the remembered dark winter, and 1943 was the latent spring. These days, as soon as the air raid siren blared out its warning, the people outside the window simply expected the all clear to follow with the immediate inevitability of an exhaled breath. In Alice's mind they were beginning to get blasé about the whole thing; she would never let that happen to herself.

She decided to stay put. She went back to bed and listened out for the sound of aircraft engines, but none came. Eventually the all clear was sounded and her wandering thoughts returned to the letter.

Alice hadn't allowed herself to think about her husband for the last twenty-eight years. Way back, not long after she was first widowed, she would have seen him in the crowd whenever she looked out into the street. A single Jack Tar, conspicuously still, amongst a sea of people, grey-faced, but always there. She had fought hard to resist his presence, always looking in the opposite direction, often with liquid help, but she had eventually won the battle. The toughened skin of her emotional scars had served her well since.

Some memories, of course, still had a way of making themselves known when she least expected them, popping into her mind in moments of weakness, when she was tired or in the deep of the night. She had even become adept at spotting the first signs of this happening, so that she could quickly reinforce any cracks in her armour; but now she knew that it was time to let Bert back in.

Eyes closed, she forced herself to remember. It was harder than she thought it would be. Her memory had been well trained by the strict taskmistress she had become. Painful reminiscences were shackled firmly away in its deepest, darkest and most remote places. Then, out of nowhere, the light came and she saw his face again, hazy at first, but then with complete clarity. Her eyes flickered in fear for a moment before relaxing and allowing her mouth to break into a gentle, joyful, smile as she began to remember a brilliant warm Saturday afternoon almost exactly thirty years before.

Chapter 6.

England: 1913.

Bert Kingdom was wondering why on earth he'd agreed to play in this bloody stupid game. He was twenty-one years old and as fit as any man on the pitch, but it was far too warm an afternoon, and the freshly mowed field they were playing on was as hard as a rock. To make matters worse, pebbles and boulders of various sizes were scattered like skin-ripping shrapnel across its surface. Between them and the animal shit, keeping his eye on the ball was the least of Bert's worries.

The pitch lines were marked out with sand and the goals were formed from wonky wooden poles hammered into the ground. Some old rabbit netting was tied loosely – and optimistically - behind them. The sturdy panelled-leather football they were playing with weighed roughly the same as a cannonball, so no one gave the net any chance of stopping it. It was already flapping around precariously in the barest of breezes.

Bert was playing in shirt sleeves and wearing his working boots. His trouser bottoms were rolled up and tied in place with string. It was late into the game, and his feet hurt. He could feel the rawness of burst blisters and he was pretty sure they were bleeding too. If that wasn't enough torture to put a man through in the service of his mates, he was pouring with sweat and his lungs burned like they were going to explode at any moment. Someone kicked the ball out of play and he dropped to his knees, gratefully seizing the opportunity to try and recover some breath.

"You still alive Bert?"

It was Stan Cooper, the younger brother of Old Oak Farm's manager, who asked the question.

"Just about," Bert wheezed, his chest heaving.

"Come on, we've got to win this, we'll never hear the last of it if we don't."

Bert knew that Stan was right. This was, after all, the annual grudge match against the neighbouring farm: Gorse Field Hall. For the Old Oak Farm boys, it was an away fixture. Gorse Field had won it for the last three years running, and with victory came the privilege of playing the next game on home soil. Pride might have been the only trophy at stake, but the owners were long standing business rivals. They were fiercely competitive in all things and rumours were rife that the Gorse Field lads were on a bonus to win… and that would never do.

The opposing teams were differentiated by the neckerchiefs they wore, red ones for Old Oak and green for the opposition. Forty or so partisan supporters of both sides, wearing similar favours, roared on their teams. There was five minutes still to go and the result was on a knife-edge, with the match tied at two-goals-all. The tension, on and off the pitch, was palpable in the early summer air.

The ball was thrown back onto the field of play and Gorse Field immediately went on the attack, rushing the Old Oak penalty area in numbers. The ball broke out of a scrum of legs and fell to the home team's tall inside-forward, but he mis-kicked it badly. George Pike, Old Oak's youngest player, took the loose ball and belted it high and hard upfield. It landed somewhere close to the nimble feet of Stan Cooper and he ran alongside the bouncing ball over the uneven surface, sometimes controlling it with his shins or knees as it bobbled. His speed took him beyond the Gorse Field half-backs, before a crunching tackle launched him into the air, leaving him sprawled on the ground with his face in the dirt. He watched the ball squirm away and bounce erratically across the dry earth.

Contrary to what his body was telling him, and against his better judgement, Bert had kept on running. With each agonising stride the sound of his heart pumping at full pelt echoed even louder in his ears. If he had had a gauge fixed to his chest, the needle would have been oscillating furiously in the red. His insides were raw, and every breath magnified the pain.

As the ball looped languorously towards him, dull thud by dull thud, he could see that not one player from Gorse Field stood between him and the goalkeeper. The spinning leather moved in a way that was almost out of time with the rest of the world, until it hit a large stone and reared up sharply, hitting Bert on the side. It dropped softly and settled perfectly into the stride of his right foot. He could sense a collective intake of breath from the spectators. There was only one thing to do.

"Oh, bugger it."

He put his toe-end through the ball with as much power as he had left in him. Just as he did so a Gorse Field player launched a late tackle which ripped down Bert's leg and sent him tumbling through the air. He landed with a crunch on the hard ground, which winded him slightly, but left him facing the goal. As he raised his head, he was just in time to see his shot bounce over the out-stretched arm of the goalkeeper and rip away the remaining netting behind his flailing dive.

Before the keeper had landed, the referee blew the whistle signalling the end of the match. Old Oak players and supporters rushed to where Bert lay and hoisted him above their heads. Every inch of his body was aflame, inside and out. His trousers were ripped, a gash along his leg bled profusely, but he didn't care one bit. It was one of the few times in his life that he'd experienced that feeling of pure, unadulterated, elation, and he could not stop grinning.

"You lucky bastard! You'll be suppin' free ale for the rest of the year!" Stan Cooper roared into his ear, "… and odds on a promotion too, for my money!"

"Well… I reckon I've earned myself a pint at least," said Bert to anyone who was listening.

Players and supporters from both sides were invited to tea after the match. They took their places on benches either side of two long trestle-tables, squeezed in between the farm machinery inside one of Gorse Field Hall's outbuildings. The excited din of conversation drowned out the chatter of the chickens that busied themselves around their feet.

Bert and his teammates cleaned themselves up by throwing buckets of cold water at each other in the stable yard. Then, to a fanfare of cheers from the Old Oak contingent and reserved applause from their opponents, he took his seat at the table with a mock salute.

Rivalries were set aside, and each captain raised a toast to the endeavour and skill of the other team. Then the ale flowed, dulling their aches and pains, before empty stomachs were eagerly filled.

"Come on then Kingdom, you've heard enough toasts... and supped enough ale... what about givin' us a speech yoursen?" implored Stan.

Bert shrugged his shoulders.

"I suppose it's a small price to pay."

With the room spinning a little, he scrambled up to stand upon his bench seat, prompting jeers from Gorse Field and another ovation from Old Oak. The verbal jousting lasted for a few minutes. Bert waved the palms of his hands in the air to quieten his audience, and then tapped a fork against his tankard. The gathering fell into a hush and he cleared his throat.

"Well, what a day!" he began.

More 'hurrahs', 'boos' and the raucous banging of tables and tankards resumed for a moment, each contingent trying to outshout the other.

"Now I know how Mr. Hobbs felt when he bashed that ton against the Aussies! How bloomin' often is it that you can say that you're the hero of the day?"

"You're usually the zero of the day!" somebody retorted, causing laughter to erupt from all sides.

"All I can say is that one man doesn't win a football match on his own. As you all know, it's a team game... just like running a farm is a team game. And there in't no better team in these parts than the lads at Old Oak Farm. So, raise up whatever you've got in your hands in a toast... to me mates!"

He lifted his tankard. As he did so the room spun a little more and he staggered backwards. He tried to adjust his balance, but this just unsteadied him further and he fell from the bench. He crashed against one of the girls serving the food, launching the plate she was carrying into the air. The platter smashed onto the stone floor at precisely the same moment as Bert landed on top of it, showering him with fragments of broken crockery. The room was now in uproar. The mirth became uncontrollable when his painfully heavy landing was followed by a downpour of ham sandwiches, which slapped down like strange rain upon his prone body.

Bert looked up at the startled girl.

"You appear to 'ave dropped your sandwiches Miss."

He peeled one of them from his chest and took a bite.

"And very tasty they are too!"

He picked out a fragment of broken plate from his mouth.

The hand she held over her mouth couldn't disguise that fact that she was now doubled up with laughter, fuelled further by the uncontained merriment around the table. She eventually composed herself enough to reach a hand down towards Bert.

"Is everything alright... I mean there's nothing broken is there? Apart from the plate that is!"

"The only thing that's broken down here Miss, is me pride... I expect I'll not hear the last of this."

The girl spotted the injury to Bert's leg, which was beginning to bleed again. She stopped laughing.

"Dear Lord!"

"Oh, that's nothing... just a souvenir from scoring the winning goal today, a small price to pay."

"Well, you've got to let me clean that up, come with me."

To a chorus of wolf-whistles from the tables behind her, she took Bert by the hand and led him out across the yard and into the farmhouse. In the kitchen, she sat him on a chair at the large oak table, whilst she filled a bowl with water from a jug. She pulled up a chair beside him, rolled up what was left of his trouser leg and began to gently bathe his wound with a cloth.

"So, you're the one then... Old Oak's match-winning hero?"

"Yes, Miss... I am. I'm not too sure how it happened though... Bert Kingdom's the name," he held out a hand and she took it.

"I'm Alice... Alice Oxton. Am I allowed to fraternise with the enemy?"

Bert took a closer look at his nursemaid and he liked what he saw. As she gently dabbed the damp cloth onto his leg her long, glossy, coal black hair draped across his leg. It was cool and tickled his skin, sending shivers through his body. She was perhaps a little younger than him, but there was devilment in her brown eyes.

"You can fraternise with me anytime you want," he found himself saying, half-regretting it as soon as the words had left his mouth.

Alice blushed a little and flashed him a look out of the corner of her eye,

"Was that you offering to take me to the church picnic just then?"

It was Bert's turn to blush.

"I would like to, yes Miss... I bloomin' well would," he stuttered, "Do you work here?"

"The farm manager is my uncle."

"Alice Oxton! Of course, I should have realised."

She dropped the cloth back into the bowl of water and patted Bert's leg dry with her apron.

"There's a bit of bandage here somewhere... wait here."

Bert watched her intently, an unconscious smile on his face, as she emptied the bowl into the sink and rinsed out the cloth. She dried her hands by rubbing them up and down her apron, as she did so she pulled it tight against her, accentuating the shape of her body. Then she opened a cupboard and took out a tin box from which, excitedly, she produced a roll of bandage.

"Told you so!"

She looked pleased with herself and skipped back over to Bert, carefully wrapping the bandage around his shin. She split the end of the bandage and tied it in place with a bow.

"I'll be at the Church on Sunday for morning prayers. So, if you happen to bump into us there... then perhaps you can walk back with us?"

The following Sunday morning Bert set out from The Meadows to walk the four miles to Wollaton. It was a lazy stroll of about an hour; a journey he made every day to go to work at Old Oak Farm. He followed the gently meandering course of the River Leen, through Lenton, before skirting the parkland around Wollaton Hall. He arrived just as the communion was beginning and slipped inside as quietly as he could to sit in the back row, straining his neck to locate the spot where the Oxton family were sitting.

He spotted Alice at once in a middle row, she was easily the prettiest girl there, and a beam of light from the nave window seemed to pick her out. She occasionally turned her head to scan the faces of congregation. Bert dared to hope that she was searching for him, but she didn't appear to have noticed him. At the end of the service he slipped out before anyone else and waited outside, leaning against the wall of a cottage which faced the entrance to the church tower. He twiddled his cap nervously between his fingers.

The Oxtons were the last family to emerge. Bert recognised big Jack Oxton, the farm manager at Gorse Field Hall, and following closely behind him was Alice. She skipped over to where he stood, unable to hide the radiant smile which beamed her pleasure at seeing him.

"You look happy," Bert observed, gripping his cap so tightly that his knuckles almost bust through his skin. He could barely keep his feet still.

"I didn't think you'd come. I was looking for you, but I didn't see you in there."

"People like me should be invisible in those places."

Jack Oxton spotted them talking. Although engaged in a conversation of his own with another member of the congregation, he made sure that his gaze monitored proceedings. As soon as he was able to make his excuses, he walked stiffly across to where Alice and Bert stood.

"Well, if it in't Old Oak Farm's match-winner… in the flesh."

Bert and Jack met eyes and shook hands.

"I've never seen you 'ere before." Oxton was blunt and to the point, eying Bert with some suspicion.

"No… I don't usually come here, to this church that is, Mr. Oxton," he felt like he needed to offer more of an explanation, "But I'm working up at the farm this afternoon, helping to fix one of the wagons. I thought this is as good as place as any to hear the word of God on a Sunday morning."

As he spoke, his eyes sought out Alice's and she pressed her lips tightly together so that they would not betray a smile.

"I see," mumbled Oxton, not able to conceal his doubt.

"Uncle Jack… can Bert walk back with us?" asked Alice.

"Hmm... happen he can, it's not out of 'is way back to Old Oak after all, is it?"

As the family meandered along the lane that cut through the pastures north of the village, Bert and Alice lingered at the back, deep in discussion. The occasional voluble giggle was returned with a sharp glance from the watchful eyes of her uncle, who was leading the group from the front. When they reached the canal bridge, Oxton stopped and waited for the couple to catch up.

"Alice, your aunt Jane needs a moment of your time... run on ahead."

Alice glanced nervously at Bert and did as she was told.

"Mr. Kingdom... I'll cut to the point. I'd like to know your intentions with regard to our Alice."

"Intentions? We've only just met."

"So, is it your intention to see her again?"

Bert nodded slowly.

"I like her company I suppose".

"I thought as much. Look 'ere... Alice is a good girl... you may know that she's my brother's lass. He were a wayward sort and he came to a sticky end. After it 'appened, I made a promise to myself that I wouldn't let her go the same way. I want only the best for 'is daughter... do you understand me?"

Bert indicated that he did.

"Are you a wayward sort, Mr. Kingdom?"

"No... no, I'm not wayward."

"Do you work hard?"

"Yes Sir, I do."

"Well you certainly put some bloody effort into that football match. Have you any prospects though, Mr. Kingdom?"

"I've been promised the head wagoner's job when Dick Wigley retires."

"Well that's a start... but I hope you've got your 'ead set on summat more than that in the fullness of time. You need to make the most of the life you've got ahead of you. Do you believe in God, Mr. Kingdom?"

Bert nodded. Oxton stared down at him through narrowed inquisitional eyes,

"Well, I expect we'll see how things go. The track forks just over the bridge, you can tek your leave of us there. The path'll tek you up to Old Oak right enough."

"Yes, I know it. Thank you for letting me walk wi' you and your family."

Oxton nodded the briefest of acknowledgements.

"I'll fetch Alice back over... then you can mek arrangements, if you want."

After the Church picnic the following Sunday, Bert saw Alice as often as he could. This usually meant that he walked home via Gorse Field Hall after work. Sometimes the lateness of the evening meant that they had only a few precious minutes to chat, but it was always done under the watchful eyes of Jack and Jane Oxton. Bert also became a regular churchgoer at Wollaton. Eventually he was invited back with the Oxtons for lunch, and afterwards he and Alice walked together unchaperoned in the fields behind the farmhouse. They held hands for the first time but, by then, it felt like a natural thing to do anyway.

Every Sunday afternoon they walked in the woods near Strelley, where they sometimes they would play hide and seek or pretend to be trees themselves. On occasion, in the fields around Bilborough, they would lie on their backs looking up at the sky, trying to feel the earth moving through the heavens. Often, as they talked, their lips came within a breath of meeting, but it was Alice who pulled back, even though it was like fighting back the force of a powerful magnet, her heart beating heavily with the effort. Being in love, thought Bert, was like the careless elation of freewheeling on a bicycle down a very steep hill. And this was a ride that he didn't want to end.

***

As the indolent summer transformed into to an industrious Autumn, the Oxtons hosted their annual farm-workers dance. Bert's ticket to the party came courtesy of his standing as Alice's young man. It was a ticket that now extended to most of the Oxton family gatherings.

At the outset the dance was a polite affair. Couples promenaded to the sweet airs and gentle rhythms coaxed from a couple of fiddles, a banjo and a dilapidated upright piano, by an unlikely looking quartet of whiskered musicians, who seemingly managed to both play and sup their ale at the same time without missing a beat. Occasionally, someone would join them to sing *An Ode to Burton Ale*, or the *Maiden of Bashful Fifteen*. Then Jack and Jane Oxton took their leave and, as everybody joined in with a chorus of *The Foggy, Foggy Dew*, the festivities really got underway.

Bert and Alice stepped outside for some air. He slipped his jacket over her rose-coloured blouse and she took both of his hands in hers. Their hands were clasped in silence for a few minutes before Alice whispered softly into Bert's ear, her misty breath cutting through the Autumn chill and warming the side of his face,

"I will let you kiss me now... if you want to."

The moment was disturbed by a loud crash behind them as young George Pike staggered out into the yard. He wobbled unsteadily in front of them.

"Look at you two lovebirds! We know what you're up to...," he slurred, "I won't tell your Uncle Jack... don't fret."

Then he threw up.

"George Pike! Why are you even here?" demanded Alice, stifling her anger as best she could.

Bert held up a hand.

"My fault. Sorry. He was small enough to smuggle in."

"Come on," instructed Alice, gripping Bert's arm and pulling him away, "let's go somewhere warmer... and quieter!"

She pointedly addressed her final two words in the direction of the figure slumped on the cobbles at her feet.

Alice led Bert to the rear door of the house. Holding a finger to her lips, she carefully opened it, stopping to listen intently at intervals as she did so.

"Shhh!"

"Careful Alice. What if your Uncle Jack is still up and about?" Bert whispered. He felt like a trespasser and the prospect of running into Jack Oxton didn't bear thinking about at all.

"Stop whittling, he won't be... did you see how much ale he was knocking back? It dun't take much to see him off."

Once the door had been closed gingerly behind them, Alice led Bert into the parlour. They stood, momentarily hesitant, in front of the fireplace, where the dampened embers still crackled and glowed in the hearth.

"Now, we can be alone."

She dropped Bert's jacket from her shoulders. They kissed.

"I love you," said Alice as their lips finally parted, "so, so much."

Before Bert could respond she kissed him again. The kiss lingered.

"I think I must be dreamin'," said Bert, fighting to speak between kisses, "you're the best thing ever Alice…"

He touched her dark hair and the soft skin of her face, and then his hands dropped to trace the shape and feel the warmth of her body. He could feel her breasts pressed against him and, he imagined, he could sense her beating heart. He liked how her breathing became more rapid as his hands traced the contours of her side, down over the roughly pulled-up hem of her fluted skirt, to the top of her legs. They slipped behind her, and his fingers followed the curve of her back from her hips up to her shoulders. The kissing became more intense, wetter, and her breathing had turned into subdued moans and unintelligible whispered words of pleasure.

Bert's fingers reached her shoulders and their voyage of discovery continued as they caressed a line around her neck, until they came upon the end of a silk ribbon protruding from underneath her collar. They gently pulled it until it became loose and could be discarded with a gentle flick of the wrist. Then, finding the first in a row of embroidered buttons, they unfastened it, before moving on to the next.

Alice suddenly pulled her mouth away from his and she looked deep into his eyes, almost questioningly, but without focus, as if she had fallen into a trance. Her wet lips quivered, wanting to speak, but instead they pressed back upon his.

The buttons were proving fiddly, so Bert dropped his hands down to the top of Alice's skirt. He found a buckle, which came undone surprisingly easily. His hand had come to rest on the warm, soft, flesh of her belly. Gravity led him irresistibly downwards to the top of her panties. It seemed as if they both had stopped breathing as he slipped a finger between her skin and the elasticated band. Beneath it, something soft brushed against his fingertip and he froze.

Alice regained her breath and let out a stifled squeal. His face dropped until it rested against her hot, salty, neck. She offered no protest and, once he was sure that the silent permission had been granted, he pushed on, until his finger became wet and she squealed again. This time she inhaled deeply and pulled herself away. As she backed off, her gaze locked onto his, he could see tears trickling from her eyes.

"No Bert, I can't... not here".

Feelings of exhilaration, disappointment and shame crashed together in waves to pump Bert's heart almost beyond what it was capable of. He felt unsteady on his feet and very, very hot. Then Alice's cool hand took hold of his and led him gently towards the door.

***

"Oh my God! What have we done... what on earth have we done?"

Alice shook Bert awake. She spoke in strained whispers. Panic was etched into her face and tears were beginning to well in her eyes.

For a moment as Bert emerged from his slumber, he thought he was in his own bed and then, after a few seconds of confusion, shameful realisation struck. He lay on the floor of Alice's bedroom, his head resting on a cushion. He was clothed in only his shirt and socks. Alice was in her nightgown and had a blanket pulled tightly around her. He checked the insistently ticking clock which hung on the wall. Quarter past five.

"Uncle Jack will be up," said Alice her panic rising even more.

Bert thought quickly, adrenalin beginning to feed his senses.

"I'll slip out through the window... I can get across to Old Oak easily enough from here."

He eased himself to his feet and dressed himself. His throat was sore, and his heart was racing. Tiredness separated his mind from his body. He tried to understand why he was there. Flashes of memory pulsed in time with his headache. His recollection of the previous night was a hazy and fractured dream, but there was no time to linger whilst connecting the pieces together. The dream had just turned into a nightmare. He pushed up the lower window carefully and quietly, before surveying what lay outside. The bedroom was at the gable end of the house. Below the window there was an adjoining outbuilding used for storing wood. He could see the pitched roof clearly enough in the pre-dawn moonlight. He worked out that if he hung from the brick window-ledge it probably wouldn't be too much of a drop onto the tiles below. He just hoped that the roof was strong enough to take his weight... and that he could land quietly.

"I'm scared," said Alice feebly, "... I don't want to lose you now. Be careful won't you Bert?"

"I will," he kissed her on the forehead. "I'll leave it a couple of days before coming over again, just in case. If you need me, just send a message over to Old Oak and I'll be here."

She nodded.

Bert pulled himself up onto the window-ledge and carefully manoeuvred his body so that his legs went out first. Running his feet down the bricks on the outside wall until he was hanging, he gripped tightly onto the window frame. As he looked up he could see Alice, fearful and watery-eyed, with an anxious hand covering her mouth. Then he looked down to his target and let go.

His body caught the wall as he dropped, causing him to spin round. He stifled a cry as he hit the wood-store tiles back first, before rolling down the length of the roof. His fingers clawed frantically at the tiles, but they couldn't get any traction and he slipped off the edge. His fall was fortuitously broken by a large pile of twigs and branches shorn from the trees around the farm the previous day. He lay for a moment gathering his breath and to make sure that he'd suffered no serious damage. He wrestled himself free of the prickly twigs and found his way to the solid ground. As he edged rearwards, Alice's bedroom came back into view and he could just about make out her shape through the still open window. He waved and imagined that the shape waved back to him, then he turned and walked swiftly away from the house. Somewhere nearby a dog barked and so he quickened his step. He couldn't see that the shape in the window was sobbing.

True to his promise, Bert stayed away from Alice for a few days. When he braved Gorse Field Farm again, they resumed their courtship as if nothing had ever happened. There was no hint at all that Jack Oxton had any suspicions about Bert and Alice's behaviour, but they knew that it had been a close call and they conducted themselves impeccably from that moment on.

They saw little of each other over Christmas; the Oxtons had travelled to visit a dying family member in the north. Then, a couple of weeks into the new year, a cold snap began, and the frost arrived and took hold. The ground was hard and there was little for the wagoners to do at Old Oak Farm. Joel Cooper, the farm manager, told Dick Wigley, George Pike and Bert that they should stay home until the ground thawed. If it went on for more than a few days, he told them, then he'd be happy if they managed to pick up work elsewhere to tide them over.

After a couple of days with no news, Bert contemplated asking Jack Oxton there was any work available at Gorse Field, but he always trod carefully with Alice's uncle, feeling that he had not yet been wholeheartedly accepted as a suitor for their niece. He made up his mind to wait a few more days, to see what came up.

Wednesday was wash-day. Whilst Bert was making himself useful by cleaning up Tom's old bicycle in the back yard, Edie Morton had just finished washing clothes in the dolly tub and had begun to run them through the mangle. Edie had taken in her younger brother when he moved to Nottingham from their home village of Calverton. She and Tom had no children and, with her mother dead and father estranged, they had assumed the role of Bert's parents for all practical purposes. There was a loud knock on the front door.

"Hold your 'osses," Edie called out in response, "you could knock a bit quieter; I'm coming as fast as I can."

She unfastened her apron and went through the motions of tidying her hair, glancing, as she passed, at her reflection in the mirror. The knocking continued insistently. She pulled open the door.

"Is that commotion really necessary?"

"Mrs. Kingdom?" queried the shorter of the two men revealed to her by the opened door.

"No, I'm Mrs. Morton... but I used to be Miss Kingdom five or six years back."

"My apologies Mrs. Morton, and good morning to you. Then you must be Bert's sister?"

She nodded.

"Joel Cooper madam... I'm the manager up at Old Oak Farm."

He gestured to the taller and more serious looking man standing behind him.

"And this is Mr. Oxton, who manages the farm at Gorse Field Hall."

Oxton tipped his hat but the scowl on his face didn't diminish. Edie's expression remained unchanged.

"So, what's our Bert been up to then that brings you two to my front door?"

"I wonder if we could trouble you to let us come into the house, Mrs. Morton... we have a rather delicate matter to discuss," Cooper suggested.

Edie invited them in. She glowered at them as they took seats in the front room, before calling for Bert. As he entered the room, still wiping the oil from his hands on a piece of rag, an icy chill ran through his body as he set eyes on Oxton.

"What can I do for you gentlemen?"

Bert was praying in his head that this was a business visit, although he could sense that it wasn't. Oxton rose up from his seat.

"If your sister weren't present in this room, lad… well, I'd tek you outside and knock six bells out of you."

His rage was barely contained.

"What's this about?" pleaded Edie.

"It's about Alice in't it?" asked Bert.

"Your young lady?"

Bert nodded.

Oxton's face began to turn mauve.

"Your bloody 'young lady' indeed! Why you… you villainous scoundrel."

He took a step towards Bert, but Cooper leapt up and blocked his path, pushing his hands against the taller man's shoulders. Edie moved over and put her arms around Bert.

"Let me handle this Jack, you're in no state," said Cooper. He looked to the ceiling and then scratched his head.

"Bert, you're a good lad, I know that… I look upon you like one of my own family," he paced over to the wall and back. "There's no easy way of saying this... but Alice is in the family way."

Edie gave out a muffled yelp and Bert grabbed her hand tightly.

"Don't deny that it's your doin' lad," raged Oxton.

He extended a bony finger in Jack's direction, his mouth forming words that he couldn't speak, before dropping back down to his seat and letting his head fall into in his hands.

"My house is such a place of upset that I can't bear it," he croaked from between his fingers.

"I don't deny it Mr. Oxton... and, believe me, I'll do right by Alice," Bert announced stoically.

Calm slowly descended upon the room and no words were uttered for several minutes, until Oxton spoke quietly.

"Mrs. Morton, I'm sorry that you had to witness my rough behaviour just now, and in your own home an' all."

"No apology is needed Mr. Oxton, the upset is quite understandable."

"Can I request that I entreat with you to make the arrangements, as the boy's father is not present?"

"Arrangements?"

"Aye... for a weddin'." His eyes shifted towards Bert. "You've no choices left laddie."

Tears started to roll down Edie's face.

"Oh, Bert! Lord 'elp us, what have you done?"

She turned back to face Oxton and wiped her eyes.

"Mr. Oxton, you can be sure that we will do everything necessary."

Bert offered his sister an awkward smile.

"Gentlemen," Edie continued, "I think we're all about ready for a cup of tea, don't you?"

Chapter 7.

England: 1914.

A heavy shower was enough to render Shakespeare Street completely deserted. Its passing left the heavens patterned with fast-flowing grey clouds and still blue sky in equal measure. Beneath the dying squall two figures emerged tentatively from the entrance of the Nottingham Parish Guardian's office. They had been to see another occupant of the well-appointed red-bricked building: The Superintendent Registrar. Their eyes were fixed only upon each other as they descended arm-in-arm to the base of its rain-washed stone steps.

"So then, what do we do now?" asked Alice, leaning forward to settle her nose against that of her new husband.

"Tek your ring off, duck," Bert demanded mock-seriously.

"But we've only just wed!"

"Come on duck, you did promise to obey me in there."

"I didn't."

Bert raised a querying eyebrow.

"Oh, alright then if I must! Nobody told me that husbands could be this bossy... I thought that was my job."

Alice pulled the ring from her finger and held it up in front of Bert's face with a defiant glare. He removed his own ring and lifted it up so that it hovered in the air alongside Alice's.

"Look inside."

She did as she was told, her mouth and eyes widening together as she read the words engraved inside the nine-carat gold band.

"Oh Bert... you didn't tell me you were going to have something written in it."

"Read it out then girl."

"Your heart is my Kingdom!"

Alice spoke the words with theatrical exaggeration, whilst fluttering her eyelids. They fell into an embrace and kissed.

"Oh Bert! It's beautiful... it's like poetry!"

"I did both of em' the same. That means that, whenever we're apart, you'll be able to look at them words and know that you have my heart and I yours. Sometimes it's quite handy having a surname like mine!"

Edie and Tom appeared from the pilaster-framed doorway behind them.

"Look at you two lovebirds. Do you remember when we were like that Tom?"

Tom looked to the sky.

"I don't know about that love, but I reckon that rain'll be back sharpish."

"Well, in that case, we'd better get you two sweethearts' home... I'm ready for a nice cup of tea and some cake anyway."

"Perfect," agreed Bert.

The four of them linked arms as they crossed the street, walking in the direction of the city centre and home. Around them the raindrops became fatter and started to quicken, just as Tom had predicted. Alice squealed and giggled as the deluge resumed, forcing them to break into a run. Already drenched, they found shelter under the ornate portico of the Guildhall and stayed there until the cloudburst subsided. They were unknowingly watched from above by the benevolent ashlar eyes of Equity and Justice. Under their protection, in that moment, and even beneath the passing storm, the world was indeed quite perfect.

***

The Man Who Found Treasure

Before the month was out Bert had been promoted to head wagoner, meaning that he and Alice could afford to move out of their cramped bedroom at Edie and Tom's. They rented a two-up, two-down terraced house, which stood a couple of doors away from the Morton's home. After the hectic and exciting few weeks between their wedding and finding their own place to live, their world became a closeted one, bounded by what was close to home. The tensions that had begun to invade the world around them, borne on the echo of gunshots from afar, largely passed them by. Neither were they dismayed by the dark clouds that ushered in the first day of August, for Alice was finally ready for her confinement and the colour of the skies was merely a backdrop to the enormity of events that were taking place inside their little house.

With their focus narrowed, Edie took charge of the household and supervised arrangements. She recruited a neighbour, Mrs. MacDonald, and her friend, Florrie Atkins, to help. Bert was sent up to Gorse Field Farm to fetch Jane Oxton. Upon their return, however, they found Edie standing guard at the front door and, letting only Mrs. Oxton pass, she turned Bert away.

"Get yersen off up to the Queen's my love... we'll send word when the time comes," she ordered, clasping a hand onto each of his shoulders and planting a peck on his cheek.

"Will it be long?" asked Bert, as fear began to shiver through his body.

"Mrs. Mac says it's happening quick enough for a first 'un," Edie replied with a wink of her eye and the hint of a smile. "Don't forget, I'm not used to this lark either."

The night was muggy and feathery drizzle hovered in the air. Bert walked the long way around, weaving through the humid streets of The Meadows, his excited mind unable to settle. Eventually, wet through, he found himself at the Queen's Hotel where he secured a resting place at the bar.

"Pint o' mild please, Arthur," he said to the man behind the counter.

"You look like you've been for a swim in the Trent lad."

"I might as well 'ave been, me head's all over the place."

"Trouble with the young lady?"

"You could say that, Arthur. My 'young lady', as you call 'er, is just about to 'ave our first kid!"

"Well, in that case, you're in the best place. There you are… get in early to wet the young un's head, that's what I say. Sup up!"

He pushed a pint of mild across the bar before continuing.

"You're Tom Morton's brother-in-law, aren't you?"

Bert nodded.

"I didn't know you'd been hitched?"

"It was what they call a 'whirlwind courtship'," Bert chuckled.

As the night wore on, more and more pints were supped. Bert didn't have to pay for most of them, as his story was passed from table to table in the bar room. Then a territorial soldier of the Robin Hood Rifles came in. Voices became hushed and the talk turned quickly to war.

"I need this bugger," the soldier said, downing his pint in one, "I've just got back from a day trip to Skeg with the missus n' kids and, blow me, if there in't a note waitin' for me when I get back tellin' me I've been called up to join the bloody regiment! They're up in Hunmanby playin' at fightin'. I'm off to catch the train now. So much for my bloody Bank Holiday weekend."

"You reckon it'll be war for real then? It doesn't sound good… well not if you read the papers. The lace factories are having orders cancelled from Europe, and the churches are praying for peace already. And now you're saying you've been called up!"

Arthur pushed a copy of the Nottingham Evening Post across the bar towards the soldier.

"I reckon they'll sort it out… I mean, who wants a war anyway? The King don't want to be fighting his bloody cousins does he?"

"God, I hope that you're right," said Bert.

Arthur bent his head in Bert's direction,

"You can forgive him that face… he's just about to become a father."

The soldier slapped Bert hard on the back.

"Don't worry mate, it's only a spat… politics, it 'appens all the time! Congratulations though, have one on me…"

"No lad," said Arthur, "these two are on me… just in case you're wrong."

The Man Who Found Treasure

Upon Arthur's call of last orders, Bert tottered unsteadily out into the night. As he got within a couple of streets of home, he saw a familiar figure striding swiftly towards him. He did a doubletake, to make sure that the alcohol wasn't playing tricks on him.

"Edie?" he called out.

Sobering up quickly, he ran to meet her and was relieved to see a huge smile on her face. She smothered him within an enthusiastic embrace.

"Do you want to know?" She asked.

"Course I bloody do... tell me."

"It's a boy, Bert... a beautiful little boy. He looks just like you did when you were born."

Bert crumpled into her neck.

"Now, now Bertie boy... you're supposed to be 'appy at a time like this." Edie stroked his head softly as she spoke.

"I am happy Edie... but..."

"But what?"

Bert didn't reply. A clap of thunder rolled across the sky and proper rain, at last, started to fall.

"Typical... in the middle of bloody summer too. Come on brother of mine, let's get you home."

***

Bert sat on the bed and looked at his son, cradled in the arms of the woman he loved. He'd never felt prouder or more sober.

"He's beautiful."

"Teks after his old man then, don't he?" Alice beamed.

"Have you thought on any names?"

"I quite like Walter, what do you think?"

"Well, if you quite like the name Walter... then Walter it is. Come to think of it he looks like a Walter," Bert gently rubbed his son's nose, "... you do, don't you?"

"Are you alright Bert?"

"Yes, why?"

"Edie said you seemed upset."

"It's nothing."

"It's this war talk in't it?"

Bert shrugged his shoulders.

"We'll be alright Bert, I know we will."

"I know it too," he stroked the baby's head, "and anyway. Even if there is a war, he won't have to fight in it will he?"

As clouds continued to hide the sun and a warm breeze blew through the streets, Alice and Bert braved the outside world for the first time with their new son. They pushed the pram down to the embankment, and then along the river, where they watched the bathers at the Trent Baths and ate sandwiches on the riverside steps.

"We might not be able to do this again on the Bank Holiday, for a while at least... if there's a war," said Bert.

"Don't say that," replied Alice with a frown. "Let's just enjoy it. It's Walter's first day out."

She leant across and planted a kiss on her husband's cheek. Bert looked around at the bathers, the boats on the river and at the other families who were picnicking, just like they were.

"Don't you think it's strange that everyone is enjoyin' themselves."

"What else can you do Bert?"

He shook his head.

"I don't know love... I really don't know."

The following day, back at the farm, Joel Cooper called Bert over to him.

"Look, the military were here yesterday taking details of our horses and machinery. You'd better make sure that the wagons are ship-shape, just in case."

"You'll have no problems there Joel."

The atmosphere amongst the men at Old Oak was subdued. Bert worked later than usual, doing as Joel had asked. As he walked home, he became aware that there were more people than usual on the streets, some with serious faces and others seemingly more excited. It was dusk as he passed the Queen's Hotel. He felt uneasy again. There was a group of men that he knew standing outside talking. As he passed, one of them shouted out to him.

"Bert... wait on. Have you heard the news?"

"No."

"We've issued an ultimatum to Germany. If they don't back away from Belgium before eleven tonight... well, we'll be at war right enough."

"So, it's finally 'appened. Bloody politicians."

"We're going into town now... up to the Express, or maybe the Guildhall to see what's cookin'... are you comin' wi' us?"

Bert shook his head, "No, I don't think so. I need to be with me wife and baby tonight."

The man nodded.

Alice was oblivious to the drama unfolding in the world outside as the clock ticked past eleven. As she slept, Bert stood by the window, rocking Walter in his arms whilst observing the street below. The beam of a streetlamp angled across the dark of the room. Suddenly, the number of bodies who were milling about outside began to grow, there were cheers and the general hubbub became louder. Some people began singing the national anthem.

"That's it then mate, war it is."

Bert sighed and kissed the baby's head.

"Not that you'll know much about it, you lucky little bugger."

As rising apprehension stiffened his body and quickened the beat of his heart, he sought comfort in the soft warmth of his infant son and in the scent of the child's hair and skin. His senses became amplified and, as he gently tightened his embrace, Bert knew that he needed to imprint that moment... those sensations... deep into his memory.

"What's the point in being here?" Bert asked Stan Cooper as they stood in the courtyard of Old Oak Farm the following day.

Stan was sitting on the edge of a stone trough wrestling with a newspaper which was being unfolded and tugged by the light breeze.

"Life has to go on Bert. Look... it says, *'Your King and Country Needs You'... 'Will you answer your country's call'*?"

"I know what it says, Stan. It also says it's looking for unmarried men... so that counts me out."

"But not me and George."

"George is only seventeen!"

"He'll be eighteen in a few weeks. I talked to Joel about it and he wants me to stay here, he says he can't run the farm without me, especially now. That's important to the country too in't it?"

"I suppose so... and anyway it'll probably all be over before too long."

"I hope so... what does Alice say?"

"She doesn't say anything. She's blocked it out... it's like the war in't 'appening at all. She dun't like bad stuff like that."

Bert had been considering his options. As August passed by, several of his neighbours had joined the ranks; others were talking about doing so. He knew he needed to do something. It was clear what was expected of him, but when he broached it with Alice, she changed the subject or blanked him completely. Their first argument of any substance happened when he pushed her on the subject, and she snapped back.

"Don't you understand... I don't want to talk about it. I *can't* talk about it."

"Well who the bloody 'ell can I talk to about it then?"

"Go and talk to your sister."

He stormed over to the Queen's where similar agonies were being felt by other men. He could talk to Edie and Tom, and they had listened to him on many occasions, but their advice was always the same,

"Just do what you think best and we'll support you lad."

As August became September, Bert and George were harnessing one of the wagons in the stable yard when Stan sprinted in; running so fast that he lost his footing and went sprawling across the floor. It didn't perturb him though and he was breathy and excited.

"Bert... George, there's a soldier riding up the track!"

As he spoke, they heard the lazy clip-clop of equine hooves and then a man in uniform, on horseback, appeared in the yard.

"Good day to you men!" he exclaimed and saluted.

They greeted him back. Joel Cooper, who had been watching from the front window, came running across from the house.

"Can I help you Sergeant?"

"I'm sure that you can sir. I'm here to tell you that a great opportunity awaits to serve your king, country and the empire, we need men just like you... why don't you come and join us today and help put an end to this war?"

It was a well-practiced speech.

"I'm sorry sergeant, but I can't spare any of them."

"But surely you can, sir... for the defence of your country?"

"But the country needs to eat too?"

"Would you rather your country was hungry and free, or well fed and under the yoke of the hun? The young men can best serve in the line... there are many others who can tend to your cattle. Think of the question Mr. Kipling posed, sir... *What stands if Freedom fall? Who dies if England live?*"

"Are you a Sherwood Forester, sir?" asked George.

"No laddie... I'm a sergeant of the Northumberland Fusiliers. We are recruiting in Nottingham today and then off to camp in the south."

"Why are you recruiting here?" asked Joel Cooper.

"Ah! ... because experience tells us that the fittest, bravest men work on the farms... and we need the fittest, bravest men. Are you with me lads?"

"Yes... I am."

George Pike jumped down from the wagon.

"Good lad! I've got a cart down at the farm gates with some other stout fellows aboard, they'll be glad of your company."

The sergeant turned back to Stan and Bert,

"What do you say lads? Will you be bested by your young friend?"

"No... I'm with you sergeant," Stan answered.

As he spoke, he looked across to his brother, who stood open mouthed.

"Will you speak to mother for me Joey?"

Joel heaved a resigned sigh and then nodded reluctantly,

"Yes Stan, I will, but come back in one piece for God's sake."

"What about you sir?" the soldier addressed Bert.

"I'm a married man Sergeant... and I've just had a kid."

"So am I son... and I have three kiddies myself. In my experience married men make the best fighters, they don't take silly risks... they're more mature I reckon. NCO material a lot of 'em. You look the part, come on and join us."

"I need to speak to me wife."

"Once you've signed up, you'll have a few of hours to square things with the good lady... I'm sure she'll be as proud as punch."

Joel Cooper grabbed Bert's arm.

"Bert, don't do this," he implored.

"As someone else once said to me Joel... I have no choices left."

Bert, George and Stan marched behind the horse as the soldier turned and trotted off slowly back down the track. Joel Cooper pulled himself up on the seat of the wagon and turned his face skyward, before throwing his cap angrily onto the floor of the yard.

"Sergeant... will we be goin' back up north?" asked George.

"We might."

"I've never gone any further away than Nottingham. Will we be able to go and see Newcastle United play?"

"Wait and see laddie... you never know."

The sergeant led them to the end of the track where a long horse-drawn wagon awaited. A handful of other men were already aboard. By the time, two hours later, that it trundled to a stop outside the Territorial Drill-Hall on Derby Road in Nottingham, it unloaded thirteen passengers in total.

"Join the queue lads," called the sergeant, "and remember that you're Northumberland lads now."

The queue snaked out of the archway at the centre of the buildings' grand stone facade and out onto the street. It contained mostly young men of all shapes and sizes. Some were hopping about or chattering excitedly, others were pale and quiet. The column moved slowly. Once consumed by the archway, it shuffled into a small courtyard and through a doorway which led into a dimly lit room. Inside it the nascent warriors were ordered to strip off their clothes. Their height and weight was measured by a stony-faced military doctor, who then listened to their chests and recorded its expansion without comment. Next, he donned a pair of cotton gloves, slipped his hand between their legs and asked them to,

"Turn away and cough please."

Then, finally, their eyesight was examined.

A few of the lads were gathered to one side and told that they couldn't be taken on. A couple more were referred for further treatment of medical conditions that had been uncovered, but Bert, George and Stan were given the news that they had been passed fit for service. They barely had the chance to put their clothes back on before a well-worn bible was thrust into their hands by a gruff sergeant. A white-haired officer with a tired expression and only one arm then asked them to,

"Repeat after me gentlemen..."

The group cleared their throats and repeated the words as instructed.

"I... speak your name... do make oath, that I will be faithful and bear true allegiance to His Majesty King George the fifth, his heirs, and successors, and that I will, as in duty bound, honestly and faithfully defend His Majesty, his heirs, and successors, in person, crown and dignity, against all enemies, and will observe and obey all orders of His Majesty, his heirs and successors, and of the generals and officers set over me. So help me God."

After being taken through the completion of the attestation form and some other paperwork, they were handed a shilling, and told to report to the recruiting office the following morning to pick up their travel warrant and further instructions. It was also made clear that they should be prepared for a long day of travelling. Once back outside, the three lads shook hands, slapped each other's backs and felt fleetingly both relieved and very pleased with themselves.

"I'm sorry boys, but after the doc had checked me credentials, he said that I should expect me first medal in the post... you know for havin' the biggest jigger," announced George.

Stan pretended to make a quizzical face and scratched his head, "Hmm... so why does everyone call you 'little' George?"

George pushed him hard in the back.

"And anyway... one of the other lads told me that the doc was checking for hernias," added Bert, immediately changing the mood.

"What do you reckon Mam'll say when I tell 'er I'm a soldier?" asked George, apprehension suddenly subduing his excitement.

"She'll be the proudest mam in Notts, I'm sure of it," Bert reassured him, ruffling the younger man's hair.

"At least you can tell her that you won't be fightin' overseas for a while... and you've signed up for the duration, so if it only lasts 'til Christmas, you'll be back home in no time."

George bowed his head ruefully,

"No, I can't say that Bert... I told 'em that I were nineteen. They gen me a bit of a funny look, like, but they believed what I told 'em."

"I'm not sure how you got away with that 'un, you only look about twelve, you daft bugger. You'd better not tell your mam that."

"We should get off, lads," said Stan quietly, "I'm not sure that Joel will be all that happy wi' me either. He might kick up a bit. I'll see you tomorrow Bert. Give Alice my love."

Bert nodded solemnly, knowing that he was just about to have the most difficult conversation of his life.

Bert closed the front door behind him as quietly as he could. Alice was in the kitchen whilst Walter was asleep in his cot in the living room.

"Hello love. I wasn't expecting you back this early," she said.

Bert's expression betrayed that he had something important to say, but he said nothing. Instead he took off his cap a walked across to Alice and hugged her tightly, kissing her a couple of times on the cheek.

"I love you girl."

She pushed him away,

"What is it? What's wrong?"

There was fear in her eyes and she lifted her hands to cover her face.

"No... no, don't tell me that you've signed up?"

Her voice quivered and broke. He went to hold her again, but she stepped aside.

"How could you! How could you! What about Walter, what about me?"

She fell to her knees and started to cry.

"How can you leave me now?"

Some water had been left on the stove and it began to boil over. Bert grabbed a towel before reaching across to lift the pan into the sink. He dampened the stove and then lifted Alice gently to her feet, pulling her shaking body close to his.

"Come on girl, let's sit you down."

He moved her over to the armchair and waited for the tears to subside. With her face now wet through, she attempted to repeat her plea between stuttering hiccoughs of shock, as her body convulsed again.

"How can you leave me now?"

"I'll be back soon love. They say it'll all be over by Christmas, don't they?"

He wiped her eyes and nose with a handkerchief.

"And what if it's not?" she panted.

"Then I'll be back as soon as I can... and soldiers get leave and things like that."

"And little Walter, *your son*, what about him?"

Her voice broke again.

"I'm doin' this for him don't you see? I'm doin' this so there's a future for him. When he's older and he asks me what I did when our country needed me... how could I answer him... how could I hold me head up proud if I didn't go?"

Alice shivered and said nothing. Walter stirred and she rose to her feet as if in a trance and picked him up, clutching him close to her body.

"Just come back to us. That's all," she croaked, wearily.

They spent a restless and wordless night, in turns holding each other tightly and tending to their baby. A chaotic myriad of thoughts, of all shades of dark and light, fought off any pretence of sleep. At the dawn, Bert gathered his things and packed a small haversack. He told Alice that he wanted to say his goodbyes before he left the house and not at the station. Edie and Tom joined them.

"Do your duty son. I wish I were two inches taller and didn't have a gammy leg, or else I'd be coming wi' you," his brother in law said, gripping Bert's arm firmly. Edie hugged him, pecked his cheek and smiled stoically. Holding the baby's tiny hand, Bert kissed his son's head.

"Look after your Mam Walter. You don't know it yet... but she's the most precious thing in the world. I want her ship shape and in one piece for when I get back."

As he and Alice hugged for a final time, he pressed his forehead hard against hers.

"We'll be together again soon my darling. It'll seem like two minutes, I bet it will. Remember the words you've got engraved in that ring."

Then he slipped through the front door out onto the street. As it closed behind him Edie enveloped Alice in her arms.

Bert strode purposefully into the city centre, up the hill to Derby Road and on to the Drill Hall. He was relieved to see Stan and George standing outside having a smoke before they went in. They greeted each other enthusiastically, as if they'd not seen each other for several years. Several groups of men were being lined up in the courtyard, some were already in full kit. A recruiting sergeant beckoned them over.

"You lads interested in the navy?" he asked.

"We signed up with the army yesterday," replied Bert.

"That's not a problem lad. Hear me out. There's a new army division just been formed called the Royal Naval Division. Some bright spark at the War Office realised that we've got all these Navy and Marine reservists knocking about who won't be use nor ornament... 'cos we won't be fightin' the hun on the sea. Get my drift?"

The lads nodded.

"So, they thought, 'let's get 'em in the army so they can fight on the land'. Now, here's the thing...," the sergeant leaned towards them and spoke in hushed tones as if it was a shared secret, "they'll be in the army for sure, but still subject to navy rules, rank and culture."

"Does that mean wearin' a sailor's uniform?" asked George.

"You got it lad... you're a smart 'un! Trouble is, they 'aven't got enough men, so they've asked us recruitin' sergeants to get some of you new lads over to 'em. So, what do think... do you fancy it?"

"What about the Northumberland Fusiliers?" asked Stan.

"Don't worry about them... I'll square that with the bigwigs and off you can go to London."

"London?" George's eyes brightened.

"That's right lad, the Crystal Palace no less!"

"I'll do it sergeant!" George replied.

"Good lad! What about your mates 'ere?"

Stan and Bert looked at each and shrugged their shoulders.

"He needs lookin' after," said Stan.

"That's just what I were thinkin'," agreed Bert.

"Your country is proud of you lads... come on then, let's get your travel warrants sorted out."

Bert, Stan and George joined the rear of another line of men in the courtyard, just moments before it marched out onto the street and in the direction of the station. As they paraded, passers-by wolf-whistled or applauded. Some shouted, "Good on you boys," or "Stick a bayonet up the Kaiser for me lads!"

To his surprise, Bert found himself enjoying it, and he regretted that Alice wasn't there to see him off.

"I can't wait to tell Walter about this," he said to Stan.

"No talking in the ranks!" yelled a voice from the front.

At the Midland Station the inceptive army was led down the stairs to the platform. The front group came to a sudden halt when their path was blocked by another line of men. The recruits at the rear collided with them, sending a few sprawling on the steps. Before he saw it for himself, Bert could hear and sense the chaos that had been let loose on the platforms. There were hundreds of newly recruited men, flag-waving wives and sweethearts and their children, jumbled together with all kinds of service personnel and whinnying horses. Hassled porters were fighting to manoeuvre tottering mountains of luggage, piled-up on rickety trolleys, through the constantly shifting throng. The stage upon which this drama was unfolding was sandwiched between steaming leviathans, which stood ready to eat-up the new recruits and ferry them on to their place in history. Patriotic songs floated in and out of the steamy air between the impatient hissing of the engines and blurry station announcements, which evaporated instantly in the noise and general pandemonium. Bert's brain reeled as it fought to follow the commands of the sergeant amid the confusion.

After a cramped and uncomfortable three-hour ride south, standing or sitting wherever they could, the men met equally chaotic scenes at St. Pancras station. They were led outside to omnibuses, which were lined up on the roadside, and then packed into their even more confined spaces. A short ride to London Bridge station followed, after which they were put on yet another train, this time to Penge. The final leg of their journey consisted of a short but, by now, weary march to the vast grounds that housed the Crystal Palace.

"Bloody hell!" exclaimed Bert, excitement briefly breaking through his exhaustion.

"I've never seen anything like it," added Stan.

"It's like a giant bird cage," George chirped.

Once rollcall was completed, the men were lined up outside the grand façade of the Canada Parliament Building, before being led to makeshift beds deep inside the great cast iron and glass pavilion itself. There was no welcoming party for them and only dry bread and water on the menu, but it didn't matter. The only thing on everybody's mind was sleep and, for most, unlike the night before, it came easily.

In the light of early evening on the following day, Bert sat on his bunk and surveyed the great structure that encased the tired and still bewildered men within it. It was almost too busy and intricate to look at for long. Instead he trained his eyes on the blank piece of paper resting on his knee. Slowly and carefully at first, trying not to press on too hard and rip the page, he began to scratch out words upon it with the stubby pencil he held between his fingers.

Crystal Palace,
London
10 September 1914

To my darling Alice and my little soldier Walter,

You will be surprised to find me in London at the Crystal Palace no less. What's more I'm in the navy now. I expect that this will be as much as a shock to you as it was to me. When I say I'm in the navy it don't mean that I'll be serving on a ship, because the Royal Naval Division is still part of the army, but this whole place is like being in a ship without any sea.

I'm all signed on now and you can tell Walter that I shall be getting my sailors uniform and rifle in a few days. When we first got here there was no food to eat other than bread and water, but today the Lyons tearoom have given us boiled eggs and bread and butter for breakfast and a roast beef dinner, it's not as good as yours or Edie's mind you. There are some apple trees next door still with a few nice big ones on the branches and me and George managed to sneak off and have our fill of them yesterday.

Today we are moving out of the big old palace into the Australia building which will be my new home. We slept on the floor at first but one of the petty officers said we will be slung in hammocks in the new place. They are putting flags all over the place too and we've been told we've got to salute them or face a charge. It takes some getting used to believe you me. Soon we will be sent on a training camp down south to turn us into real fighting men, but for now there is only square bashing and phissical jerks to do. We have lights out at ten o'clock.

I expect you think this all sounds very exiting, but it seems strange not having you my darling or little Walter at my side and I am missing you both more than I can tell you with only pencil and paper. I wish my words could truly say what I am feeling. You know that I do this for you both and for the country and it is for the best. I will send a photograph of me in my uniform as soon as I can if you promise not to laugh and make sport of it in front of Walter.

I am wishing away the days until I can see you and touch you both again. By the way this letter is being sent to you with the help of the YMCA who are also here doing laundry and such like.

Your ever-loving husband and daddy
YHIMK
Bert.

Chapter 8.

India: 1943.

Mam's reply to my letter eventually found its way to me after we had been taken out of the line for some rest and recuperation. This entailed a five-hour train journey up to Chittagong, steaming through the lush, deep green, wet carpet that made up the western edge of Burma. Mere words won't let me fully convey how much of a relief it was to be shipped so far away from the fighting. All of us visibly relaxed and I felt a gripping tightness, one that I hadn't even realised was afflicting me beforehand, fade away from my body.

The basha camp that was our new home was comparatively luxurious, so things looked promising all round. Amongst other things, we used the time in Chittagong to get down to the serious business of comparing the number of insect bites we each had. Slowcoach won the prize, partly down to a nasty looking abscess on his leg. It wasn't a popular victory though; the bugger had been moaning about how much his bites itched for the last couple of months. Still, despite the general air of relaxed informality, it was with more than a little trepidation that I opened that letter from home:

The Man Who Found Treasure

Nottingham, England,
20th August 1943.

My Dearest Walter,
I was so pleased to receive your recent letter and I am happy that you are safe and well. I hope that this letter finds you in that same state. Life here in Nottingham does not change much and Edie and Tom send their love and best wishes. We are still getting the odd air raid siren, but thankfully there's been nothing like the trouble we saw in '41.

But I do feel so far away from you my darling and I curse this horrible war - just as much as I did the last one.

I must say that the things you asked of me in your letter were unexpected. But I should not have been too surprised as I realise now that you deserve to know more than you do. Edie and I have talked about it and I now know that I have been selfish by not wanting to reopen my own painful wounds, not understanding how much I have wounded you in turn. I hope you can forgive me? I do have two or three photographs of your daddy, and some letters also, but I locked them away a long time ago - in more ways than one. If I can find them, I will send them to you as soon as I can.

I must thank you too, for forcing me look back to those years before the last war once again. Beyond the sadness I had forgotten that there are some treasured memories that were locked away as well. Now that these have been unlocked again I will try to keep them close always.

You know that I only knew your daddy for a very short time? It was not very long at all in fact, but I still loved him very much and I know that he loved me, and he doted on you so so much. He called you his little soldier and how true that has turned out to be.

I have never talked to you about it before and I am sorry for that - I don't know what Edie has told you about her brother. There is much for me to remember concerning the details, but the simple story is that I met your daddy the year before you were born, at a football match, and we fell in love and soon married after a whirlwind courtship. We were so happy together and then you were born and we were happier still. Then that wretched war came and your daddy never came back from it. There is little more to tell than that. It broke my heart and it is broken still.

Walter, you must know that you brought his light back into my life, which is why I was so frightened at the thought of you joining the army, especially when war broke out again. I don't need to tell you why I felt like that. As far as his service is concerned, I can tell you only that your daddy served with the Royal Naval Division, but I think you already know that. Of his death I know precious little and that is enough for me. I do not want to know any more. If I let more memories back in it will only ever be the good ones.

Please write again soon.
Your devoted
Mam

P.S. You will be sad to hear that Arthur Atkins has been killed in North Africa.

I was relieved that Mam had taken my questions in good heart, although there were many more of them left to be answered. Still, there was clearly a thaw in her attitude to re-opening the wounds of the past. The prospect of seeing a photograph of my dad for the first time filled me with a great deal of excitement, but it failed to dissipate the anger I still harboured from her locking so much away from me, for so long.

Eric, laying on his bed, had been watching me read the letter and had put up with my surliness for a while afterwards. He can't have failed to notice the tear that I wiped away as I read those words.

"How old are you Wally?" he asked eventually.

"Twenty-nine... thirty this coming summer."

"You're no spring chicken then, are you? How many years have you done in the army now?"

"I joined in thirty-five... I'd just turned twenty-one."

I was fully aware that Eric already knew the answers to his questions, so I wasn't quite sure where this chat was leading.

"Why did you do it?"

"Why did I do what?"

"Join the bloody army?"

I thought about my answer for a moment.

"To live up to up to the example set by my dad I s'pose, although I didn't have a clue what I was meant to be living up to. I know that I really wanted him to be proud of me though... wherever he is."

"And to piss off your mam a little bit too? For keeping you in the dark about your old man I mean?"

Eric's analysis didn't offend me, I was just surprised that he was able to read me so well.

"Piss her off? Maybe. To get away from her - you bet. Anyway... what's with the third degree?"

"Because your service will be up when the war's over won't it... whenever that happens. I've known you for a few years now, and I know you've got no ambition to climb up the ranks... you're still a fuckin' private for Christ-sakes! And Smitty did let slip that you've been offered a stripe before and refused it."

"He can never hold his tongue that one, which is bloody useless for a corporal."

"I've seen the stuff you write for the regimental rag, and that script you're putting together for the Boxing Day concert ... it's good... very good, but don't let that go to your head."

"Well you would say that, wouldn't you? ... You're a mate."

"It's not just me Wal', everyone says it's good."

Eric turned himself round to sit facing me directly.

"I know you're not asking for my opinion... but I think you need to get shut of the bloody army at the first chance you 'ave, go off and marry Dinah, God knows she's been hanging on long enough... and get yourself a proper bleedin' job. All this moping around don't do anybody no good... least of all a soldier."

"Thank you, Uncle Eric! Your advice has been duly noted... not that I've got much of a choice about it while this bloody war's on."

Eric then dropped another bombshell.

"Smitty wants to put me up for a stripe."

"And?"

"And I said yes. You don't mind then Wally?"

I picked up a fag packet and threw it at him, catching him square on the forehead.

"No, of course I don't bloody mind... Lance Corporal bloody Newton."

***

The letter, and the conversation with Eric, stirred up more fragments of long-dormant memories. As I dozed off that evening my mind travelled back to a chilly autumn day standing on the empty grey platform of the Victoria Station in Nottingham. I was shivering like a baby and fully kitted out for my new life in the army; pink-cheeked and well-scrubbed behind the ears, as Edie used to say. Any conviction I might have had about being single-handedly ready to save the Empire was exposed for all to see as the sham that it was. I felt, and must have appeared even more so, small - weighed down by my pack, and a uniform that looked like it was wearing me.

Edie was there of course, and so was Dinah. She blubbered away like it was my bloody funeral. Her magnificent friend, Elizabeth, stood beside her, somehow managing to look radiant through the greyness. How she managed this with Dinah clinging grimly onto her arm I don't know, but then again, radiance was a particular talent of hers.

To my surprise and private relief, Mam came to see me off too. I wondered, and I wonder still, if she knew how much I needed her there, despite everything. Beforehand, she had been fiercely adamant that she didn't want to come. I went along with that position quite happily and feigned indifference. After all, it was only to be expected given the coolness that had long existed between us. In the end, Edie had virtually dragged her along.

On the day I had told Mam that I wanted to sign up with the army, she seemed to sink into a dark place of her own inhabiting. She barely spoke to me, or even acknowledged my existence for a few weeks afterwards, hiding away inside the house, as if she had joined forces with the shadows to wrestle with some unseen foe of her own. By then, though, our relationship had been difficult for while... ever since I had started asking serious questions about Dad.

I'd got by as a kid without too much trouble, by creating an image of Dad as the man who'd won The War all on his own. Other boys seemed impressed that my dad was killed in action, and it carried a kind of kudos with them, and pitiful looks from other adults. It also elicited maximum sympathy from girls, and I milked that as much as possible. My imagination was bursting with invented stories of heroics, hun-bashing and other acts of his derring do, some of which I still find myself thinking about even now... often to the point where I can't easily separate fact from reality. But, eventually, as I became older... well then, I just wanted to know the truth. Why wasn't he here, and not just in the flesh? It was like he'd never existed.

There were no photographs anywhere in the house, no medals, no letters from overseas and nobody ever talked about him either. All Edie and Tom could tell me was that he was a good man, and Edie was happy to regale me with hundreds of stories about what they got up to as kids; but never in Mam's presence. Edie said that, other than knowing that he was a marine and that he had died in the Dardanelles, she could tell me very little about his war. It wasn't enough for me.

Whenever I tried to start a conversation with Mam about it, she became sullen and changed the subject, or left the room. The whole thing soon became a no-go area. Me joining the army just made it worse. Whatever demons she was battling with... well, she kept them to herself. Locked behind the doors that she always made a point of firmly shutting. It got to the point where I was seething with resentment and I took it out on her.

I didn't feel any guilt about my feelings at first. By the time I joined up home had become nothing more than a prison to me. The army offered freedom, with the added beauty of allowing me to follow in Dad's footsteps. I was very well aware of what that would have meant to Mam.

But things changed when I saw Mam's face that morning at the station; stoic and tearless, teeth-gritted, but with her eyes betraying something else too... fear. I know that now, I've seen it in on plenty of other faces since. Fear can sit deep in a person and it did with Mam. When war broke out in thirty-nine whilst I was in India, my guilt sunk to new levels. It has never left me to this day.

***

Christmas in Chittagong came and went. For a short time, any thoughts I had about Johnson or Dad drifted into the background, behind other occupations. My script for the Boxing Day concert, which I helped direct from the wings, went down surprisingly well. It wasn't anywhere near ENSA standard of course and looking back now I know that it wasn't much of a concert either, but it did the job of adding a bit of joy, or something akin to it, back into our lives, before our inevitable return to action.

The tunes remain in my head now as a faded soundtrack to the memory of it. From what little I recall the show was built around the story of a mermaid who washed up on a beach in the Bay of Bengal. She falls in love with her rescuer, a British army sergeant major. When he goes off to fight, she unleashes her magical powers to keep him safe, with the help of a friendly tiger. I'm not sure where I dragged up that rubbish from, but it gave plenty of opportunity for a multitude of japes, singsongs and cross-dressing... the staple of any concert party. Slowcoach brought the house down, in drag as the mermaid, singing 'Moonlight Becomes You' as a duet with the tiger. We finished the show with a bit of audience participation, everyone linking arms to sing a rousing re-worded version of 'As Time Goes By' together.

"You must remember thish, a fish is just a fish, a guy is just a guy, we'll meet again in old Rangoon, as time goes by..."

I can't imagine old Herman Hupfeld being too pleased about it – but the song must have touched some primal yearning in all of us and I was amazed to see strapping blokes all around me with tears running down their faces.

I wrote a review and sent it off to the SEAC newspaper. To my surprise they published it, which gave me the courage to send them other bits of writing. Very soon they were asking me to write for them... you know the sort of thing... a postcard from 'our boys' in the jungle and all that stuff. It gave me an inkling that maybe there were things that I could do that didn't involve killing human beings or being eaten alive by bugs.

Come January, though, it was back to the real war... and with a vengeance. We were ferried back into the jungle to be put through some strenuous attack training. I guess that was going to be necessary anyway, as a way of getting rid of our ring-rustiness, but we all sensed something brewing, and it wasn't long before we found out what it was.

Jap had been on the move once more and had made more gains in the Arakan, in the area around our old stomping ground: the Mayu River. So, they put us on a train and then loaded us into trucks, which took us down to the Mayu mountains. From there we marched over the hills with supplies loaded onto mules. We were still travelling as light as possible and had to have our supplies dropped by the RAF boys. We lit signal fires and prayed that the Jap air force wasn't looking too closely in our direction. Just seeing one of those Jap Zeros buzzing round in the sky above you, covered in menacing red circles like a bringer of plague, well... it really dragged your heart into your mouth.

We eventually found ourselves emerging into a long valley. The ground was soft and obscured by a strange mist which lapped and probed around the bottom of our legs. Its long milky fingers caressed our ankles and it felt like we were being sized up, maybe even by Death himself. At least that was the thought that came into my mind. We didn't know what we were walking in really, but the whole scene was like a ghost-world to me and we all sensed it. Everything and everyone stood in silence, including the mules.

Then we heard Jap.

We saw him too. The darkness rising up to our left was patterned with tiny splashes of flickering orange. They were like evil eyes… maybe the multiple eyes of a giant spider, all trained in our direction, burning through the black night to strike fear in our bones. There was a hushed exchange of nervous voices around me, pointlessly expressing what we had all already worked out,

"Campfires!"

"Jap must be dug in up on that hill."

We moved quickly into the shadow of the hill on the other side of the valley, trying to make ourselves invisible to those prying eyes opposite, but we could feel that our boots were treading in something other than Burmese earth. It didn't feel right as our feet sunk and squelched into whatever was beneath us. It sent more shivers of dread through me. It's funny how your subconscious knows when something isn't right. Only when the mist cleared could we make out what it was. The ground was littered with carcasses of the recent dead.

They were our men, Indian soldiers, together with their pack animals. Strange and oddly fascinating expressions of surprise were etched into their bloodied faces. Bulging, wide-open eyes recorded their final moments of shocked astonishment. It was clear that they'd been ambushed and that the whole thing had been done and dusted without too much fuss. I'm not sure how long the bodies had been there, but the warm perfume of fresh death, and maybe the sight of it too, caused a couple of the lads to throw up.

For some reason I never did feel nausea at those moments, but I did become, at once, extra-vigilant. My senses sharpened. I felt it straight away… in the awareness of my own breath, and the sensitivity of my skin to the night. It made me feel that I was ready for whatever was coming next. I can clearly hear Slowcoach's voice, even now. He was at the back of our group as usual, and he was prophesising doom.

"This ain't good lads!"

He had a succinct way of putting into words exactly what we were all thinking.

Then one of our mules whinnied. Almost immediately machine-gun fire rattled at us from the winking spider's eyes, its deathly fire-trail disturbing the mist and kicking up earth and dead flesh from the ground just in front of where we lay. One of the mules was hit and went charging off into the darkness, we could hear its cries of pain for a few moments, until it was quietened by another burst from the gun. We responded with a volley of mortar fire aimed in the vague direction of the onslaught. Our company was then told to ready itself to rush at the orange patterned darkness and, with no fanfare, we were on the move.

The dark ground flashed by quickly under my feet. In every direction swirled an aural kaleidoscope of heavy shuffling footsteps, laboured breathing, and the shouts of men in God knows how many languages. Fast whirling mutable shapes danced around me in the blackness. Soon there were short sharp exclamations of pain and then screams too. The human sounds were clearly heard, even despite the torrent of machine gun and rifle fire that rattled through the air. I was too scared to feel empathy. There was a voice in my head… my dad's voice?… that urged me to keep going… You're still alive, just keep bloody moving! Occasionally, a burst of light would illuminate single acts of the drama, turning the spotlight onto individual cameos of bravery, self-preservation or the exhalation of a final breath.

It all moved so quickly that everything was bewildering, and nothing was clear or certain. Instinct, not other men, commanded your actions. Running around on that hillside in the dark, I felt like we weren't actually doing any fighting. Instead, the feeling was one of being trapped underneath a thick black blanket of confusion. I wanted to rip through it with my bayonet and feel the comforting presence of sense and order.

Now and then I collapsed to my knees and fired my rifle at where I thought the enemy was positioned. After one of these moments, as I got up to move again, I stumbled. It was a long stuttering, drawn out fall, like it was happening in slow-motion, as they call it these days. I landed heavily on top of a pair of boots. Above the boots were trousers, tucked neatly into their puttees. Jap puttees. My eyes followed the soft contours of the prone body until they eventually made out a youth lying on his back. Even in the colourless dark, I could see a single bullet hole, seeping red, in the middle of his chest. He was barely a teenager I reckoned, with soft, beardless, features. He wore spectacles, but these were now hanging from his face and one of the lenses was shattered. Then, as my panic rose off the scale, I realised that he was still breathing. The faintest hint of mist crept from his nose and mouth. I heard myself saying aloud,

"What do I bloody well do now?"

I had some choices of course. Do I make sure he's dead? My bayonet could do that easily enough; but the lad was no more than a kid… and I'd have to do it close-up.

Whilst I was deliberating, his eyes opened. They were dark and intelligent. They looked at me and I sensed that he wanted to speak, but no sound came out. I knew then that I couldn't do what was expected of me. This was no textbook enemy. Then the boy's gaze dulled before my eyes and his breath ceased. A trickle of blood ran from his nose. I felt a guilty sense of relief that the decision had been taken away from me, but there was grief too. For a brief instant, we had known each other. I had shared eye contact with my foe and found that I was staring into the heart of a human being. I carefully replaced the spectacles back over the boy's nose and brushed way the dirt from his face, before touching the palm of my hand gently against his cool skin. I let it linger there for a moment.

As I struggled to my feet, I became conscious that the noise of battle was over. The fear was still with me though, and for a moment I was alone and disorientated. Mist was rising from the surface of the hill like the souls of the dead ascending. Then, as my eyes adjusted to the gloom, the moonlight caught the edge of Soldier's silhouette as he scrambled over towards me, his body slightly crouched as he moved, like a crab. For the second time that night I let myself feel relief.

"Looks like you've been getting closely acquainted with the enemy Wally."

Soldier was at his happiest after a fight, and he had a big grin on his face.

"Enemy? He's just a kid."

The words didn't come out easily, my lips seemed like they didn't want to move.

"There are kids on our side too, don't forget that."

A shrill cry on the wind, no doubt from some distant animal or bird, stiffened Soldier's senses and he dropped to his knees and instinctively surveyed the surroundings. His voice carried a hint of impatience.

"Look, you're on one side or the other... it can't be any other way. Come on, let's get to the top of this hill before we're chased off it... and bloody well keep as low down as you can."

We lay, sprawled out, at the crest of that unremarkable hill, in the middle of nowhere. This was our prize for killing the children of our adversary. I looked around for the rest of the section but, apart from Soldier, I could only see the dark outlines of unknown men against the night, some crouching, some laying down like us.

"Listen," instructed Soldier.

I heard my teeth chattering.

"It's quiet."

"Listen again."

Then I could just pick up the barely audible sounds of movement, of machinery clicking ready for action, of voices. They were nothing more than whispers on the breeze, but they were there.

"Is that us or them?"

"Them... they're regrouping on the hills around us."

"It's not over then."

He looked at me as if I was crazy.

"It's never over Wally. Don't ever think it is. At least not until you've jumped on the charabanc back home."

"What?"

"I always think of a shoot-out like this as a day-trip to hell. Your only way out is that charabanc back home. Keep that image in your head... and make sure that you're alive enough to catch it."

I could sense the suppressed smile in his voice. He knew full well that I wouldn't be able to get that image out of my head now.

A sudden burst of automatic fire from the hill in front of us kicked up the dirt to our left, then another came and then it became constant. Fire-trails and mortars came over from the hill to our left and then the high ground to our right. We were sitting ducks, caught in a crossfire. I could hear men screaming; our men this time, for sure.

Smitty crawled over to us, "Let's move laddies."

He pointed back down the hill from where came and slowly our line retreated backwards. Jap had got close enough to start lobbing grenades and the force of an explosion to our right toppled me over. With my ears still ringing, Soldier grabbed me by my webbing and dragged me down the hill. I could see his mouth moving but couldn't hear his words. To me he looked like a warrior-king in the moonlight, snarling, heroic, clear-thinking and resolute; I was glad that he was on my side. They make statues of men like him.

We retreated down the hill, back to the valley where we started, and made sure we kept on moving. Grenades and gun fire were still being hurled in our direction and our paltry attempt at a defence, from our rear as we withdrew, was not enough to repel Jap. We managed to fall back into a large dry chaung where a makeshift first aid post was being set-up. Eric and Smitty were already there and we fell onto the welcoming ground beside them. Not long afterwards, Podge and Errol stumbled in amongst us, before Slowcoach and Coggins rolled up together. Slowcoach was limping and Coggins supporting him.

"You in one piece 'Coach?" inquired Smitty.

"Aye, just a stone in my shoe Corp... no bother."

"Where's the Sarge?" asked Soldier.

Smitty shook his head in a way that immediately told us that Sergeant Dickinson hadn't made it.

"What about Fred Bailey?" added Coggins.

We all looked at each other.

"He were next to me at the top of the hill," offered Slowcoach. "… cracking mermaid jokes. I can't remember seein' the bugger after that."

I felt a stinging sensation on my left leg, and I rolled up my battledress trousers see a couple of leeches attached to my calf. How they had managed to get up there I don't know. I grabbed Podge's cigarette from his mouth and burned them off. Then the ground started to shake in harmony with a deep bass growling sound which seemed to prophesise the end of the world. We looked nervously at each other until we made out a familiar chinking of metal upon metal that could only mean one thing. Slowcoach announced their arrival in typical fashion.

"Fuck me... it's tanks!"

They came out of nowhere and, as they trundled towards us, we wondered for a moment if they were Jap tanks. None of us would have had the legs left to run, or the energy to fight, if they had been.

"Halle-bloody-lujah! It's jungle green... they're Lees tanks... they're our fuckers lads!"

Smitty's voice was thick with relief.

They were Dragoons and they had stumbled upon us accidentally. They carried with them much needed water and some more medical supplies. When you are as parched as we were at that moment, and you only have the taste of dirt, blood and cordite in your mouth - then you'd give up your most prized possession, or maybe even your best mate, for a single sip of water.

As time passed, it became clear that Jap had backed off. Perhaps, like us, he had taken enough casualties for one day and, anyway, he still held the ground he started with. Somebody pulled out a mess tin and started brewing tea, and we all started to relax a little. In time we dragged ourselves to our feet and began the long march back, supported for some of the way by the tanks. The walking wounded came with us, but it was a slow business. At one point we lost our original trail and had to hack through virgin jungle with our dahs and kukris for some of the way. Finally, at dusk on the following day, we arrived at our destination, a place that must have sounded like 'Banana' because that's what we called it.

***

Fred Bailey was never seen again. Eric replaced him as Lance Corporal, and Smitty was promoted too, in Sergeant Dickinson's stead. In our new digs, the temperature was now becoming almost unbearable whilst our discomfort was compounded by the amount of dust which was simply everywhere. It was in your hair, on your kit, in your pants. You drank it in your tea and ate it with your Bully Beef. Because it was so hot, you sweated profusely and so the dust stuck to you even more.

"What are we doing here?"

I'd finally plucked up the courage to ask Soldier that unanswerable question one humid night whilst on guard duty. He responded with a now familiar look of incredulity.

"We're fighting a war... what are you talking about?"

"I was thinking, the other day... we marched for miles through the night to take a position that nobody cares about. Jap fights back, we withdraw and then march back here. People died. Where is the sense in any of this?"

"It's a bit late in your career to start questioning things now. You should know better than to do that anyway. Look... what we did on that hill might have been a diversion for all you know, tying up Jap long enough for him not to take an objective elsewhere... or for us to win a fight in another place miles away from here. You've got to remember Wally that we only have a narrow field of vision. We're given a job, we do it as best we can. It's not our job to see the big picture. We have to trust the top brass to do that."

"Do you trust them?"

He gave me that look again. It lingered for a moment longer this time.

"It's not about what I think is it? Our job *is* to trust them... without question. We can complain about it, that's our right as soldiers, but that's a different thing altogether."

He locked his eyes on mine.

"You start thinking too much about all of this and, one day, you'll hesitate... just for a second maybe... like you did over that Jap kid. Or else self-preservation suddenly becomes more important. Either way you'll be fucked. Dead meat... like Bailey and Dicko."

"They might have been taken prisoner."

"Still dead meat. Jap don't take prisoners... only for bayonet practice or worse."

My state of mind was not improved when I received a letter from Dinah. I read it with a mixture of both apathy and hope, disappointed and frustrated to find that she had not recognised any coldness in my words to her. I was sure that I had left enough indifference on show for her to detect it. Neither did she mention the war. Instead, I learned from her that the sky in Nottingham was the bluest she'd ever seen and that she was wearing that pretty green dress that I liked so much. She told me that her friend, Elizabeth, was going to send a letter to me too, but beyond that there was nothing that lingered in the memory. I imagine that she finished it by telling me that she was still missing me terribly and that she was counting down the days to when we were to be together again, or words to that effect.

Whilst I knew that some of the men around me would kill for a letter like that, I just felt guilt and confusion. I couldn't shake the feeling that we had both wasted a big part of our lives, and I regretted that I hadn't had the courage to end it all a couple of years before, or even in my last letter.

My guilt was exacerbated by the letter from Elizabeth which arrived at the same time. Guilt mixed with immeasurable pleasure that is. It made me smile the sort of stupid dreamy smile that you don't realise you've got on display until somebody points it out to you. And Eric did just that. Elizabeth declared that she was writing to cheer me up because, she imagined, it must be hell being stuck in the jungle with nothing but monkeys for company. She'd clearly met Slowcoach and Errol, I thought. Then she told me that she'd recently joined the NAAFI, as a waitress, and that she was hoping that one day she could serve me. I presume that I must have blushed at those words and I knew that I had to keep that particular line hidden from the rest of the lads.

Unlike the images of Dinah that I called up, I found that I had no difficulty in picturing Elizabeth's face and, I admit, the thought of her stirred all sorts of other feelings in me. I had been thinking about her A LOT, since recalling my departure at Victoria Station. Outwardly, Elizabeth might have been one of those girls who did regular things in a regular way, like any other girl anywhere in the world, but, inexplicably, when *she* did them, she cast a spell that drew you to her like a magnet. One side effect of this, when I was back home, was that I was generally reduced to speaking gibberish in front of her. She completely made me lose the ability to string a coherent sentence together. Whenever this happened, I felt like the world's biggest imbecile and I bet she thought I was a bit of a prat, but she just smiled coolly, as if nothing was in any sense awry and I immediately felt better. She was also by far the best-looking girl I knew; having something of the young Elizabeth Taylor about her... an Italian darkness, inherited from her mother, no doubt. Next to her - even in my imagination - dreary Dinah resembled the outline of something familiar that was now lost beneath the shadow of something bright, shiny, exciting and new.

The Man Who Found Treasure

After reading the letters I made the mistake of telling Eric and Errol what I was feeling about Dinah, without mentioning Elizabeth. They commiserated with me as much as they could do, but the conversation touched the boundary of what mates could comfortably talk about. Looking back, despite it never occurring to me at the time, I'm sure my small worries were replicated in the minds of men right across the battalion, but if any of them were going through such private dilemmas of their own - or worse, then they never troubled me with them. We lived in tiny bubbles of our own making, inside the larger, forgotten, bubble that the war in Burma both created and occupied.

To drum some sense into my brain, I told myself sternly that now was not the time to be thinking about matters of the heart. I mean, why should I waste time agonising over a future which might never exist anyway? But, oh… those images of Elizabeth! They still managed to creep into to my mind from time to time.

Errol tried to cheer me up by saying that he would "sort me out" the next time we were in Calcutta, if I wanted it. That took me back.

I had visited one of those places before, not long after I first came out to India. I was naïve enough then to let an old soldier drag me up a flight of stairs, above a barber's shop, right in the middle of Sonagachhi. We were greeted by a large woman who talked continuously and shook her head a lot. She wore a choli beneath her sari that was almost stretched to breaking point.

The old soldier whispered in her ear, stuffed some rupees into her cleavage, winked at me and then wandered off whistling, hands in pockets, along a dark corridor with an intricately patterned red carpet. The woman babbled at me impatiently with a face like thunder and I wanted the floor to break open and swallow me up.

Finally, she seemed to register my obvious discomfort and her features softened, her mouth breaking into an upward curve that might have been a smile.

"Come."

It was less an order, more of an invitation. She gently took hold of my hand and led me down the corridor, stomping over creaking floorboards, past a parade of doors that made me think that the place used to be a commercial hotel or something similar, years ago. We came to a halt in front of room number six, I remember the number clearly, and she opened the door and pushed me inside without a word, closing it firmly behind me.

The dim windowless room I found myself in had seen better days. From what I could make out, it contained a single bed with bare mattress and, incongruously, several items of rather scuffed oak furniture. On one of these, a chest of drawers which was missing the middle drawer, stood a flickering candle which was the room's only source of light. I wondered what I was supposed to do next. Perhaps I had been sent into solitary confinement for the crime of first-degree innocence. Perhaps I had just been locked out of the way until the old soldier had completed his business.

As my eyes adjusted to the gloom, I soon realised that I wasn't alone. Curled up by the bed, almost lost in the shadows cast by the candle, lay the sleight but just about recognisable figure of a human being. It stirred, and I found myself being stared at by a pair of wide, bright eyes. It slowly got to its feet and shuffled towards me like Marley's ghost; I saw then that I was in the company of a girl who couldn't have been much older than thirteen or fourteen years old. She said something softly in her native language. The words floated timidly towards me, and I shook my head to indicate that I didn't understand.

After a nervous stand-off where we just gazed at each other, I sat down on the floor. I don't know which of us was the most scared. Then, out of nowhere, I just started crying, and huge sobs just poured out of me. At that moment, I don't think I'd ever felt lonelier. The girl came over and sat down beside me. She rested her head gently on my shoulder. We stayed like that until the candle had run down and the old soldier's rupees had run out. I often think of that young girl and wonder what became of her. I hope that one day she found the solace that she gave to me that night.

For a fleeting second, even despite my haunting memory of the young girl, I almost resolved to take Errol up on his offer, to make a statement, to show Dinah that I was in control... not that she would even know of course. But I didn't, and I wasn't, and I knew deep down that I never could cheat on her, even as I wished more than anything that I'd never met her in the first place.

"I wouldn't mind givin' some of those native girls a go," chipped in Slowcoach, eagerly, "them ones with the big brown eyes... you know. I think they're the most beautiful girls I've ever seen."

"I'm all for big eyes!" Exclaimed Errol, making the shape of a different part of a woman's anatomy with his hands.

"You wouldn't last two minutes 'Coach," cautioned Eric, "I reckon most of them Burmans aren't keen on us English, what with all that colonial crap we've thrown at 'em. Who's to say she wouldn't make you all lovey-dovey, and then get her Jap mate to slit your throat when your eyes are off the ball."

"That's as may be, but, I can think of worse ways to meet your maker out 'ere" winked Slowcoach.

***

Things began to quieten down for a time in the Arakan after that, and the fighting became concentrated further north and around the border with India. As time moved on, the complexion of the battle for Burma began to change. Suddenly it didn't feel like we were running away anymore and our confidence, slowly but surely, returned. It was like a switch had been flicked overnight.

We were picking up a greater number of Jap prisoners too, some of whom weren't in great physical shape. It gave us another inkling that the tide of the war was turning our way. I tried never to get too carried away though. For one, it just wasn't ever comfortable enough in the jungle to do that and, secondly, my brain was indelibly stamped with Soldier's warning about our narrow field of vision.

When the monsoons came again, in late May 1944, we were once again pulled out of the line. On the eve of our withdrawal, though, we were told that there might be enemy movements close by. Jap had clearly been sensing our new-found confidence. That night, before we could properly ready ourselves, he attacked our camp in force. We didn't see him at first, but we heard him.

"Hey, Tommy... Tommy Atkins... come out and meet us," he taunted from the dark cover of the trees in broken English. He must have been there for a while, listening to our conversations, because he threw in the occasional real name too,

"Corporal Smitty... Private Errol... how are you?"

If it was designed to put the willies up us, then it worked a treat, but it also enabled us to be ready for the fight when it came.

They ran, screaming like wraiths, out of the trees. Hundreds of them. They streamed from the blackness, eyes bulging, with faces grotesquely contorted, possibly in an expression of the same fear that we were experiencing. I might have frozen on the spot out of sheer terror, if it wasn't for the fact that they ran straight into our line of fire. It was suicide. Pressing my finger on the trigger was no more than an automatic act of self-preservation. I don't know where my gun was pointing or even if my bullets hit any of them, and I don't really want to know; but they were mowed down as they raced towards us. Weight of numbers meant that some of them got very close to breaching the perimeter, before they crumpled to the ground in a brief halo of red mist. Amazingly, our lines remained unbroken. It was a sad and desperate act, but it was also a timely reminder that we shouldn't take anything for granted. This pointless slaughter… this waste… wasn't over yet.

Afterwards, I couldn't take my eyes off the twisted and lifeless wasted flesh that was left behind. It was over far too quickly, and I felt the leaden weight of guilt on my shoulders. They had come out of nowhere; out of nothingness. Out of silence; to this. If life is worth anything, I asked myself, then surely it should come to an end with more significance… and with more reason?

"Rather them than us Wally," said Eric, reading my mind, as he stood beside me. There was no hint of triumph in his voice. For him it was enough that our section, depleted though it was, was still together.

"Do you think it was like this for my dad?"

Eric nodded, "I can't see them Turks ever bein' as stupid as Jap though. They won their battle, didn't they?"

"… and Dad never caught the charabanc back home."

"What are you talking about Wally?"

Those of us who were left had survived another year and, as we fell gratefully into our new bashas at a place we called 'Tung Po', we thanked our lucky stars. With Mam's promise firmly fixed in my mind, I felt that I now had an extra reason, if I needed it, to remain focussed on staying alive.

***

The Man Who Found Treasure

By October the rains had begun to fade. One morning, after the section had returned from a patrol, we sat together in the open, preparing a brew as usual. A few of the lads were flicking through the SEAC newspaper. Errol was making his usual observations about the heroine of the 'Jane' cartoon. She was one of the few women who ever made it into our ranks on the front line and so even her two-dimensional black and white image was enough to stir a man's yearnings. Gradually, one by one, our attention was captured by the hint of a crowd gathering over towards a hut used by our commanding officer. Hovering above the crowd was the unmistakeable buzz of excited voices, and our eyes strained to see above the bobbing heads.

A group of officers appeared, including some of our regimental top brass. Our Lieutenant-Colonel, who always stood out from the throng because he was so blooming tall, was in conversation with a slightly shorter, stockier, square-jawed man as they strolled through the forest of troops standing to attention around them.

"Bloody hell, it's Desperate Dan," observed Slowcoach none too quietly.

Then a name was carried on a whisper through the ranks, passed from man to man until it reached our ears.

"Slim!"

We instinctively rose to our feet.

"That's no character from a comic 'Coach," said Soldier, "That's Uncle Bill... our bloody army commander."

So, there he was in all his glory, Lieutenant-General Bill Slim, Commander of the Fourteenth Army. I suppose he didn't look much like a commander; he wasn't scrubbed up and perfectly pressed like they usually were, but you noticed him that's for sure. He stepped onto an upturned wooden crate that had appeared at his feet. The act of rising above the crowd had the effect of drawing our eyes towards him and silencing our conversation. He didn't have to call us, we just gravitated to where he stood, following the herd, jostling with each other to gain the best view of the sermon he was about to preach. He waited for our motley troop of sweat-stained jungle green and sun-reddened bare chests to settle. There was a palpable air of expectation. And then he spoke.

"How are you men?"

We told him that we were in fine fettle in the only way we could, with a volley of shouts and other appropriate noises. His eyes scanned our ranks from beneath the rim of a rakishly angled slouch hat, arms folded resolutely.

"Good... good. I wanted to come here, first of all, to thank you for all that you have done in this fight so far. You have done everything that has been asked of you... and more... and you are a credit to the army, the King and your country. Most of all, you are a credit to yourselves."

I remember him pausing and adjusting his belt around the back of his jacket, before folding his arms again to stand like a statue looking down upon us. There might have been a practical reason for this, but it certainly added an element of suspense as we eagerly waited on his next words.

"They call you the 'forgotten army' don't they?"

We made a kind of grumbling sound; we didn't like being called 'forgotten'.... I mean the war hadn't even finished.

"Well... if they do call you that, then don't worry, you'll soon have the opportunity to be remembered by the annals of history. You'll be the soldiers that small boys will want to mimic in the playground or read about in their monthly magazines, like the heroes I used to idolise as a child.

At this moment you may feel that you are far away from the worst of things, but I can tell you now that the fight still goes on all over this land and, very soon, each of you will be asked to go into battle for your country again. When this campaign began two years ago, you will no doubt have believed that we were up against it. Well, I can tell you in, all honesty, that at times our backs *were* up against the wall. Hard and tight! Even though we ... or rather *you*... fought doggedly and with great valour, there were times when we had to take a few steps back and regroup. Through it all, however, we have never been defeated... *never*."

We listened, spellbound.

"Now though men, the tide has turned with a vengeance. Your steadfastness, your tenacity in battle, your morale and your skill as soldiers, has seen us take the upper hand. We've kicked our enemy out of India and, all over Burma, we are now pushing him backwards. Our brutal opponent... our *so-called* invincible foe... is losing his hope and his will. We are stretching his supply lines to breaking point and, as a result, he is hungry and thin, and his morale is cracking. All the time we, however, are growing stronger and stronger.

That strength is what will enable us to continue pushing on... to harry and pursue our enemy. If he turns to bite us back, then we will stubbornly hold-fast. We will keep on his shoulders until he runs away before us, like so many of those ants you see a lot of out here, fleeing into the jungle and into the sea, if that's what it takes... and we will be treading on him, squashing the him with our boots, as he runs!"

Well, that broke the spell, and the assembly around me released the pent-up pressure of its approval with a raucous cheer. Remembering my recent encounters with Jap, I must admit that I felt a little uncomfortable about some of the imagery Slim used, and the enthusiasm with which my comrades lapped it up, but it was easy to get carried away. I saw Slim's face crease into a slight and uneven smile before he ended with an understated but reassuring flourish that made my spine-tingle.

"You all know who I am, men... you can't fail to with my ugly mug, that's for sure! Yes, I am your commander, but first and foremost I am also one of you... a simple soldier ... and I will be standing at your side all the way to Rangoon. I'll see you there!"

As he stepped down from his makeshift podium, we cheered wildly but with one voice. We waved our hats, mugs and anything else we had to hand in the air. It was true what he said, he came across as being one of us, not like the usual top brass at all.

I'd been there when the Supreme Commander, Mountbatten, spoke to us. He was entertaining enough, but it was all very superficial, a bit like you were a guest at the Captain's table. With Slim, though, it felt more like you were rolling up your sleeves and getting your hands dirty together in the engine room. We really sensed that we were in good hands with this man.

The crowd dissipated and we wandered back to our stoves feeling excited that we were part of it all, but Slim didn't disappear. He strolled through the ranks, chatting informally to the men as he went, even speaking to the Indian cooks, sweepers and water carriers in Assamese or Hindi or Bengali or whatever it was.

In no time at all, there he was, standing right at my side. I guess that he wasn't that much taller than me, but he seemed bigger. He had a presence, you know, these days some might call it an aura. If it was, then it was one that I have rarely encountered in anybody since... and I've met a few so-called top people in my time. So, after that build up, what do you reckon was on the fourteenth army commander's mind?

Tea.

"Ah, I'm just in time for a brew I see."

There was a glint in his eye.

"You're welcome to join us sir," offered Errol.

"I would love to," said Slim, with meaning, "but alas, duty calls. How's your morale men? Is the food up to scratch?"

We nodded and told him that it was good and, for that moment at least, it was.

"I'm pleased to hear it. Remember, take pride in what you do, and look after each other won't you?"

We nodded, but just as he tipped his hat to move on to the next group, I found myself doing something unthinkable. I blurted out to his back,

"Somebody told me that you fought in the Dardanelles, Sir?"

I heard my voice sure enough but, for a moment, I didn't realise that it was me speaking those words. They came out of nowhere; I have no recollection of even wrestling with the idea of speaking before those words emerged from my mouth. Straight away my stomach turned over, my throat tightened, and I felt colour rushing to my face. I wanted to dive into the nearest basha. I caught a glimpse of Eric's overly widened eyes communicating telepathically to me the unmistakeable phrase,

"Why the fuck did you say that?"

Slim turned around almost mechanically and peered at me with squinted eyes that seemed to drill into the furthest recesses of my mind. If he was taken aback, he didn't show it. He stroked his moustache.

"Yes, I did... why do you ask soldier?"

He had the bearing of a man who was very interested in knowing the answer.

"My dad, Sir... he served there too."

"Oh, yes? What regiment?"

"I'm not sure Sir, all I know is that he served with the Royal Naval Division."

He nodded approvingly.

"What was your father's name Private?"

"Albert Kingdom, Sir."

"Kingdom?"

"Yes, Sir."

Slim's sharp hazel eyes continued to burrow into mine for a few moments longer and then he nodded almost imperceptibly. He turned to whisper something into the ear of the adjutant standing next to him and then stepped away and merged again into the crowd of soldiers around him.

"You're in for it now Wally," was Slowcoach's verdict in a doom-laden voice, "You wait 'til Captain Ross hears about this."

He affected a sharp intake of breath and ran a finger slowly across his adam's apple. I offered an apology for any embarrassment caused. There was a ripple of laughter and shaking of heads.

"You're a right daft bugger," was Eric's final word on the matter.

We sat down to drink our tea and relaxed back into our gentle micky-taking. Of course, it was mostly at my expense. It didn't last long though. Just as I thought I'd got away with my faux pas, both the smile and the colour abruptly drained from the face of Coggins who was sitting directly in front of me. His gaze levitated to a place somewhere above my head and the chatter died away mid-stream. Slowcoach was the last one to realise this and he only shut up when Errol dished out an elbow to his ribs. I became conscious of a looming shadow behind me.

"Which one of you is Private Kingdom?" it demanded.

I turned my head to see the legs of an officer, so I scrambled hastily to my feet and saluted.

"Sir!"

It was the adjutant who had accompanied Slim a little while earlier.

"Captain Synge, general staff," he sneered, before casting a disdainful eye up and down the sweaty, stubbly specimen before him.

"Will you follow me please?"

He led me over to the abandoned native hut that our officers had commandeered and ushered me up the bamboo ladder, without following me up it himself. Inside I found Slim sat on another upturned crate, he was striped with thin watery light and reading from a sheet of paper. He sipped from a mug of tea. His hat was now nestling beside him. He folded up the paper and slipped it into his jacket pocket.

"Stand easy Private," he ordered. "I was intrigued by your question out there. As we are currently fighting a war against Jap in a place that is five thousand miles away from the Gallipoli peninsula, it is not a question that comes up very often."

"Sir."

"However, it would seem that the Dardanelles is still of some concern to you?"

"Sir."

"I like to pride myself in remembering the names and faces of as many soldiers as I can. It's not easy, of course, and some of them stay with you more than others... for different reasons. In your case the name Kingdom is unusual, and it has stuck in the memory."

I was surprised at how softly Slim spoke and, as he did so, I thought I could pick out a slight West Midlands twang in his voice. He sounded like no commanding officer I'd ever encountered before, and it was like having a chat to... well, an uncle I suppose. He pursed his lips and his countenance became very serious.

"I did come across a man called Kingdom in Turkey... but I only recollect that because I was close by when he was killed, on the beach at Cape Helles."

My breath quickened.

"Sir... how?"

He nodded.

"He was with a group of..."

At that moment the adjutant entered the hut and interrupted the revelation that I hoped Slim was about to make.

"I'm sorry Sir, you need to see this," he drawled.

He handed over a scrap of paper. Slim read it quickly, nodded to the adjutant and grabbed his hat.

"I'm sorry private, but I have to go now... this war never stands still does it?"

My heart sank.

"I suggest that you seek out a man called Johnson, a lieutenant in the Royal Engineers. I understand that his field company is with us in the Arakan somewhere. He can tell you what you want to know."

"Sorry sir, but I have met Lieutenant Johnson… in fact he was responsible for telling me that you served out there. He wasn't able to tell me very much else."

Slim smiled mischievously.

"Then I would suggest that he has not told you the whole truth. Tell the old bugger to cough up next time… and tell him that's an order, from me!"

With that he left the hut. I felt badly cheated. Here was my moment of revelation with a man who was actually there when my dad bought it and, just as he was about to spill the beans, somebody decides the bloody war is more important than me getting the answers to questions that had plagued me all my life. I mean, what sort of flipping cheek is that? Of course, there was little chance of me seeing Slim again… in the flesh at least, so I had to pin my hopes on tracking down Johnson. Burma was a big place, but I wasn't going to give up now.

Chapter 9.

Burma: 1944.

An open-backed Bedford truck skidded to a halt on the slim verge with a clattering protest from the engine and a toe-curling screech from the brakes. The discord had a terminal feel to it, and the cloud of dust kicked into the air by the skittering wheels lingered over the stationary machine like a shroud. As the air cleared the dust was replaced by hissing clouds of steam pouring through the radiator grille and from underneath the chassis. The driver leaped down from the cab and inspected the damage. He tilted back his beret and wiped his face with a handkerchief.

"We're buggered Lieutenant", he shouted. "Kaput!"

The recipient of his diagnosis emerged from the other side of the cab. He too was wiping his face with a handkerchief and limped as he walked.

"Can you fix her?"

"I'm not sure. I can have a look, but…"

"Do what you can my man," the lieutenant patted the driver on the shoulder. "If you can't mend the old lady, well then we'll just have to flag down the next empty truck that comes along."

The Man Who Found Treasure

He flashed a weary smile and stroked his moustache and then tapped his swagger stick against the side of the truck.

"Better get out and stretch your legs men. We might be here for some time."

The vehicle's cargo of sappers jumped down from the tailgate, one by one. They lit cigarettes, and some of them relieved themselves in the scrubby vegetation that lined their stopping place. In time they sat on the ground in groups of three or four, with the odd one removing his shirt to reveal a well-defined sun-bronzed ribcage.

The lieutenant moved to the edge of the road and surveyed the scene. It was a busy route, and today was no exception. An unending line of military vehicles flowed in each direction as far as the eye could see. The trucks, jeeps and armoured cars occasionally had to negotiate a native ox cart, or a barefoot farmer pulling a load of coconuts on a home-made barrow. This took place usually to a fanfare of blasts on the horn or swearing from frustrated drivers. The whole panorama smelled of petrol, burning rubber and the overwhelming scent of warm dust.

The sappers became so engrossed in their small-talk and cigarettes, that they didn't notice the lieutenant edging ever closer to the highway. A few were lying back on the ground and shading their eyes from the burning sun anyway, oblivious to what their officer was up to. The old soldier took another step. As he did so, the wing mirror of a passing truck whipped the bush hat from his head.

"Watch it Grandad!" yelled an angry Australian accent from the truck's cab.

It didn't stop. The lieutenant was unmoved.

By now the sappers' interest had been piqued. They started to nudge each other and point as they saw their officer step out into the stream of vehicles, as if in a trance, his eyes seemingly focussed on something in the distance. As he walked in an unerringly straight line across the path of the traffic, brakes were rapidly stamped on, more horns were sounded, and curses were liberally aimed in his direction. A jeep screeched and swerved off the road, narrowly missing the sappers, a couple of whom had to leap swiftly from its path. Miraculously, the lieutenant glided through to the other side of the road and onto the edge of a wide beach without being touched once.

"Bloody hell! Somebody up there must be looking after the daft bastard," one of the sappers exclaimed.

As he emerged from the dust of the roadway, the lieutenant raised his arm to shield his eyes and squinted. As his sight adjusted, he began to make out the twinkling pale blue water at the edge of the beach, and he came to a halt. He stood like a statue, frozen in that position, for what seemed like minutes.

"Are you alright Sir?" yelled another one of the sappers, as they all gathered at the edge of the verge; but the traffic had resumed, and even if the sound of his voice had carried to the far side of the road, it was unlikely that the lieutenant would have registered the question.

"Lieutenant Johnson, sir?" he tried again to no avail.

Johnson suddenly twitched back into life and began to move forward in a stuttering walk towards the waters of the Bay of Bengal.

"Is he going for a swim?" asked the driver who had now re-joined the sappers.

"It does look invitin' don't it?"

"He's got the Doolally Tap if you ask me!"

The lieutenant pulled up at the centre of the beach. One of the sappers took advantage of a gap in the traffic and sprinted across the road and onto the beach, a couple more followed. As they neared him, gasping for breath, Johnson crouched to the floor and gathered some sand between cupped hands. He stared at it trickling through his fingers, intently, as if weighing it, before rising unsteadily to his feet and launching the remaining sand high into the air above him.

"Boom!" he roared; his face contorted into an expression of pure joy.

Chapter 10.

Blandford Camp,
Dorset,
24 February 1915

To my darling wife Alice and my boy Walter,

I hope these few simple words find you both in stout health. I have just received your letter which has cheered me up no end after the sadness of leaving you both behind again. As I put pen to paper I am proudly wearing the broach you gave me when I was home with your picture inside it. As it and the letter have been touched by your loving hands I will keep them close to my heart always. The little picture in the broach reminded me again just how beautiful you are – as if I needed reminding that is. I hope that you will be able to send me a picture of Walter next time? As I read your letter I tried to imagine you writing each word on the paper. I can see that each one was written with so much care and love that I thank God that he chose me to be your husband and the father of your son. Sometimes I think I can feel the touch of your soft skin through the paper itself but it only makes me sad to think things like that and I want to be with you again even more. Having been with you for those brief few days at new year you might say it is a bit greedy of me, but to hold you tightly for the first time in ages and then have that moment taken away so soon afterwards was the hardest thing I've ever had to take. I know now that there is nothing this war could ever throw at me that could be harder than that.

But it was the best feeling in the world to see you and Walter during my leave and the new year celebrations with all of us and Edie and Tom will be a pleasant memory to carry with me at least. Sometimes I wake up thinking it was a dream. If it was, then here's to another one soon. I hope that the new year will bring better news about the war which we all hoped would be over by now.

You will be pleased to know that I am now a proper army man. When I came back from leave we got rid of the navy uniform apart from the cap - but that is also now khaki. We have been marching a lot again. We route marched to Lyme Regis the other day where we paddled in the sea. Would you believe that's the closest I've been to the sea since I joined the navy, but it just made the big blisters on my feet sting. Do you remember that I told you that there are lots of toff officers at the camp including Mr. Asquith's son and our favourite is sub-lieutenant Tisdale who has a laugh with the boys and encourages us with the sport? Well he chucked us a pair of boxing gloves yesterday and one of the big miners from up north challenged all comers. George Pike took him on and got battered to kingdom come, but he's always game for adventure is George.

What with the new kit we've been issued and everything there are many rumours that we will soon be off overseas. I am ready to go if called because it only feels like we have been playing at being soldiers so far. It will be good to give the hun a bit of what we've been trained to do and know that the bayonet practice we've been doing has been put to good use. Some of the lads have been saying that Mr. Churchill and the King will be inspecting us in the next few days, but I don't know if that is just part of the rumours.

Dear Walter - How grown up you had become when I saw you at new year. As you are now the man of the house I will need you to protect your mam for me until I get back home. I hope that will be very soon and I can give you both another big cuddle. If God wills that I don't come back, then you must know - my big man - that I am already the proudest dad there is and I know that you will make me even prouder still.

All my love to you both
Until we meet again
YHIMK

Your Bert

***

The Man Who Found Treasure

England: 1915.

Dusk brought with it a darkening of the grey clouds that had hung over the camp all day like a quivering veil. It had been raining for an hour and Bert Kingdom stood at the centre of the troop of men who were gathered upon the sodden parade ground. After endless months of training, the battalion was finally on the move and, for most of the men, rampant expectancy overrode any concerns they might have had about the inclement weather. The soldiers of the Anson Battalion wore full tropical kit, including the new pith helmets which Bert now self-consciously balanced on his head. The helmet was disdainfully referred to under a much less flattering name by the soldiers of the battalion, using a word that sounded very similar to 'pith'. It was heavy and uncomfortable, but for now it was Bert's friend, protecting him from the downpour better than his naval cap would ever have done and the rainwater cascaded like a torrent from its rim in front of his eyes.

The raindrops tapped out an insistent beat on the hard skin of the topi. Their rhythm enchanted Bert's drifting thoughts into returning, once more, to the precious couple of days of leave he'd spent in Nottingham a few weeks previously. He was transported back to the moment he held his son for the first time in months. With his emotions unashamedly set free, he'd shed unexpected tears at feeling the softness of the boy's body close against his once again. He remembered how keenly his senses had drank in the warmth of the child's breath and the delicate touch of his skin and lips, as if those were the final moments he would know them. The vivid memory of the clear-eyed interrogating stare that Walter practiced whenever he was in the arms of his father now brought a grin to Bert's face. It was probably the only grin on show amongst the assembled troop of men waiting out in the dark in the freezing rainstorm that evening.

Bert let his thoughts roam naturally to Alice, but he didn't allow them to linger there. He could not think about her for long without the yearning it produced gnawing at his insides until it caused physical pain. Yet these thoughts were so sweet that he could not turn them away entirely and a sting of pain was a small price to pay for the effort. He remembered too the nights in the Queen's Hotel during Christmas and New Year, when he could forget that he was a soldier for a few hours and joy held sway. For Christmas, Bert and Alice had exchanged brass sweetheart brooches, identical with ornate rippled edges, each containing a tiny photograph of their beloved. Alice tried to teach him how to foxtrot, but any hope that he could master even one step was a forlorn one, let alone a whole 'trot'. On New Year's Eve the night passed away in an ecstatic swirl of ale, singing and kisses, and he wanted it to go on forever. He was surprised at how very happy he felt then; maybe happier than he'd ever felt before. That was until the last strains of Auld Lang Syne died away, and the new year descended upon them like a heavy weight.

The burden of remembering their farewell at the station was particularly painful. If, in a careless moment, the thought of that last embrace ever escaped into his brain, then he screwed up his eyes and willed himself to think of something else, with all the effort he could muster and until his head hurt. But even then, the warm whispered, breath of her parting words remained, ringing in his ears, coating them like honey so that they could never melt away... even in the rain.

"I love you Bert Kingdom. You'd better come back to me."

Not for the first time it was George Pike, standing beside Bert, who broke the spell.

"I tell you what Bert, them bloody Turks'll be running scared if they could see us now," he whispered. His new black eye, a souvenir from the boxing match, was camouflaged under the wide brim of his helmet.

"If they do, I bet they'll soon come running back, once they find out that the best the British army has got to throw at 'em is a bunch of drunken Geordie stokers and a short-arse kid from Bilborough," retorted Stan Cooper who was lined up directly behind them.

Bert joined in.

"Are we having a flutter on which one of us'll get to Constantinople first, eh lads?"

"No contest," declared George.

"I wish we were going to France to fight the hun instead," Stan replied, "I know we might have some sun and a nice bit of scenery in the Dardanelles, but it won't be like a war will it? It feels like I've been cheated, I mean what does your average Turk know about fighting?"

"I was talkin' to a scouser in the mess hall this mornin'. He towd me his old man were out in the Crimea a few years back. Accordin' to him the Turks needed us to bail 'em out back then... so they can't be up to much, can they?" supposed George.

"Well, Mr. Churchill seemed happy about it... I bet he's countin' on us nippin' the hun in the backside in no time," replied Bert, "and to think he came down to see you off himsen! That were bloody good of him I reckon."

"Aye, and the King too... so you've got royal approval Stanley lad," added George, flicking his leg back to give Stan a crack on the shin.

"Oww! You little...," exclaimed Stan.

Sub-Lieutenant Arthur Walderne St. Clair Tisdall walked down the line and stopped on the duckboards beside Bert, rain dripping from his cap. He was a couple of years older than Bert but looked younger. What he lacked in experience, he made up for by the strong bond he had with his men. When his charges found out that, despite his privileged background, he had originally enlisted as an able seaman, his stock rose even higher amongst them.

"'D' Company Anson Battalion... ready yourselves to go ashore men," he announced.

He looked at his watch. As he did so, a whistle blew at the front of the line and the command "Forward March" was intoned. The mass of men around him started to move forward as if it were a single giant organism, its boots crunching out a loud rhythm, in perfect time, on the wet ground. Combined with the rain, it was a sound which mimicked that of a powerful train pulling out of a station, and it thrilled those who marched at its heart.

As they trampled the dark muddy lanes leading out of the camp, one of the officers urged a song and the men duly obliged. A powerful tenor voice, straight from the banks of the Clyde, struck up:

Sub-Lieutenant Tisdall had a hundred eager men,
Sub-Lieutenant Tisdall had a hundred eager men,
Sub-Lieutenant Tisdall had a hundred eager men,

but the rain came down and washed the buggers away.

Tisdall grinned broadly as the whole company joined in the chorus:

Glory, glory hallelujah.
Glory, glory hallelujah.
Glory, glory hallelujah,
but the rain came down and washed the buggers away.

Almost three hours later, the soaked men paddled into the village of Shillingstone and headed for the railway station. The singing had long since ceased, drowned out by the rain and the cold. Several ladies from the village, forewarned of their arrival, made the tired men hot drinks as they stumbled, wet-through and shivering, into the simple red-bricked station building. The soldiers each found a berth wherever they could around the platform. Here they waited, huddled underneath oil lamps, for the next stage of their journey. The tiny station looked like it was bursting at the seams.

Bert had his hands wrapped around a tin mug of hot tea, under cover of the platform's large wooden awning, when Tisdall approached him.

"Able-seaman Kingdom, I hope that you're feeling revived by the tea?"

"Yes sir."

"Look here, there's a bit of a to-do over on the far platform. The mules are playing up. It seems that they're bored by the wait. I hear that you have some expertise with horses. Perhaps you could lend a hand?"

"Will do sir, leave it to me."

"Good chap."

Eight mules had been gathered in a stockade on the end of the platform. One of them, a small grey mare, pushed at the other animals hard with her nose and scraped her hooves on the ground. She tried to run in the confined space and crashed into the wooden barriers of the stockade. The other mules became unsettled and kicked and whinnied in turn. A gruff looking petty officer and young able seaman were vainly trying to control the chaos. The petty officer whipped the

The Man Who Found Treasure

grey mare with a short length of rope, but she reared and knocked the young seaman to the ground.

"Whoa there lassie, you'll be for the knackers-yard if you deen't calm down... an' you'll be tekkin' me with you if you carry on like this."

He lashed the mule hard again, but each time he did so she became more agitated.

"Stop that mate, it'll do no good," Bert urged the petty officer, as he scrambled over the fence.

"Well, 'ave you got any better ideas, cos she'll be gerrin me boot as well as the rope in a minute?"

Bert ripped the rope from his hands and threw it over his shoulder.

"I'm more used to 'osses, but I know that if there's one thing a mule don't like it's bein' whipped. You'll get the best out of 'em if you love 'em. Like any woman."

"Well if she wants me to love her she's gooin' aboot it the wrong way... she is better lookin' than the wife mind."

"Have you got a pack saddle or panniers?" asked Bert.

The petty officer wiped the rain and mud from his face and nodded. He gestured for the young lad to go and find one. Bert waited for the mule to calm down a little and, when he the opportunity arose, he stroked her neck and back, feeding her a little apple purloined from the station tea room.

"There you are Long Ears... it's not so bad is it?"

The mule settled at last and, as she did so, the commotion in the stockade subsided. The seaman returned with a pack saddle and he and Bert fixed it to the mule.

"Well, blow me! Now I've seen everythin'. You're nowt but a magician," the petty officer scratched his head.

"If you mek friends, like, she'll do anything you ask of her. Don't forget they're workin' animals... some of 'em are happier with a pack on their backs."

"Well I reckon you've got yourself a job laddie."

Bert looked at the handful of mules in the pen.

"There's not many. We'll need a few more than this won't we?"

"Aye, we will... and there'll be a few hundred more waitin' for us at Avonmouth. Yankee mules... straight off the boot from America."

The train rolled into Shillingstone station in the early hours of the morning. With steam billowing around them, the men were lined up and obediently packed into the carriages, taking up any few inches of space they could find. The animals were less submissive and resisted to the end. After lending a hand with coercing them onto the train, Bert chose to co-habit the same carriage as the mules. Stan and George stayed at his side.

"Let me introduce you to Long Ears. She's a sweetheart."

"And you a married man Bert! Just wait 'til I tell Alice," quipped George.

Despite the continual restlessness of the mules, the three friends dropped off to sleep one by one, dozing together as the train rattled through the shadowy countryside. They were awoken by a loud horn. The petty officer who was in the carriage with them looked at his watch.

"Half-past seven lads."

The door of the car slid open to reveal the breath-taking sight of a large ship already in the dock, its single funnel steaming between the masts which stood at its fore and aft. It resembled a curtain being raised on a stage drama.

"It's like a picture in a book!" exclaimed George.

"It's a bloody noisy picture," yawned Stan.

Around the dockside there was barely organised confusion. Thousands of men, mules and horses were lined up in still straight lines or marching between transports. Stores, weapons, military vehicles and other machinery were being noisily unloaded, moved and loaded again by dockside cranes. Trains, trucks and buses were being driven in and out. Dotted around the scene in small groups men were singing, some laughing and joking, whilst the faces of others carried the hint of a shadow, as their minds drifted towards what was to come. Horses and mules, spooked by the noise and the vast crowd, panicked and bolted. One horse seemed to be screaming, and as five or six men tried to restrain it, it collapsed onto the dockside floor. In amongst it all, dockers wandered about wearing an expression of bewilderment.

On the dockside the Anson men were gathered together and formed into a line. When it was their turn, Bert's unit was marched slowly towards the steaming ship. As they shuffled alongside it their eyes widened at its enormous scale. Bert read out the name written in large black letters at the fore of the ship,

"Grantully Castle."

The Man Who Found Treasure

The ship's horn blared out, ordering the men to board, and they moved forward carefully along the gangplank. The chaos present on the dockside was gradually transferred to the deck. Horses and mules shared the open space, not only with the men, but also with vehicles and machinery that had been lashed down for the voyage.

Bert, Stan and George fought their way to the ships rail. As the time of their departure neared, the hubbub died down, except for the occasional whinnying of a horse, but even they seemed to sense the mood of stillness that overtook the men. Nobody stood on the quayside to wave them off. Instead, as the ship pulled quietly and solemnly away, it bellowed a farewell of its own; one which reverberated through the body of each man, bringing lumps to their throats or knots to the pits of their stomachs. Then, somewhere amongst the crowd of quietened soldiers, a lone voice began to sing. It echoed around the men, bare and plaintive, a fitting accompaniment to their private thoughts about leaving the old country behind and of the destiny that awaited across the sea:

Farewell and adieu to my fair Spanish ladies
Farewell and adieu to my ladies of Spain
For we're under orders, For to sail to old England
And we may never see you fair ladies again...

As the man sang, several other voices joined in, but most of the men just stood and watched as England floated away into the distance.

"It dun't look real does it, like it's meltin' into the sea?" Bert observed.

"What? England? Never!" scoffed Stan.

"Do you think we'll ever see her again?"

There was no answer, and the question simply hung in the salty air alongside the ever-present gulls.

To his surprise, Bert found himself revelling in the new experiences and sensations that he was bombarded with. He thrilled at the feeling of the wind on his skin and in his hair. He savoured the smell of saltwater and coal on the air that he breathed. The vibration that coursed through his body from the pounding engines excited him too, as did the lurch of the vessel in the waves, and at the shrieking of the seabirds hovering like kites in the slipstream of the ship. His heart skipped a beat each time the ship's horn bellowed a message to the world that the *Grantully Castle* was steaming its way to war. Each of these new experiences quickened his pulse.

"I don't think I've ever felt so alive," he eventually said, solemnly, to himself, a tingle of pride shivering through his body. "I'm ready for this."

The men slept a couple of decks below, packed in their hammocks amidships; it was uncomfortable and airless. On the second night Bert took a blanket up to the main deck and managed to find a spot close to where Long Ears was housed, bunking down on a bench where he could lie with an unhindered view of the starry sky.

As they progressed into the Bay of Biscay the sea revealed its full power and men began to suffer from seasickness in droves. They lined up at the rail of the ship and there was an almost constant hosing down of the decks. Only George seemed to be immune, and he gleefully mopped up the piles of leftover food.

Weapons and drill training continued onboard throughout the voyage. There were vaccinations to be had and, in their spare time, the men occupied themselves playing cards or singing in an impromptu choir assembled by one of the officers. As March arrived, they turned into the Mediterranean where the sea became calm and the sky brightened. When they finally reached Valletta harbour Sub-Lieutenant Tisdall arranged for ice-cream to be brought aboard for his company, a spoonful each.

"They tell me that Malta has the best ice-cream in the world men. Let's hope this is the beginning of sweeter things to come."

"I hope you're bloody well right," muttered Bert under his breath.

Stan nudged him, "Look at that Bert."

He pointed over to the starboard side where a French battleship was moored.

"It's a big bugger in't it," exclaimed George.

A member of the crew of the *Grantully* started to play the Marseillaise on a fiddle and a few of the men hummed along, one or two of them cheered. Some of the French sailors waved their hats in the air and yelled across unintelligible greetings to their new comrades in arms.

"I reckon it won't be the last un you see," speculated Bert as he was handed his spoonful of ice cream.

Chapter 11.

Turkey: 25 April 1915.

The swarthy armoured body of the *SS River Clyde* shudders as she steals through the water; her forging red blade eagerly peeling back layers of the cold sea. Beneath riveted skin she is a living moaning creature of the emerging dawn; her lifeforce conceived in the fires of her nine furnaces, nourished by a trio of boilers and made alive by a shuddering, whirring, three-cylinder engine. A steady repetitive metallic throb pulses pervasively through the bones of those held captive inside her dark heart; regardless of whether they are human or not.

The deadness of her insistent drone threatens to numb your brain into a stupor, but you know that you can't let it prevail, so you fight hard to stay the right side of alert. You can hear other sounds too – they beat a steady rhythm - booming, muffled… distant. They add a discomforting harmony to the strident thrumming of the engines, stretching the unsettled membrane of your ear drums to its breaking point.

The stifling gloom which encases you doesn't help either, though there is the merest promise of light. It comes from the rising sun which trickles through into the bowels of your steel coffin, showing itself in tantalising flashes in between the other shapes packed around you. Its watery orange glow has seeped in through an open sally port which can only just be made out through the swaying bodies. They are the bodies of Soldiers, moving in involuntary – some would say inhuman – jerks and twitches. Occasionally the orange light is caught on the point of a bayonet, fixed and ready for action. You welcome it, hoping desperately that it will bring an end to the shivering icy cold that descended along with the night and which has taken root in your bones despite the proximity of those bodies around you.

Though the breaking sun has managed to find a way in from the outside, the oxygen hasn't been so lucky. The sheer number of men crammed inside the hull has broken its will, and what little of it there is soon becomes devoured by the odour of several days of stale sweat, fresh urine and even more recent vomit. Its broken remains are finally washed away by the drifting fumes of oil and coal which weave congenially, like the host at a wake, through the thick air.

To some of the occupants of this underworld these are precious perfumes to be savoured - that is in comparison to some of the more recognisable human odours which are harboured in the darkness. You rock gently back and forth, feeling both the forward motion of the ship and the gentle rise and fall of the sea. There is a sudden lurch, and you fall hard into the man next to you, bouncing back like a skittle in a pub alley. You take it in turns to perform the same dance with the other men at your side. No cards are marked, nor apologies exchanged. A sense of unease can be felt by all present, as if it were a physical entity doubling your number.

Your own fear, though you might deny it exists, is indisputably there in the tightness of your chest and in the coarse sandpaper dryness of your mouth. Your heart taps it out in the insistent pitter-patter of Morse Code. Shivers of cold serve to spur it on. You try to convince yourself that everything will be alright. *It has to be*, there is no turning back now and, *surely*, sheer force of willpower will be enough to get you through... *won't it?* Losing your life at this moment just wouldn't make any sense. Meanwhile, you have to remind yourself how to breathe, with each breath re-constructed and learned again. Knots gather in the deep hollow of your stomach, the size of the pith helmet weighing down your head; a head which is already burdened beyond its capability with questions that have no answers, and a deep desire not to be here.

You desperately want to retch. For now, you manage to hold it off, but you know that it's only a matter of time.

This was not what Bert expected the landing to be like.

He'd been ready to land once before, but it was all so very different then. That was a few weeks ago, after the *Grantully Castle* had steamed out of Malta and docked at the island of Lemnos within tantalising sight of the Dardanelles. The battalion was packaged up for the invasion and then hastened towards the Turkish coast. He had quickly scribbled a last note to Alice and left it aboard ship. His fingers were so tense he could barely think or write anything legible. The usually excitable George was the personification of calmness, but he sensed Bert's apprehension.

"I'll stick by you Bert... don't you worry about that."

"Are you scared George?"

"No... I don't know why, but I'm not. I'm ready to fight though."

"What do you reckon it feels like? ...You know... dyin'?"

George shrugged his shoulders as if it wasn't even worth thinking about. Bert continued,

"I wonder sometimes what it might be like... to be hit by a shell. Would you get time to think... to know what's happenin'... to remember things, even for a second, before you pass over like?"

George shook his head.

"I've tried not to think about it, but I can't seem to help m'self. I know one thing though... I don't wanna die. Not now, not here."

George lay his hand on top of Bert's and smiled.

"Give over. You won't die, Bert. You can't... me and Stan'll see to that. We'll keep you safe for Alice and Walter, eh?"

"Eh, lads... look at this!" whispered Stan, choosing his moment to puncture the tension. He loosened the flap of his breast pocket to reveal the top edge of something dark inside. He raised his eyebrows and was met with quizzical faces.

"It's a pocket Kodak!" he dipped his chin a couple of times in its direction, just in case they hadn't grasped what he was referring to.

"Joel sent it on to me. Should come in handy to record our triumphant march into Constantinople."

"You're for the bloody high jump if they catch you," George spat back out of the corner of his mouth.

"Will they 'eck as like. They'll have bigger fish to fry than me I reckon."

Just as they had steeled themselves for their climb into the lighters that were waiting to take them to the enemy coast, there was a shout from an officer which that told them they were turning around.

"Change of plan men... we're goin' back to Lemnos."

Bert didn't dare declare his relief, as other men around him cursed their lost opportunity to go to war.

From Lemnos the battalion had sailed back across the Mediterranean to Port Said in Egypt. Whence forth they were packed on trains and shipped to the Mustafa Pasha Barracks in Alexandria. It was only a brief respite from the action though, and they were soon parcelled up again, and ordered back on a boat to Lemnos.

This time it felt different from the start. The battleships of several nations were crammed into the busy harbour at Mudros, bobbing uneasily on the water, their mooring ropes tightened as if straining at a leash. Adrenalin seeped into the air for everyone to breathe, and the many other hormones that steel a man for battle pulsed through ten-thousand veins. It raised the voices of some and quietened others.

The battalion was carved up and shared out between the hastily assembled landing forces. Each one destined for a beach on the Gallipoli peninsula; none of them knowing what would be waiting for them there. This time there was no turning back.

Tisdall had explained the plan on the deck of the *Cawdor Castle* in Mudros harbour the previous evening.

"Men, we're going to use an old coal steamer called the *SS River Clyde* as a kind of Trojan Horse. It'll be packed full of our chaps and run aground at one of the beaches at the tip of Cape Helles. This is our beach... V Beach. Our Irish friends will float in ahead of us to secure the ground and we'll use the steam hopper, which is coming in behind us with the lighters, to form a bridge. Once we've come to a halt we'll disembark from the ports they've cut into the side of the ship. Using the lighters as a pathway, we'll make our way onto the beach and then up into the village beyond. Our objectives, other than securing V Beach, will be the old fort... fort number three on your maps... and hill one-four-one at the top of the village. The Turks will be bombarded until they're senseless before we arrive there, so they won't know what's hit them... they'll be overwhelmed in no time. It should be a satisfying mornings work."

"Whose bloody stupid idea were that Trojan Horse?" grumbled a Scots voice from the back of the company.

Tisdall smiled.

"Well actually it was the Greeks. Troy is just over on the other side of the Dardanelles you see. It worked very well for them I seem to recall."

"Aye, but they weren't packed inside a blooming gret coal ship were they?"

Bert was pressed tightly up against George and Stan who stood either side of him. His legs, swollen from the heat in Alexandria and not cured by the frigid air of the hold, ached badly. The pith helmet was making his head itch. He felt nauseous and said nothing. He could hear rapid and strained breathing, before realising that it was his own. There was a whispered prayer intoned by an unknown voice somewhere in the darkness.

"I am the resurrection and the life, saith the Lord: he that must believeth in me though he were dead, yet shall he live: and whosoever liveth and believeth in me, shall never die."

Some of the men joined in with the speaker and a few more responded with "Amen." The same word spilled, involuntarily, from Bert's mouth too. Somewhere close by, a gruff scouse voice repeated the words, "Hold fast lads, get yourself ready," over and over again. Then the words, "Brace yourselves!" snapped and growled their way urgently through the crowd, carried on a thousand breaths.

The ship slowed and stuttered; its engines died. A long yawning growl announced landfall, as the hull ran first along sand, before making contact with the rocks beneath. It shuddered briefly before becoming gently still again.

A wave of clicking sounds rippled through the jagged forest of men and then... just silence. Hands reached to adjust helmets, but no one dared to breathe as they waited for an order. A tense stillness bound the invaders, until a lone quivering voice observed,

"It's quiet... we must have surprised 'em."

"Or they're all dead from the shelling," sputtered another.

After an age had passed there was a clamour of sound from somewhere towards the front of the ship. The clanking of metal was followed by a sharp whistle, muffled orders were barked out and men began to pour from the sally ports out into the light, their voices raised determinedly towards the enemy.

And then the gunfire began.

"Rapid fire! Machine guns!" Stan cried out.

Bert vomited.

The shooting did not subside. The shouting and yelling grew louder. After a few hours, they had not moved. Bert became aware that his whole body was shaking; a coldness had moved through it from his toes upwards. Then the message was passed from man to man that someone had managed to get the lighters together to form a bridge to the beach. There was a shuffle of bodies ahead, and the many-headed shape began to move cautiously forward to the front of the boat.

Bert could see the open sally port ahead with men stumbling through it directly into a makeshift gangway. He could just about make out fragments of the boats pulled up alongside. Stan pushed Bert forward.

"Come on lads, let's do this for Old Oak!"

"I'm comin' for you Johnny Turk," roared George.

As they emerged into the daylight, Bert baulked momentarily. The sky was unbelievably blue, and ray of strong sunlight blinded his eye. He raised a hand to it, but as he readjusted his sight he could barely comprehend what he saw playing out before him. Men were scrambling over the lighters, but as they moved beyond the *River Clyde's* bow they were being hit with machine gun fire from the fort to the right and from the high ground above the beach. The maxim machine guns on the boat were firing aimlessly towards the source of the gunfire, but the Turks were not aiming their guns at the boat, instead they were targeting the men as they came out into the open. Soldiers were falling into the shallow water in droves, and the lighters were already filling up with bodies. The beach ahead of them was already decorated with scores of dead.

"The hopper's in the wrong place," Stan observed, spotting that the steam hopper had drifted away from the *River Clyde* and was floating, uselessly, parallel to the beach. His voice was barely able to carry his words above the din of battle.

"It dun't matter Stan... look over there, the lighters have been tied together somehow, we ought to get a shift on," urged Bert, his ears buzzing from the sheer volume of noise around him.

He felt a sharp push in the back.

"Keep bloody movin' laddie!" a Scot's voice bawled from behind.

The gangway wobbled unsteadily under foot. A bullet cracked and whooshed past Bert's ear, and he dropped to his knees.

"Snipers!"

There was another crack. It caught Stan in the shoulder and spun him round. Further unbalanced by the weight of his pack he toppled backwards, frantically pulling at the straps with his right hand in an effort to release it, but as his left arm hung uselessly at his side he was unable to grip it. Instinctively George and Bert each made a desperate grab for him, but he was already out of their reach and he fell backwards into the azure sea. As he foundered, for that moment, time seemed to slow almost to a standstill, even as the battle continued to rage around them. Stan appeared to make a grab for the pocket containing the camera with his good arm, but his hand just slapped against it as if he were gently waving farewell.

George fell to his knees and reached toward the water, grasping vainly towards his sinking friend. Bert stood transfixed, his eyes following the expression of startled terror on Stan's face as he descended into the clear-green space beneath. He saw other bodies too, lining the seabed like monstrous fish, some frantically blowing bubbles to the surface as they convulsed and writhed in a frantic and forlorn dance. Others spewed out clouds of dark ink.

"It's the packs... they're too heavy," Bert heard himself crying out, now shaken from his trance, and with the noises of war crashing back into his ears.

Very soon Stan wriggled no more and he sank serenely, eyes wide open, to the bottom. Bert couldn't tear his eyes away from his lost friend. Even as he watched, he knew that he was witnessing the unfolding of an incipient nightmare; one which would haunt him for the rest of his life.

"Can you move men?"

It was Tisdall. He too came to a shocked standstill at the sight of the chaotic panorama ahead of him and exclaimed,

"Good Lord!"

He turned to Bert who was nearest to him.

"This is madness, utter madness, I can't stand here watching this slaughter. We've got to do something to help the men in the water... here, take this."

There was no time to linger and, now acting on nothing but instinct, Bert took his officer's cap and gun and helped the sub-lieutenant strip his jacket, before Tisdall jumped into to the surf. Unquestioningly Bert then removed his own pack and did the same. George followed him, angrily growling out threats of revenge for his dead friend, even as saltwater filled his mouth, making him sputter and gag.

There was an empty lifeboat already in the water. With bullets flying around them churning up the water like a hailstorm, Tisdall swam over to it and pushed it forward in front of him. Bert and George and other men who had joined them, swam to his side. As they came across men who were still alive, they heaved them up into the boat. When they'd loaded five or six men they turned and pushed the boat back to the *Clyde*. The men still on the gangways helped lift the wounded men back through the sally ports. Bert swam back exhausted once the second load had been deposited and then watched in awe as Tisdall went back for more with George still at his side.

After several hours of fighting, the gunfire had not died down. It felt like a lifetime since they had run aground, and they had achieved nothing, other than being massacred. The wire beyond the beach remained intact. Another attempt was made to break through by a company of Royal Munster Fusiliers. They rushed past Bert who found himself, involuntarily, following in their wake back out onto the gangway. They were mowed down in front of him. He threw himself down into one of the lighters as the crossfire enfiladed over the shoreline towards him, landing on bodies. Even putting his hands over his ears didn't block out the incessant rap of the machine guns, *chu-chu-chu-chu, chu-chu-chu-chu-chu-chu-chu*. He wanted badly to block it out. He felt he would go mad if he didn't.

There was an explosion that sounded as though it came from deep in the bowels of the ship, he tried to turn his head, but he had no control over it, and it stayed stuck between his hands. The shockwave from the explosion rippled through the dead flesh beneath him.

As the blast subsided, a different sound caught his attention. He heard it even through the strident and incessant whistling in his ears, and it made him feel sick. It was the sound of sobbing. He tried to block that out too. There was nothing he could do for the poor mangled wretches around him, and his soldier's intuition told him that he couldn't waste time trying, so he grabbed a rifle and some ammunition from one of the corpses. As he did so a hand sprung up and forcefully clutched his wrist. Bert dropped the rifle and lowered himself to the side of the man who held him. It was a young Munsterman, his chest and face soaked with blood. Bert instinctively stroked the boy's forehead with his free hand and a momentary calmness settled upon them both, as if the battle was holding its breath just for them.

"You lay still young fella... you don't wanna be attracting more attention from them Turks do you?"

As if to make the point a bullet thudded into one of the still bodies next to him. Bert got down as low as he could until he was almost touching the Irishman's face. The boy tried to speak but could only gurgle wordlessly as pink foam dribbled and spattered from his mouth. Bert forced a reassuring smile and stayed with him for a few moments, as bullets continued to hiss and thud around them. Gently releasing the man's grip, he picked up the rifle and slithered carefully over the remaining bodies to gain a better view of the beach.

He didn't move far. He shivered to a halt at the sight of a thick foaming red line running across to the far end of the beach. The horrific thought struck him that maybe a small part of it was made up of Stan's blood. His vantage point provided a better view of the boats nearer the shore too. The cutters that had delivered the first wave of Royal Dublin Fusiliers bobbed up and down on the ravaged surf, they too were full of bodies. He gritted his teeth to control the anger that was now rising within him, but it was also stiffening his resolve. Further up the beach more bodies lay strewn over the sand and around them the sounds of war were being played loudly from all corners of the small bay. Machine gun fire continued to pour from the heights above it and smoke, together with the smell of cordite and death, hung over the amphitheatre-like bay like a proscenium arch.

He realised he didn't know where George and the rest of his company were. Then artillery fire began to hit the beach, its reach extending to the edge of the waterline. Huge geysers of sand, seawater and body parts erupted into the air with each ear-bursting explosion.

"I've had enough of this lark," Bert said to himself and scrambled back towards the safety of the *River Clyde*. He crawled the last few yards until he was claimed by welcoming oily-damp hands from above and was dragged back into the dark safety of the hold.

The survivors of the failed landing on V Beach hunkered down for the night inside the hull of their Trojan Horse, its secret cargo now well and truly revealed. Exhausted and hungry, Bert sipped frugally from his water ration. Sleep wouldn't come to him. His mind calculated that, if they wanted to, the Turks could saunter down from the high ground and finish off the remnants of the army now cowering inside the decoy ship with ease.

"We're here for the taking, aren't we?" he enquired of George, but he found that the younger man *was* asleep.

Instead he shared his fear with only himself. He considered the possibility that, if the Turks didn't counter-attack, the divisional commanders might attempt to rescue them under the cover of darkness. It was a forlorn hope. Eventually exhaustion finally claimed him.

Unbeknown to Bert, and the other soldiers at his side, their misfortune wasn't unique. Out in the icy night, the invasion force was spread thinly around the rocky headland. It was trapped in pockets, in similar situations, in coves and gullies and on beaches, fully engaged in fighting off an unexpectedly wily defender, whilst wondering what the hell to do next.

The darkness dampened the gunfire. Neither rescue nor annihilation came to pass. Some men took tentative steps out into the night, dancing around the occasional searchlight or hopeful volley of bullets. As no horror befell them, others followed. Impelled to do something ... to do anything they could ... they moved their feet in the shallow water, amongst the rocks that formed a causeway to the beach, feeling for anything that might be a body that they could drag up onto the sand. They didn't have to search for long. In time a deep orange sun began its ascent from a calm and clear blue Aegean Sea, just as it had risen over other scenes of carnage in that place through millennia gone by.

A distant cockcrow had heralded the onset of a new firestorm alongside the breaking dawn that morning. As those still imprisoned within the *Clyde* stirred their aching bodies, they might have been forgiven for thinking that the enemy was unleashing their final *coup de grâce*. Some were ready for the inevitable and prayed that it would be over quickly. But then rumours drifted through the dark that the Hampshires had gone on the offensive, even pushing the enemy back. Many didn't believe it, but however incredulous, men were starting to stream out of the stranded hulk. A loud explosion vibrated the metal around them. Tisdall sauntered into the still trembling hold clutching a steaming tin mug and wearing a wry smile.

"I thought that you might want to know lads… the Hampshires have taken the fort."

There were no cheers then. Men buttoned up their shirts and grabbed their rifles. A chorus of coughing rippled through the void as chests were cleared. They knew what was coming next.

In the scorching heat, the fighting beyond the fort was intense. Following the Hampshires lead, Tisdall led his men up the hill adjacent to the fort to support the rear of the attack. Soldiers were fighting hand to hand, ruined house by ruined house; through a shattered ghost-village that had been emptied of its population. The air around them burned with the hiss and crack of rifle fire and echoed with the shouts and screams of men. Bert's company hung back, feeling like they were onlookers, until they were finally called to join in the push, as the battle raged away from the village itself. They moved along the vertical and straight main street, through wrecked houses and shops on their way up the hill, checking that they were clear. The dusty street was full of the contorted bodies of both sides, laying where they fell. Bert was relieved to see that they were mostly Turks. It was the first time that he had seen the enemy in such proximity, he struggled to resist the temptation to look a little more closely. These were the men who had murdered Stan after all, and now they had reaped their reward for the horror they had unleashed the day before. But, then again, yesterday seemed so long ago now.

As the sun reached its zenith, at the top of the hill, loud battle-cries exploded into the air as the Hampshires and the Irish regiments charged in to mop up the last remnants of Turkish resistance. A tall officer, who wore no hat and carried no more than a swagger stick, led the assault. The sun glinted from his bald head as he surged forward, seemingly unconcerned and untouched by the bullets flying around him, even as he towered above the combatants amid the melee. Bert came upon the scene just as the moment of victory was secured, but in its last act he witnessed the tall officer take a bullet to the head and fall to the ground like a felled oak in a forest of men.

For now, the beach was secured and, barring the odd sporadic rattle of gunfire, a relative peace descended at last. Bert glanced over to his right and saw the twinkling blue waters of the Dardenelles Strait in the distance. As he did so, birdsong struck up a chorus of liberation in the branches of the cypress trees that were dotted around him, as if they had been holding their breath for this moment. It seemed a far cry from the bloody horrors of the previous day and, as feelings of relief enveloped him, he let himself wonder if the hardest part of the task they'd been given to do had now been achieved.

There was no time to savour the success of their plan, however. 'D' Company were soon set to work recovering bodies from the boats before being detailed to assist with bringing ashore stores both from the *Clyde* and the other boats that now poured into the bay. The beach was now a hive of activity. There were burial parties to form and a casualty clearing station to set up. The bloodied and bullet-riddled dead were pulled from the deep pools of red seawater where they rested and lined up on the beach to await being handed over to the burial parties. Bert helped carry the body of the young Irishman he'd encountered the previous day. Whilst doing so he saw, to his great relief, that Stan was laid out close to the spot where the Munsterman was placed gently down. There was no time to linger in the company of his private thoughts though, despite the guilt he felt that he couldn't sit with his friend for one last time.

Along with the cold, the evening brought with it a relative quiet, broken only by the occasional gunshot or machine gun burst. Bert and George made their new home on the scrubby ground above the beach. They dug shallow fox holes using empty Bully Beef tins and laid ground sheets across the top. Conversation was muted at first as they tried to make sense of the last couple of days and come to terms with a confusing myriad of feelings they'd never experienced before. It was George who broke the awkward silence, his breath misting in the cooling air.

"I'm fed up wi' this bloody sand already... it's bloody everywhere. Look, it's even in me tea... I'm going to be pissin' sand at this rate."

Bert turned tired eyes towards his friend,

"Sand! Why are you rabbitin' on about bloody sand? Just thank the bleedin' Almighty that you're alive enough to get fed up about stuff like that."

George bowed his head,

"I know, I know... and I'm grateful for it, don't think I'm not. I'm hit hard about Stan too Bert... he were my mate as well as yourn. He won't be the last of us to die here though, will he? It could be you tomorrow... it could even be me. I can't wait to get away from this fuckin' place and off to bloody Constantinople, then maybe they'll send us home after that. That's all I'm thinkin' about now... gerrin' bloody home."

To his own surprise, Bert found a smile from somewhere.

"You know, you're startin' to sound just like an old man George... where's that cocky short-arsed bogger who I know and love gone, eh?"

"I think he walked into that coal ship yesterday, but never came out again."

"So now there's just two of us Old Oak boys left," Bert mused.

After a moment of contemplation, George suddenly sat upright as if hit by a moment of revelation.

"Look Bert, I've got something to show you... I'd forgot all about it."

He rummaged around in his pack and eventually pulled out a battered old pocket watch.

"That's Stan's watch... 'ow did you get hold of that?" queried Bert.

"He must've shoved it into my pack when we were on the *Clyde*. I reckon he din't want to get it wet, and it was easier to stuff it into mine than 'is."

Bert thought for a few moments, before announcing,

"George... I've got an idea."

The two friends followed the track back down to the beach and sat down on the sand. Bert had brought with him one of the empty Bully

Beef tins. He cleaned it out as best he could by rubbing sand around it with his fingers and tapping it on his thigh. He then placed the watch inside. They dug a small hole in the sand with their hands and lowered the tin into it. Each of them then threw a handful of sand onto the tin, before they refilled the hole. George had lashed together two thin twigs, pulled from the scrub around their bivouac, to make something that resembled a cross. He stuck it into the ground where they had buried the tin. Bert heaved a sigh.

"We remember our good friend Stanley Cooper."

He hesitated.

"Did Stan 'ave a middle name, George?"

George shrugged his shoulders and shook his head.

Bert nodded and continued,

"He was a lovin' son to his mother and a dutiful brother to Joel. Whilst he was a lanky bastard and crap at football and a few other things... we're damned sure that he were the best of us, and there in't no doubt about that. He were meant for bigger and better things, I reckon. We'll miss you Stan, rest in peace lad."

Bert and George shared a moment of solemn quietude and then they shook hands.

"Well said Bert," said George, rubbing his eye. "I've just realised that Joel won't know that he's gone, will he? Neither will his mam. That makes me feel just as bad as losin' Stan in the fost place."

"Likely as not it'll be months before they find out. Bastard war."

"This dun't feel real does it? It's like Stan were never really here wi' us at all."

Bert raised his aching body to his feet and offered out a hand to help his friend do the same. He felt himself shivering.

"If you're sayin' we just dreamed all of this... well then, I hope to God you're right."

"Amen to that."

"Anyway, I don't know about you George, but if Johnny Turk'll let me, I'm ready for some bleedin' kip."

Chapter 12.

Turkey: 1915.

Just a year ago Bert would have savoured the sensation of the sun's rays caressing his face. He would have eagerly looked forward to the next precious day of baking summer heat, knowing that the life-giving radiance it would dispense could not be taken for granted. There was something else it gave him too… the promise that good times might be on the way.

But those days were long gone.

Here, in this barren place, the sun was just as much the enemy as Johnny Turk. It burned and blistered his skin until raw, it swelled his joints, and it magnified his thirst. Worse still, it intensified the smell of decay which hovered around him, as it rotted the flesh of the unburied corpses carpeting the ground of no man's land.

Bert mused upon this change in his circumstances as he stood on the fire step of a trench now occupied by the shattered remnants of 'D' company. On its own he might have been able to overlook the burned skin and warmed through death that surrounded him and simply get on with things; but what he could never forgive, or forget, was the black plague of flies which had also been unleashed by the sun's fire. Fat from their fill of flesh, they grew to the size of marbles and were everywhere. Even if he no longer gagged when he drank them with his tea or ate them with his fatty bacon and Bully Beef, he still panicked when he opened his mouth and breathed them in, the flies buzzing in protest as they wriggled around on his tongue.

He never thought it possible, but the flies were even worse than the lice that crawled fearlessly within the seams of his shirt, and inside his underwear. Their plentiful maggots burrowed through the walls of the trenches, pale, squirming packets of consumed putrid flesh; a reminder, as if he needed it, of what lay in store for the soldiers of Gallipoli. He had given up trying to burn them to death with his cigarettes, there were just too many of them for that and anyway, unlike the soldiers, most of them appeared to be immortal.

Flies brought with them the dysentery too. Every man had suffered with it at some point since the early days on the peninsula. The latrines, despite the vile combined smell of diseased excrement and quick lime, attracted large queues. It was so bad that, often, Bert took a chance by digging a pit of his own, some distance away from the trench. There was also that nagging thought in the back of his mind that 'Johnny' was bound to target the latrines one day; he could knock out half the company in one go if he dropped a whizz-bang on top of them, that's for sure. Today, it was George's turn to be under the weather. Not very long-ago Bert might have made a joke about it, but the laughs were wearing thin now and any attempt at a diarrhoea-related wisecrack would most likely result in a black-eye.

Still, it was not all bad.

Today was quiet, monotonous even. Bert had come to treasure monotony. There hadn't been a full-on battle for a while, apart from the odd half-hearted Turkish attack or short-lived skirmish. He had told George that morning that they were due a bit of boredom, after all they'd had more than their fair share of its alternative. There was something else too which made him feel less miserable than he usually did; something more than the simple the joy of monotony. Bert tried to work out what it was, and then it came to him: Silence... stillness. It took him a while to fully comprehend it, as if learning precisely what it was all over again; it was just that rare on Cape Helles.

Once he tuned into it, it was almost deafening, but he knew it wouldn't last more than a few seconds. It was enough though to allow him to think... to remember what had happened to him in these few short turbulent weeks.

If the landing was his baptism of fire, then there had been little time to catch his breath, even after that frenzied rite of passage into the sordid business of being a soldier. The battle for V beach had been bad enough on its own, without having to spend the following couple of days helping to bury the dead. His job was to rifle through their pockets to find any personal effects and to recover pay books and identification disks, if they were there. He got through it in a nauseous daze, but the smell of death had not left his nostrils since, and he feared it never would. At first his face had openly betrayed his revulsion, a fact which was not lost upon the Sergeant of the Royal Munsters standing next to him.

"You might not feel it now laddie... but it could be worse... a hell of a lot worse."

"Worse? How?" disbelief heightened the pitch of Bert's voice.

The Sergeant held up a calming hand.

"Well, just think on laddie, you could be one o' these fine gentlemen for a start. Remember you're the one doing the buryin' here. And, even if you disregard that agreeable state of affairs, then take note that these gentlemen still have a certain freshness about 'em. Now then, I remember I was on a burial party during the late South African War. We were lookin' after some of our lads who'd fallen in a spat a few weeks before. The bodies looked a bit bloated, but they were... you know... in one piece, so to speak. When you went to pick 'em up though... well, then they turned to nothing but stinkin' putrid slime that dripped through your fingers. We had to scoop em' up into sacks with our bare 'ands. Aye, laddie, if you make it through this, then... mark my words... you won't be rememberin' this as the worst day of your war."

Bert's first experience of trench warfare came a week after the landings, although he had already lost count of the number of days that had passed by then. The company had been moved to the east in support of the French front line and they soon came under heavy attack from the Turks. He found himself sharing a claustrophobic trench with some of the fearsome looking Senegalese troops whom he had previously only seen from a distance. They regarded each other suspiciously at first. The Africans, silent and dour, watching the British soldiers intently and with an unconcealed wariness. Bert had never seen black-skinned men before, and it brought back to him the tales he'd heard in his childhood about Gordon of Khartoum and marauding, murderous black dervishes, their faces screaming from the pages of ancient storybooks. It gave him nightmares then. Now these dark warriors put him on edge, almost as much as the Turks did. He told himself that, this time, they were on the same side, but however much he hid his unease his magnetised eyes and stiff self-conscious movements gave him away.

He found that fear was an all too willing companion during the waiting hours. If you gave it free reign, that is. It would gnaw at you and fester, like the lice. This was not the case once the fighting began, for then fear wasn't the driving force - staying alive was. Bert's fear was not of death itself. Perhaps it was at the start, in the days before the landing, but now he had seen it too many times already, close-up; enough for it to be an intimate acquaintance. There were no surprises. Its inevitability was understood. The incontinent, jabbering fear of some of the other men simply drew his pity. Instead, the fear that Bert carried was the sheer terror of not seeing his wife and child again. *Even worse*, it was the fear of forgetting what they looked like, or of *them* forgetting *him*. It was in those waiting hours, when he tried to summon up face of his son and the image would just not form, that he opened the door to its full force.

On that occasion, his fears remained conquered. As the Turks unleashed their army, black-man and white-man melded to form a single, desperate, defending force. Together they fought off unyielding waves of attacks, until the soldiers on all sides were too exhausted to carry on.

When the time finally came for the Ansons to be relieved, a stocky Senegalese soldier tapped Bert on the arm so forcefully that it was almost a push. Bert turned towards him, his blood still up from battle, mentally readying his rifle, but the soldier shot back only a wide grin and he offered out his hand. Bert replied with a relieved smile of his own and they shook hands, heartily, with each other.

"Nous sommes fréres, oui?" the African asked, waving a finger between the two of them.

Bert nodded enthusiastically, without understanding anything of the words and only knowing, with pride, that he had witnessed the sharing of respect between men of different colour, and of continents that were thousands of miles apart.

Then, all too quickly, it was 'D' Company's turn to attempt to capture the low hill that Bert could see from the position he was now occupying. They called it 'Achi Baba'. He didn't think it was much of a hill at all, but it was what passed for high ground on this part of the peninsula. He couldn't be sure how long had elapsed since they left the French lines, it may have been the same afternoon, or few days later; for time had become blurred though lack of sleep and the hazy timelessness of battle. However, on their first attempt, they had got as far as occupying an abandoned Turkish trench. The company had led the assault in the first wave, charging forward under long-range fire with Tisdall leading from the front as usual, until they came across some trigger-happy Turkish machine gunners, and that was that. They fell into the empty trench. Tisdall, however, did not do monotony and, as soon as the shooting had died down, he made the mistake of easing himself up to get a view above the trench parapet so that he could assess the situation. His reward was a sniper's bullet full in the chest.

As Bert saw the sun-tinted redness drain away from the officer's face and flood, instead, into the khaki drill of his shirt, he imagined that Death must be proudly observing his handiwork from somewhere close by, perhaps even smiling with sinister satisfaction from beneath the shadow of his hood. If he was watching, then Tisdall's demise was his grimmest and most spectacular joke yet. The loss of the company's talisman, a man overflowing with so much talent and life-force that he was bound to be indestructible, was a crushing blow. On the day that the Lieutenant's life was wasted, the Anson Battalion had gained only a scant few yards of bare ground.

More recently, just a few weeks ago, their next attempt on Achi Baba and the village of Krithia that stood in their path to the hill, had resulted in a something resembling a cull of the Anson's officers. It had been a whole lot worse for some of the other RND battalions though. The rumour was that the Collingwoods had been virtually wiped out as the enemy enfiladed the British lines, cutting them down like wheat in a field during an Indian Summer harvest. Johnny Turk, Bert concluded, had his sights lined up perfectly on that glorious, cloudless, Friday. He knew that his company had been lucky by not being in the thick of things this time, but his relief was tempered with questions. The division had lost many men on June 4th and for what? Would it be their turn to lead the attack next time? Surrendering precious and hard-won ground, piled high with the corpses of your own dead, seemed to be the way of things in the Dardanelles. "Pass the parcel," George called it. Bert just didn't want to be there when the music stopped.

After limping away from the carnage of what soon became known as the third battle of Krithia, the battalion had been withdrawn from the peninsula for a week to a rest camp on the island of Imbros. A 'holiday' their commanding officer called it, with a patronisingly straight face. It didn't feel much like a holiday. It was true that the men swam in the sea, free from the threat of Turkish shelling, some of them flirted with the Australian and Canadian nurses who had made Imbros their temporary home. They practised bayonet charges against an imaginary, docile, enemy across the sandy ground; but there was no time to rest their shattered minds. The battalions were hastily reorganised and patched up. The men, mourning lost comrades and dispossessed of their innocence, remained fractious.

Bert felt numb inside, but he couldn't put his finger on exactly what was missing and he was unable to settle his wandering thoughts. For the first time he had the opportunity to properly reflect on the previous few weeks. This was not done voluntarily, and the emotions that the flashbacks aroused were as viscerally raw as they were in the moment he first experienced them, tensing his body rather than relaxing it. The edginess he felt never left him on Imbros and the respite of sleep, which exhaustion had previously coaxed his body into accepting, was kept at bay by sweat-inducing terrors in the middle of the night.

He did have the time to write a letter to Alice, but this brought with it different terrors. What should he tell her? The truth, or a version of the truth made just for Alice? In the end his pen wouldn't, or couldn't, compose any words about Stan or Tisdall, or the other bloody slaughter he had witnessed. Instead, he reassured her that he was safe and well, and told a tale of sun, sea, sand and smiling dervishes.

And then, before he knew it, he was once more on a boat heading back into the battle. On board, he and his fellow passengers were silent and pensive, as columns of dark smoke presided over their welcoming party.

***

"You look deep in thought," observed George in a croaking voice.

He was curled up, almost at Bert's feet, inside an alcove dug out of the trench wall, a blanket pulled up to his shoulders.

"Not really... just admirin' the view."

"You'll get a better view at the abattoir."

"How's the Gallipoli trots?" enquired Bert.

"It'll pass."

"It'll pass... right through you!"

George threw the dry biscuit he was reticently nibbling. It hit Bert in the midriff.

"When you think about it, how much manure do you reckon we've shat out here? I should ask 'em if we can box it up and send it home, it'll do wonders for the cabbages on the farm," said Bert.

"Manure? You're full of it, that's for sure... and anyway our shit'll be too maggoty for any cabbages."

"I was thinking of what I'd be doin' at home on a day like this un," Bert confessed after a solemn pause.

"Well I know what I'd be doin'... I'd be fishin' in the pond at Wollaton," offered George. "You know, I'd just be lyin' there on the bank, in the sun. Then I'd drift off to sleep and do nothin' else but listen to the watter plop with the insects buzzin' round me head. Thinkin' about it... I'd tek them gnats buzzin' round that pond over these fuckin' flies any day." He chuckled, "I never thought I'd be pinin' for those bitin' bastards. In't it funny what bein' away from home meks you think about?"

"I'd be walkin' in the arboretum wi' Alice and Walter. Else we'd be on the embankment... holding 'ands like."

Bert closed his eyes and pictured Alice's face. This time the image came to him immediately, her cheeks rouged by the sun, beaming and effortlessly happy. He heard her laughter and felt the tickle of her hand run down his arm until their fingers entwined. He reached out a finger to trace the shape of her in the air. He imagined feeling the heat of her sweat-sheened, sun-blushed skin. He wanted to feel it for real, so badly.

"You could have a dip in Trent Baths if it were really hot," interrupted George, "I'd kill for a swim in ice cool watter just now."

Bert forgave him for breaking the spell, and the residue of happiness that his daydream had unlocked prompted him to laugh out loud.

"Do you remember that old bloke who used to tek 'is dog with 'im to them baths. He used to sit the bogger on 'is shoulders like it was a towel or summat... bloody ugly thing it was."

"That bloody scrag-end of a dog! I remember! I would've drowned the bastard mysen."

"You know what Georgy? I miss the sound of a game o' cricket too," the words were spoken wistfully as the thought burst into Bert's head without displacing the image of Alice that was now lodged there.

"Me an' all," agreed George. "It just in't the same wi' out the sound of a cricket ball bein' whacked on a hot summer afternoon, is it? Eatin' ham cobs and suppin' ale while you're watchin' it too."

"Suppin' ale? At your age?" Bert mock-admonished.

"I bet there'd be a few smartish lookin' gels about too, layin' on the grub like." George closed his eyes to conjure up the image, before devilment opened them again. "Hey Bert, what do you reckon the Turkish gels are like 'ere?"

Bert shook his head, unable to think about any girl other than Alice.

"If they're anythin' like them gels we had in Alex, then they'd be summat that's for sure. Them dark eyes cud get me to do anythin'. Bet they're not a patch on them though," continued George with enthusiasm.

"*We* 'ad in Alex? Speak for yoursen, you randy bastard, I'm a respectable married man."

The realisation immediately struck Bert that his diminutive friend - the hapless, youthful, figure of fun on the farm just a few short months ago - had now become a man. What's more, he was one of the bravest soldiers in the company's ranks. Despite George's new-found uncouthness, Bert felt a surge of almost fatherly pride.

The smiles disappeared from Bert and George's faces as a command was relayed at pace down the line of the trench. They knew it was back to business.

"Kingdom... transport!"

Since Bert had demonstrated his prowess with the mules back in Shillingstone, he had been allocated to transport duties when the battalion required it. This also meant that he'd had a joyful reunion with Long Ears and she, in turn, had been made an honorary member of the company. He'd grown so attached to her that he viewed her as just as much a friend to him as his human comrades. Sometimes he told her things that he could never share with the other men. He reckoned too that he could tell that she was always pleased to see him.

"Her ears prick up, and she does a little dance," he once told George, but he regretted that as soon as he said it. Discretion was a stranger to George, and so Bert's relationship with Long Ears became a source of much amusement to the other lads. Every time he was called to work with the mules, the men of the company pursed their lips and blew noisy kisses or offered more graphic interpretations of the nature of their forthcoming liaison.

A few weeks before, Long Ears had become ill. Bert thought that she'd been bitten by an insect or maybe a scorpion. She lay down and wouldn't be roused, only occasionally raising her head to peer at her carer with sad eyes. Bert spent whole nights making sure she was comfortable, feeding her with hay and water, and softly stroking her neck. Even when she was well she wouldn't eat as much as the other mules; Bert was convinced she would die.

"Come on you stubborn Jenny-Mule, you've got to eat summat. I'm relying on you to help get me through this bloody war. Who's gonna fetch our grub from the beach if you don't... eh girl?"

To his surprise, she pulled through, and was soon as right as rain. It was the best feeling he'd had since stepping onto the beach at Cape Helles and he became even more protective of Long Ears after that. It was almost like an obligation, given now that was the second time he'd got her out of trouble. Not that he'd tell the other men that.

"They'll want me to fetch up some more stores from the beach. I'd better fill this in before I forget," he sighed to George.

Bert pulled a field postcard from his pocket. Across the top was written:

'NOTHING is to be written on this side except the date and signature of the sender. Sentences not required may be erased. <u>If anything else is added the post card will be destroyed</u>'.

He crossed out all the pre-printed options apart from *'I am quite well'* and *'Letter follows at the first opportunity'* with a pencil. Then he dated it and signed it simply *'Bert'*. He addressed the front of the postcard to Alice.

"I'm due a letter from her, I've not had anything back since I wrote home from Blandford. I dunno what the army's playing at."

"They probably can't keep track of you. There'll be one on its way for sure... Alice is no slacker."

"I know that. What about you... are you sendin' anything?"

George shook his head.

"I've nowt to say... well nowt that they'll let you say anyway."

Bert made his way down the trench and waved a hand in his friend's direction,

"I'll see you later. Be good."

"I will mate... and don't forget to give Long Ears a kiss from me," replied George. He planted an imaginary peck on his upturned fingers and blew it in Bert's direction.

Chapter 13.

The island of Lemnos: Two days earlier.

Close to the eastern shoreline at Mudros, a lone British Second Lieutenant eyed the landscape. The incline rising gently behind him was speckled with white canvas tents and, as he watched, men in uniform bustled between them and the harbour. His eyes drifted up to the crest of the hill. It was lined with windmills, their sails still for want of a breeze. They seemed to be watching too, but disinterestedly; war was nothing new to them after all. Over to his left, the village – a scattering of mostly low buildings, many wooden, some with corrugated roofs - fell haphazardly down the slope and almost into the water itself. They stood under the deprecatory gaze of a grand white church which dominated the skyline, but which seemed out of place all the same, like a cuckoo sitting atop a nest full of its discarded 'siblings'.

This was the officer's first posting abroad, but he was unimpressed by what he had seen so far. He was already pining for the rolling hills of the Forest of Dean, and he'd only been on the island for two days. What's more it was much too hot, and his head ached constantly. At first he'd put that down to the nagging sense of destiny that he'd felt as soon as he boarded the boat to come here. It was a calling that had kept him awake for nights on end. There was only one way to release that pressure, and now the chance to fulfil that destiny would come his way with the dawn. He took out a handkerchief and wiped the sweat from his forehead.

Between him and the village a group of men were playing a boisterous game of football - or might it be rugby? He wasn't quite sure, it appeared to be a hybrid of the two. He studied them for a moment before turning his head back towards the water. The still bay was decorated with waterborne craft of all shapes and sizes, from steaming battleships to busy tugs, lighters and dinghies, all of them seemingly packed with human and animal traffic. Around its rim seabirds waited patiently for the wind to come.

His attention was captured by two red-caped nurses of the Australian Army Nursing Service. Their scarlet figures stood out amongst the predominant browns, greens and whites. He watched them walk down the hill towards the village, winding between the obstacles like a trickle of blood, oblivious to the scenes around them and engrossed in their gossiping. As they passed behind him, one of them stumbled on the uneven ground and fell. He was soon at her side. Another man joined him almost as instantly; he had jogged over from the direction of the football match. The officer took immediate note of the man's grey slacks and pristine white shirt, the sleeves turned up above the elbow.

"Are you injured Ma'am?" The soldier enquired stiffly.

The nurse laughed,

"No, not at all, it was a soft landing, no damage done ...but thank you so much for your concern Lieutenant."

The two men simultaneously reached down an arm to pull her to her feet and she dusted herself down.

"*Two* gallant knights! How lucky I am!"

"It's a pleasure Miss," said the other man, doffing a light-brown fedora, "a fellow Victorian I believe?"

The nurse nodded cursorily before turning toward the lieutenant and holding out a hand, which he took. She shook it exaggeratedly.

"Once again, I must thank you for your help Sir," she giggled.

She maintained eye contact whilst waiting for a response that never came, before she and her friend went on their way in giggling conversation.

The Australian removed his hat and brushed back his hair. The two men shook hands,

"Lachlan Greene."

"Johnson... Royal Engineers".

"Yes, I can see that from your insignia. Pretty little thing wasn't she, even for a Victorian? I think she liked you. I reckon she has a thing for the two stripes."

Johnson shrugged his shoulders and wiped his brow again,

"I didn't notice... I'm not very good with that sort of thing. You're a civilian?"

"Reporter...Melbourne Herald. Have you been over there yet?" he gestured beyond the hill behind them, in the direction the of Gallipoli peninsula.

"No... not yet... tomorrow."

"They say it's not going so well."

The sound of a distant field gun firing turned their heads. It was soon followed by another burst.

"No doubt you're in a better position to know that than me."

"Maybe I'll catch you when you come back here? Then you can tell me all about it," said Greene, flicking his hat playfully at Johnson.

"Yes, well, I've heard all about you reporter chaps. You're never off duty, are you? You should know that neither am I."

Greene laughed.

"Spoken like a true Brit! So where are your mates Lieutenant? Have you lost your company?"

"Mates? Oh, I see... Well, 'mates' are overrated if you ask me, especially given where I'm going in the morning. It's the job at hand that matters, rather than ones 'mates', don't you think? At least that's what's exorcising my mind just now."

"Well, if I were you, I'd probably be a little bit scared of the job at hand."

Johnson guffawed heartily in response, throwing back his head, and making Greene rock back on his feet at the unexpected outburst.

"There's nothing to fear my man! I've been well trained for this show. If anything, this is my chance to make a real mark on the world, to earn these stripes... in fact it feels like my whole life has been leading up to this moment. No, I'm not scared, but I am expectant".

The smile faded from Johnson's face and he turned his eyes towards the boats in the harbour.

"Tomorrow I know my life will change forever, and to tell you the truth, I can't bloody well wait to find out how."

The stillness was suddenly broken by the gust of a breeze, which disturbed the officer's fine sand-coloured hair. Flying low over the bay, beside the boats he spotted a Shearwater making the most of the returning wind. It dipped from side to side and, as it ascended and rotated its body, it seemed, momentarily, to make the shape of a cross in the sky. This caused a shiver to travel through his body.

"Hey, Greeney! Grab the ball mate!"

The shout came from one of the football players. The two men turned to see a leather-cased ball bouncing rapidly and erratically towards them. With an expression of panic etched into his reddening face Johnson readied himself to kick it back in the direction from which it came. He swung his leg and, as he made contact, the ball skewed off the outside of his boot, spinning high up in the air. He lost his balance and fell backwards, landing heavily on the grassy earth. The ball landed behind him with a dull thud, and then rolled tentatively into the water.

Chapter 14.

Turkey: 1915.

After winding his way through the communication trenches which zig-zagged down towards the sea, Bert scurried over to the wide stream bed where the mules were tied up, crouching down all the way as had become second nature to him. He gave Long Ears a pat on the head and kissed her on the nose.

"Good girl."

He slapped the other two mules gently on the back.

"Come on boys... work to do."

He bent down and scooped up a handful of water from the bare stream which, against all odds, still trickled through the dry ground and rubbed it into his face. The young able seaman who he'd first encountered at Shillingstone slid down the bank to join them.

"What took you so long Mac?" smiled Bert, "Didn't you fancy a walk to the seaside? I hear the view from the promenade is spectacular this time o' year."

"It's too bloody warm for a walk to the latrine Bert, let alone the seaside. It would nae be so bad if we could have a dip in the watter when we got there."

Mac wiped the sweat from his already scarlet face.

"Mebbe we can sneak a swim in, eh?" Bert replied.

Their conversation was interrupted by a distant drawn-out whistling sound and then an explosion. The two men scanned the horizon but could see nothing.

"Looks like Johnny's woken up at last."

"Aye... just our luck."

They fitted pack saddles to the two larger mules and slung a set of panniers over Long Ears' back. Bert dropped the mail bag into one of them.

"Come on then you beauties!"

He urged the animals to move and, after a couple of pulls on their reigns, they reticently obliged.

As the party wound their way along the trails that led back to the main supply beach, the smell of wild Rosemary perfumed the air, and an Eagle surfed the sky above them. Another shell exploded some distance off. The mules didn't flinch.

"Funny," remarked Bert, noticing something odd about the noise, "that one didn't let us know it was comin' did it? It were just the sound of the bang."

"Mebbe's it's our lot playing with TNT? Or else we're too far away to hear it," speculated Mac.

"Hmm... maybe."

They had a good view of the Aegean by now and its twinkling water looked cool and inviting as their insect-bitten, hot, sticky and sandy skin chafed against their uniforms with each step. The flies buzzed around their faces, occasionally plucking up the courage to land on the salty flesh, only to be chased away again with the waft of a hand or squashed by a smack to a reddened neck.

A sudden and unexpected slap of footsteps behind them turned their heads. They belonged to a young Second Lieutenant of the Royal Engineers, who was quick marching down the track towards them.

"I say chaps, can I tag along?" he called out after them.

The officer caught up with them, and they halted the mules and saluted dutifully.

"No need for that chaps, far too hot... save that for when there's a superior around. My name is Johnson, Royal Engineers... Fifth Monmouths to be precise. A little presumptive, I know, but I'm hoping you can be my native guides. You see we've only just arrived on the peninsula. I've been out scouting the lay of the land... we've been tasked with sorting out the water supply, you see. You chaps look like you might know a fast track to the beach?"

"No problem Lieutenant, just follow us," replied Bert.

"And you are?"

"Able Seaman Kingdom, Anson Battalion, Royal Naval Division... this 'ere is Able Seaman Mac... I can never get his bloody name right."

"MacManechin," offered Mac, shaking his head.

"Jolly good!" grinned Johnson, "I must say the heat out here is scorching don't you think?"

"Ye get used to it saar," Mac replied dourly.

There was another explosion and this time they felt a slight vibration of the ground.

"They're getting closer," Bert observed.

Johnson turned back to look in the direction from which the sound originated, a frown creasing his forehead.

"Yes, indeed. A chap was telling me yesterday... one of your officers I think... that our Turkish friends have a big gun over on the other side of the water that delivers a package without telling you it's coming. The first you know about it is when it hits you. Quite impressive, don't you think? 9.2 inch... or thereabouts? Big fellow anyway."

He wiped the sweat from his forehead with a handkerchief.

"I wonder who was underneath that one?"

They approached W Beach via a narrow gully, just as another explosion rent the air over in the direction from which they'd come. It was much louder than the others. One of the mules reared and then stamped nervously, momentarily unsettling the other animals. Mac calmed him down.

"Hold on laddie, they're not aimin' for you."

They heard the beach before they saw it. A drone of engines; the clatter of machinery; a disharmony of indistinct voices, animal cries and barked orders – the sounds jumbled together, rolling towards them over the undulating sandy ground like a rising wave.

They stopped short of it to pay homage to the frenetic panorama of men, horses and mules, boats, cranes and wagons, which stretched out in an unbroken haze of dust between the white cliffs which bookended the shoreline. Out at sea, boats of all shapes and sizes queued impatiently for attention or rested at anchor; or steamed along oblivious to the activity on the beach as they sailed away in search of other destinations. The hazy silhouette of a liner was visible on the horizon. As they watched, a biplane wobbled alarmingly through the air above it, finally making a fitful descent to land on the island of Tenedos.

"Let's just wait here a minute," suggested Bert.

They laid up against the banked sand, just beyond the edge of the beach, where the low dunes crowded together beneath patches of Knapweed and other scrubby vegetation. The shallow hollows between them offered a modicum of precious shade. They tied up the mules to the skeletal remains of an old Broom plant. Bert reached out and picked one of the spiky white Knapweed flowers and rubbed it between his hands before sniffing its scent. He screwed up his face and threw it to the ground, wiping his hands on his tunic. Then he lit a cigarette and slumped down in the meagre shadows cast by the undulating sand, pulling his cap down over his eyes. Mac fell to the ground alongside him.

"That sea looks more invitin' each time I look at it," he said, flicking another fly away from his lips.

There was another explosion, but the men didn't react. Johnson appeared somewhat sheepish about taking a rest with his new friends, but he lit a pipe, which he had pulled from his pocket, and paced around nervously. Eventually, he walked over to stand between the increasingly unsettled mules. He stroked Long Ears' neck and puffed on his pipe.

"What would we do without you and your long-nosed friends, eh, my girl?"

A company of Royal Warwickshires ambled wearily up the beach. They spotted the mules and gestured over to the dunes as they walked. A few of the soldiers scrambled up to join Bert and Mac, jettisoning their equipment as they climbed.

"Looks like you fella's have found the only shade on this beach," one of them called across to them, lighting up a cigarette of his own, before falling back onto the sand beside them.

"Boy, it's good to gerrout o' those bloody trenches," sighed another.

"You've just bin relieved then?" asked Bert.

The soldier who lay next to him nodded, "You'd never think it, but even a big ugly bunch of Worcesters can look good in moments like that. It weren't before time though."

The Warwickshires Second Lieutenant strode purposefully up the beach towards where the men were resting. As he walked, he turned his head and body around continually in a strange dance, one second looking up into the sky, the next ahead to his men, until another explosion shook the peninsula beyond the beach. Then he stood ramrod straight watching the blast debris rise into the air in the near distance. As if struck by a sudden epiphany, he turned and waved frantically to his men and immediately began to run along the sand towards them shouting instructions. Bert nudged the corporal sitting next to him.

"Your officer looks like he's got ants in his pants."

The soldier sighed, "What does the young buck want now? Can't he leave us in peace for just one minute?"

Bert chuckled, "He's a keen un that one. It's too hot for that, just wake me up when the war's over."

He let his head flop back to rest on the sandy bank and his mind drifted dreamily back to thoughts of home.

The officer stumbled to a halt, panting for breath, in front of them.

"Men, I want you to get over there, closer to the sea."

He pointed a straight arm over to his right.

"You mean out of the shade sir?" replied the corporal.

"Yes, out in the open... over there."

"But it's blazin' hot sir... and we haven't had any shade to rest in for hours."

The young square-jawed lieutenant fixed his sharp hazel eyes on the soldier,

"That's an order Corporal!"

The corporal sighed again and laboured to his feet.

"Men, you heard the officer... let's get your arses shifted."

There was much grumbling as they dragged their tired bodies out onto the pebble-strewn sand of the scorching beach, and they crashed into a disorderly complaining heap to make a point to the Lieutenant.

Johnson had noticed the young officer's agitation with interest and, as he looked on from his spot between the mules, he followed the line of the his gaze over to the point of the last explosion. Just as he watched the Warwickshire men reluctantly give up their shady retreat, he was struck by the same revelation that had caused the Lieutenant to act moments earlier. He too started to back away into the open space of the beach.

"I say...," he called over towards Bert and Mac.

Bert didn't hear him. Mesmerised by the deep blue diamond-studded panorama which he allowed to seep into his fluttering squinted vision, he imagined that peace had always existed here. It was so beautiful that it could be no other way. Even the heat was now a comforting friend, tempered as it was by both the hint of a breeze and the morsel of shade where he reposed. His ears processed only the distant lapping of the waves and the much closer attentions of some flying insect or other. This stubborn stillness refused to be disturbed by the muffled grumbling of the displaced Warwickshire men from further down the beach. Their protesting voices merged together to become a private hypnotic plainsong in that blissful instant.

But in the next moment there was another sound. An infiltrator; a sound that didn't fit with the others. Bert's ears slowly registered its dissonant presence, and his brain calculated its form. A sharp thought darted from the deep of his consciousness and scarred his brow, but as it did so, and his eyes opened wide, peace became chaos.

With a scream, and then a yawning wrenching roar, the beach was launched high above his head, breaking up into smoky, shooting, firework patterns of browns and reds all around him. Bert was sucked skywards by a force that he couldn't repel, spiralling and twisting until he was flying. He became a part of the air that pulsed and whooshed around him, high up in the clouds, staring down... down upon the beach; down upon the glittering sea and the grey boats that bobbed on its rippling surface; down upon men in a uniform who lay on the sand far, far below.

***

The terrible warning scream came too late. As the shell landed, the men of the Warwickshire regiment flung themselves to the ground, throwing their hands over their heads. There was a prolonged roar, and then another, as the beach seemed to buckle beneath them. They felt a sharp burst of air, before sand, splinters of wood, bone and flesh rained down upon them. The pitter-patter of sand continued to fall for a few moments after the explosion died away, the sound of its descent breaking into the buzzing nothingness that lingered; its only competition was the ringing and whistling which crowded the ears of each of the men who lay prostrate on the beach.

Their lieutenant was the first to rise unsteadily to his feet. His head ached, his ears throbbed noisily, and he was covered in sand and tiny spatters of red, but otherwise he was remarkably unscathed. The other men around him began to get to their feet. As the beach stopped spinning around him, he realised where he was and turned and sprinted over to the place where his men had been sitting just moments before the explosion.

He found Johnson. He'd be thrown several feet away from the spot where he'd been standing, and now he was lying on his back groaning. The left side of his body had a bloody gouge, the width of three fingers, running along it from head to toe. The uniform on that side had been ripped away and so had the flesh, exposing the bone in places. His left cheek flapped backwards away from his face.

The officer called over to his men, "We need a medic… quickly."

Johnson was still conscious and he tried to speak.

"Shhh!" hushed the Warwickshire man, "We are going to fetch help, just lie still."

Johnson was able to lift his right arm, and he tapped his hand against his ear. The young officer realised that the engineer was telling him that he was having difficulty hearing and nodded his head.

"It'll pass, don't worry."

He raised his voice. It was possible that Johnson might be able to hear something, but even if he couldn't, he wanted to keep the officer engaged and alert.

"You are a lucky man, Lieutenant, how you survived that blast I don't know… but you may have just earned your ticket home."

Johnson flickered a smile and then his face tightened. He tried to gesture over to where Bert and Mac had been sitting in the shaded area at the edge of the beach.

The lieutenant understood and got to his feet. His bones burned from the soreness of the explosion and the tinnitus was still chiming in his ears as he walked over to the spot where the Anson men had been sitting. The sand there was stained a deep scarlet. Where the beach hadn't fully absorbed it, blood sat in still bubbling pools. In other places the pools contained jagged islands of shapeless solid matter. The stain radiated outwards in a large circle. He winced at the sight of a detached and eyeless form resting upon the scrubby vegetation on the bank. It looked like a face at least, and the empty eye-sockets, if that's what they were, invited his gaze for a moment. More of the red shapeless matter hung from the bushes behind it, but there was not much else. He held back the urge to vomit.

A sudden and unsettling rasping noise caught his attention and he turned towards it, grateful to shift his vision in another direction. It came from a formless furry mass which was piled against the bank. His eyes took a while to work out that it was the mangled remains of a couple of mules. Another mule, intact and lying closer to Johnson, was still breathing, her chest heaving rapidly up and down. The officer knelt beside her and stroked her belly. There was a sickening gurgling sound coming from her mouth. He immediately knew what he had to do and unholstered his pistol. Long Ears large brown eyes swivelled to meet his gaze as he took aim.

"I know you don't understand any of this... I'm not sure I do either... but, trust me, this is for the best old girl," he said gently, before squeezing the trigger.

Johnson flinched heavily at the sound of the gunshot and let out a moan of distress. The Warwickshire man reappeared beside him and took hold of his hand. He looked into Johnson's eyes and shook his head. The wounded Lieutenant closed his eyes momentarily.

"My name's Slim by the way... it's probably about time that I introduced myself.'

"Johnson," his patient croaked with difficulty.

Slim's attention was suddenly caught by something winking in the sunlight at his feet. It lay on the top of the sand beside the engineer; he reached down and picked it up. It was a gold ring. As he studied it he managed to make out an inscription engraved around the inside. He read it out aloud.

"Your heart is my Kingdom."

Johnson's eyes widened instantly as he spoke.

"Kingdom?"

The words were forced out from the back of his raw throat.

"It would seem that your hearing has begun to recover already," observed Slim with a wry smile, "I think you might just make it after all my friend."

A breathless medic and a couple of stretcher bearers arrived who began attending to Johnson's wounds. Behind them, near the cliffs in the distance, men still laboured by the shoreline, lifting supplies from the boats and transferring them to waiting mules. They barely broke their stride in the aftermath of the explosion, oblivious to the human drama unfolding at the beach's edge.

"Just another day in Helles," Slim thought, aloud.

The patient reached out a shaking hand towards him, and the object he held in his hand.

"Is it yours?" asked Slim.

Johnson, grimacing with pain, nodded and replied hoarsely between struggling breaths, his hand twitching as it grasped for the ring.

"Yes… it belongs to me!"

Chapter 15.

England: 1915.

"Well... young Walter, my lad, I'd say you've grown into a stout fellow since I last saw you!"

Harry Neale patted the child gently on the crown of its head,

"I'd also say that the little man enjoys his food. Am I right?"

Alice shook her head, feigning incredulity,

"You wouldn't believe it, Harry! He's eating me out of house and home. His daddy won't recognise him when he comes back."

"Well, I'll tell you what I'll do. I'll stick in an extra sausage for the lad, on the house. Don't tell your neighbours though, or they'll all be wanting somethin' for nothin'. You never know, if you mash it up a bit, he might get a taste for it."

Harry skipped back behind the counter.

"Get the customers hooked early, that's what I say," he chuckled. "Do you reckon we'll get to see any Zepps in these parts then Alice? Papers are full of it they are."

"I hope not Harry. I've enough to worry about with them Turks shooting at my Bert without having the German's dropping bombs on me as well. Anyway, why would they come all this way? There's nowt for them to bomb 'ere?"

"Look 'ere, you can have one of these."

The shopkeeper reached under the counter and pulled out a cardboard disk. The outer part of it advertised Colman's Mustard, the inner part was made up of a smaller series of disks which were pinned together. Each disk carried a description of the weather, wind strength, barometric pressure or the phase of the moon.

"All you do is line up the conditions against point 'A'... like so..."

He demonstrated by rotating the disks. His head leaned back, and his eyes narrowed with the concentration it required.

"Then the arrow against point 'B' will tell you if the Zepps might come calling tonight! Look," he exclaimed, "...it's saying, 'Very Improbable'!"

"Thanks Harry, but I can manage wi' out that I think. It'd only scare me when there's no need."

"Aye... 'appen you might be right about that."

Harry finished wrapping up the sausages and dropped them on the counter.

"Anything else for you or the young chap, my lovely?"

"A nice pork chop please... and that'll be me done."

"I think we can find you one of them right enough."

He grabbed one of the chops from the tray in front of him and began to wrap it up.

"You mentioning the Turks reminds me... your Bert is fighting in the Dardanelles in't he?"

He dropped the parcel of meat on the counter beside the sausages. Alice nodded.

"How much do I owe you... there's some on the tab from last week I think?"

"Did you see last night's Evening Post?"

"I'm too busy with little 'un to read the papers Harry."

"Call it sixpence Alice."

Harry turned his head and shouted through to the back of the shop, "Gert... have you got last night's Post?"

Alice handed a sixpence to the butcher. Harry's wife appeared from the gloom behind him waving a newspaper,

"Last night's Post as ordered... oh, good morning Alice, how's the babby? He's just turned one year old if memory serves, an't he?"

"Good morning Gert," Alice replied, "One year old and a proper little soldier… as his daddy says."

Gert moved around to the front of the counter and started fussing the child.

"Read out that bit about the Dardanelles on the front page Gert," asked Harry.

Gert unfurled the broadsheet,

"Right, where is it... ah there it is." She cleared her throat. "It says 'The Athens correspondent of the *Petit Parisien* claims to have learned from a reliable and highly authoritative source that the Sultan of Turkey has addressed an urgent request for help to the Kaiser, declaring that the Turks cannot hold out much longer in Gallipoli'. I'd say that means that your Bert might be home soon Alice."

"I've never doubted it Gert... them Turks'll be no match for our boys, will they?"

"Have you heard from Bert lately?" asked Harry.

"Not for a while... I've had a few of them postcards, but they don't say much, and a letter before he sailed out. I'm not even sure that any of my letters have got to him, you know what war's like. I'm knitting him some socks… a little something from home."

Alice left the shop and pushed the pram lazily along an Arkwright Street that clattered with wheels and hooves, beneath its halo of grey smoke and steam. She didn't register the fanfare of near and distant train sounds that also coloured the air around her, and which she would, no doubt, only have noticed if it wasn't there. With her basket carried in her free hand, she negotiated a group of shoeless young boys playing tag, who darted around the pram and in and out of the road. She glanced at them as she passed and tutted sympathetically at their dirty feet and threadbare trousers. Walter gurgled happily, paying no attention to anything other than the wooden cut-out, shaped vaguely in the form of a horse, that Tom had made for him, and which he juggled between his chubby hands. He alternately sucked it and tapped it up and down on the thin blanket which covered his legs. It was a warm day, the warmest it had been for a while, and the confident blueness of the sky eventually pushed aside the industrial smog, making a window for the sun.

Alice felt the heat on her face, and she felt happy. She didn't need the reassurance from the newspapers that Bert was safe, or that he would be home soon. She'd had a strong conviction all along that everything would be well. A young woman standing outside one of the houses waved to her from the other side of the street. Alice crossed the road,

"Hello Florrie, how's little Arthur?"

"He's looking as round and red-cheeked as your Walter is."

They laughed together.

"You'll have to pop round for a cuppa in a bit... give me chance to sort the shopping out and get the kettle on."

A bicycle bell rang out and they turned their heads towards as it passed. Their smiles disappeared as they saw young Fred Clarke, the telegram boy, pedalling over the cobbles.

"It could be bad news for somebody," speculated Florrie.

"Don't say that," said Alice.

"I'm sorry duck, I didn't mean..."

She stopped in mid-sentence as Fred pulled up to a halt outside Alice's house. He let go of his bicycle, which clattered to the floor, before raising a hand to rap hard on the door. Alice dropped her basket and it landed on its side, spilling the contents onto the pavement. A tin rolled off the kerb and landed on an iron drain cover with a dead thud that seemed to echo along the street. Walter flinched and began to cry. Alice's knees buckled and Florrie instinctively reached out to steady her friend, guiding her unwilling and inert body towards the trembling boy. By the time Fred's shaking hand had offered the envelope to her, Alice's face had turned as grey as the smoke which spewed from the chimneys at Cammell Lairds, and a lump in her throat the size of a piece of coal blocked her speech. She couldn't lift her arm, and so Florrie took the telegram from him. The red-faced boy, his eyes focussed on the pavement, clumsily grabbed his bicycle and hastily escaped to the comfort of the road without a word.

Florrie opened the envelope and glanced curtly at the paper inside. Her eyes told Alice what she already knew and she roared out her desolation.

The commotion alerted the other women who lived on the street. Curtains twitched and Edie opened her front door, peering out to see what the fuss was about. She saw the group of women gathered in front of Alice's house and spotted Walter left crying alone in his pram. Without hesitation she walked collectedly across the road and lifted the baby into her arms, instantly calming him down. As he sniffled, she carried him into the midst of the group of women, their eyes now trained silently on her. They parted before her, exposing the sight of her fallen sister-in-law enfolded in Florrie's arms.

Without wanting to believe it, Edie had suspected the cause of the excitement and her breathing was already rapid. Blood rushed to her head and she couldn't feel her legs, but she fought to keep control. Florrie got to her feet and handed Edie the envelope, without looking inside she closed her eyes for a split second and bit her lip hard. Saying nothing, Edie handed Walter to Florrie, pulled Alice gently into her arms and calmly led her inside the house.

Only as she pulled the door shut behind them did Edie shed her armour and fall to her knees. Alice knelt beside her and began to softly stroke the older woman's hair. There, wordlessly together, they shared the private unbound rawness of their grief, at the loss of a husband and a brother.

Chapter 16.

England: 1916.

Staring at the War Office telegram she'd received a year ago, Alice carefully read the words that were neatly inscribed upon its face in blue ink:

'Deeply regret to inform you that AB A. Kingdom RND killed in action 22nd July 1915 Dardanelles. Lord Kitchener expresses his sympathy'.

For the last twelve months, it had become a nightly ritual to read both it and the regimental letter that followed in the post a few days later; together with the pre-printed message of condolence from the King that she'd also received. She read them repeatedly, several times a day, hoping each time that they were just a perverse fiction sent to torture her for unremembered sins of the past. She willed that this be true, because she *was* truly being tortured now, wasn't she?

She carefully re-folded the letters and placed them, together with the telegram, neatly back in a wooden box which she kept on the mantelpiece. In gilded metal frames, next to the box, were the only two photographs that she possessed of Bert. One showed him in his seaman's uniform; it was the same image that was locked inside the brooch which hung around her neck. The other was taken on the day they had met, picturing him stood with his foot resting proudly upon the match ball, puffing out his victor's chest and flexing his muscles. She took the frames in her hands, kissing them in turn. Each kiss lingered, before she wiped the glass clean with her sleeve. She carefully placed the pictures back on their altar, and then turned her attention to the mahogany sideboard. She opened a well-worn cupboard door, reached inside, and took out an old glass beaker. After that she carefully lifted out a bottle of gin, sighing for a distracted moment as she gazed into the deep green glass. She ran her hand gently over the bottle's embossed lettering, and then quickly pulled out its cork.

For several weeks after receiving the news of Bert's death Alice had lived in a daze. Some would say that she still did. Edie moved in with her for the first three months, keeping her sane, feeding her, dressing her; continually reminding her of the reasons that she had to carry on living. Edie did this, whilst at the same time setting aside her own considerable grief. In time, when Edie returned home to Tom, she took Walter with her. By then it was clear that Alice was not yet capable of caring for her son, or even that she wanted to.

Despite this precipitous downward spiral, the distraught widow refused to see a doctor, despite the desperate urging of Edie and other friends. When an invitation arrived, offering her the chance to stay with Jack and Jane Oxton at their new farm posting in the Yorkshire Dales, Alice tore it up and threw it on the fire. In the end, Edie considered that she had no choice but to step away from her sister-in-law, who had become a pale and dishevelled shadow of her former self.

By then, too, Alice had begun to see Bert again. It started a few months after she had received the news of his death, whilst she was sitting at the dressing table in her bedroom. She and her reflection stared blankly at each other as they did often, sometimes for hours at a time. And then he was there, standing in the empty doorway behind her; slowly coming into focus out the darkness of the landing, like a figure materialising out of the fog. He appeared often in open doorways after that, even out in the street, his grey features luminous in the shadows. He wore his sailors uniform and stood motionless as the living world moved busily around him, his gazed fix upon his bereaved wife. As time went by, he occasionally emerged from the dark margins of Alice's vision and walked silently alongside her.

In those first few days his presence was a comfort, and there were moments when it had the effect of bringing joy back to her face. However, it was a manifestation of joy that the people around her found deeply disturbing. It transformed her expression from glassy-eyed deadness back to radiant life in the merest heartbeat, leaving her gazing dreamily into nothing but vacant air. And then things began to change. The apparition's constant grey-faced presence was slowly and surely twisting the knife of her torture, deepening her pain. He haunted her relentlessly, taunting her with his loss and, even when she could not see him, she felt his heavy presence in every shadow... in every doorway. The bottle of gin in her cupboard offered up the only means of exorcism.

One leaden morning, there was an unexpected knock on the front door. Alice dreaded knocks on the door. Sometimes she didn't answer them at all, afraid of what she might find on the other side when it was opened. On this occasion, she did so without thinking. It was Joel Cooper and his face couldn't hide the shock that ran over him as soon as he saw her. The carefree young woman he had known only a short time before was now dark-eyed and unkempt. He could smell the alcohol on her breath. She looked towards him, but he could see that there was no focus in her eyes, and she didn't speak. He removed his cap and smiled,

"Good morning Alice. Do you remember me... Joel Cooper from up at Old Oak Farm?"

She didn't answer.

"Well, the truth is that I've been meaning to come over for a while, since I saw the terrible news about Bert in the newspaper. You'll probably know that I lost my brother Stan out there too? Right on the first day of the invasion it was... what bloody bad luck, eh? I know it's took a while for me to get round to doing it, but I wanted to come over and offer my condolences, and just say that if you wanted a chat about... you know," he shuffled his feet uncomfortably, "... then if you did...want to talk about it, that is... then I'd welcome that, knowing how you're feeling and all that. I wanted you to know that."

Alice remained silent and continued to look right through her visitor. Joel put his hand to his mouth and coughed awkwardly.

"You know it's not been easy on the farm of late. We had five lads fighting in the war in all. Two of 'em, Stan and Bert, have now passed on and one's come back home missing a leg. I expect it'll be my turn any day, now that they've finally brought in conscription. You know, Alice, we've got some women now on the farm doing some of the work the men used to do... if you ever wanted to..."

He could sense that his words were futile, so he shut up and pulled a bunch of flowers from behind his back. He offered them to Alice with a sad smile.

"Picked from the garden up at the farm this morning, there's some purple Astors, and a few of them big Daisies. I thought they might brighten things up a little bit."

Without taking the flowers, Alice closed the door in his face.

Edie had been watching from her window and as Joel hung his head, not quite knowing what to do with himself, she opened her front door and beckoned him over. She made a pot of tea and put the flowers in a vase. Then they talked about their brothers and laughed and cried together.

Alice placed the swiftly drained bottle of gin back where it came from. She picked up her purse and walked out of the front door, leaving it wide open behind her. The night was cool, and there was a light drizzle, but she wore no coat. She staggered through the streets until she came upon the Queens Hotel. *He* had been at her side the whole way. As she crashed in through the door all eyes turned towards her. Unseen by those eyes *he* took a seat at a table near the window.

Arthur Harrison, the landlord, was in the middle of serving a customer. Alice pushed her way to the bar,

"Arthur, I need a bottle of gin," she slurred.

"Good evening Alice. I'm just serving this gentleman. I'll be with you shortly," Arthur replied.

Alice folded her arms onto the bar and rested her head upon them. Arthur noticed that her blouse had several buttons undone, exposing her underclothes, and there was a yellow stain on the white fabric. After he'd put the payment through the till, he walked over to the tables at the front of house to collect some glasses,

"I'll be with you in a minute Alice," he called across to her.

He whispered into the ear of one of the men sitting at a table near to the door, who nodded his head and immediately left the hotel.

"Now then Alice, what can I do for you?"

"I need a bottle of gin Arthur," she raised her head long enough to speak, before dropping it down again.

"Now, are you sure that you've not already had enough gin tonight?"

She shook her head.

"Well I think you've had enough and it's my job to be a good judge of that sort of thing. After all I've got my good name to keep up."

"That's not fair Arthur... I can always go somewhere else to get one you know."

"Look at me Alice," Arthur said sternly.

She didn't move, so he repeated the instruction until she raised her head and trained her glassy eyes on him.

"There's no need for you to go somewhere else, you've had enough already. Look at you, what have you done to yourself? You're a good-looking woman Alice, you don't need to be like this. Why don't you stay here and rest for a while? I can get you a glass of water if you want?"

Alice looked up at *his reflection* in the mirror behind the bar, then closed her eyes and nodded, she hadn't got the energy to go anywhere else anyway. Arthur poured her some water from a jug. She took a few sips and rested her head back on her arms. A few minutes later she had drifted off to sleep.

The man who had left the bar earlier came back in, closely followed by Edie. She took one look at Alice and exclaimed,

"Oh, my Lord!"

"It's the third time this has happened Edie," said Arthur, in a tone that told her his patience was wearing thin.

"I know Arthur, and I'm sorry... you know how hard she's been hit."

"She's not the only one around here who's lost someone in the war, but she's the only one who does this. If it carries on it'll put off my customers... and God know there's precious few of those around with most of the men away fighting. I'll have to fetch the constable the next time it happens you know?"

Edie remained silent, and a tear trickled from her eye. Arthur sighed and shook his head,

"I sound like a bloody hard-arsed so and so, don't I? I'm not having a go at you. Bert was a good lad... I could have had a copper in here before now you know... if I'd wanted to, they're only across the road."

"I'm grateful Arthur, I'll get her home now, and it won't happen again, I promise."

"Where's Tom?"

"At home with the young un."

"I'll give you a hand then love. I'll get Hilda in here to look after the bar... wait on."

Edie wrapped an arm around her sister-in-law and guided her from the bar with Arthur's help. As the door opened, Alice cast a parting glance towards *him* before she shuffled out into the street.

***

Kapitänleutnant Hermann Kraushaar, at the helm of Zeppelin Z17, was having a good night. A smile of contentment hung on his chiselled face as he observed proceedings from over the shoulder of his young helmsman. His sharp eyes were trained on the compass, which was fixed just behind the barely moving rudder-wheel.

"Gut," he said the word so quietly that it was lost within the deafening drone of the engines and the steady rattle of the cabin superstructure.

As they had climbed into the air from their base at Tondern on the Danish border earlier that evening, Kraushaar was fully intending to deliver the full force of his deadly payload onto the city of Sheffield. He'd flown over thirty sorties during the preceding eighteen months of the war and this flight had, so far, proved to be as smooth and uninhibited as any of them. There was no sign of any enemy aircraft, but what did that matter anyway? He was ebullient in his certainty that his Z17 would easily see off even the pluckiest British pilot. The sheer speed that she could ascend to an impregnable altitude, by itself, was unmatched by anything else in the skies. Inside his head, the humming sound of the engines transformed into the allegretto tune from Beethoven's seventh symphony, and he tapped out its insistent rhythm on his thigh.

Satisfied with progress, he laid a reassuring hand on the helmsman's shoulder before moving to stand in front of the forward window panels, which sloped gently away into the darkness. He inspected his reflection in the glass, adjusted his cap, and then pulled out a tiny and well-worn photograph of a woman from his top pocket. He studied her for a moment without any change in his expression then slipped the image back into its place of safety. It had been an hour since they had made landfall over the Lincolnshire coast, and a glance at his watch told him that it was just after midnight, British time.

The thin cloud that had carpeted the night sky eventually began to break up and dissolve away. What Kraushaar saw through the glass as the mist cleared made him stand, automaton-like, to attention. He raised his binoculars to his eyes. The lights of a sizeable city lay scattered through the darkness before him, running off into the distance for as far as he could see. He was distracted for a few seconds by their mesmeric glow. Once the spell was broken, he called over to Ernst Zimmermann, his first officer. He pointed a finger ahead and raised his eyebrows questioningly.

"Ist das Sheffield?" asked Zimmermann raising his voice enough for him to be heard.

Kraushaar wasn't sure, but nodded his head gently, "Das ist möglich."

Zimmermann knew, from the grin that began to spread across his commanding officer's face, that he wasn't going to pass up on the opportunity to attack a target that was so conveniently laid on a plate for them; whether it was Sheffield or not. Suddenly the lights ahead of them started to go out, a sparse few at first, and then in simultaneous swathes, as the blackout was invoked on the ground. Even though Kraushaar knew this meant that their presence was no longer a secret, it made little difference. He had already marked his target.

As the blackout crept and stuttered along ahead of them, the two men realised, to their complete disbelief, that not every light had been dimmed. A straight line of bright beacons, dead-ahead, invited them on.

"Die Bahnlinie?" asked Zimmerman.

Kraushaar nodded, the railway line was the only thing it could be, "Muss sein."

He beckoned his artillery officer to get ready for action, "Bereiten sie sich vor die Bomben auszulösen."

"Jawohl Kapitän," came the instant reply.

"Es muss Ihr Glückstag sein," observed Zimmermann, leaning over to speak directly into his commanding officer's ear.

Kraushaar's face cracked, his head rocked back, and he laughed out loud.

"Ja... ja. Ich hab'keinen Zweifel daran, Ernst!"

There was no hesitation in his response, he *knew* it was his lucky day for sure.

***

Tom Morton slept in the spare bedroom whilst Edie and Alice shared his bed. He couldn't sleep. The old chain-sprung mattress stabbed at his side each time he changed position. Even a couple of thick blankets couldn't dampen the discomfort. He was also feeling more than a little put out that he had to give up his bed for his drunken sister-in-law. After all, up until recently, his wife had seen more of Alice than she had of him, and they'd taken in her child to boot. His anger simmered, tensing his brow more with each toss and turn. He resolved to tell it to Edie straight in the morning, knowing full well that he would do no such thing. Edie always seemed to get her own way. As the debate raged and seethed inside his mind, his ears tuned themselves into something else, unconsciously at first and then just enough to cause Tom to sit upright. There was an unfamiliar sound coming from somewhere up there in the night sky, it was constant and becoming increasingly louder, *a buzzing sound*... a drone.

He leaped out of bed, ran into the main bedroom and gently shook Edie awake.

"Tom, what are you on with... what time is it?" she asked, her eyes struggling to stay open.

"It's about half-past-midnight. Edie, listen, can you hear that?"

Edie sat up.

"I can't hear any..."

She curtailed her reply mid-sentence as her ears eventually tuned into an almost musical, mechanical sound which sounded like it was directly overhead.

"Tom, what is it? It doesn't sound like an aeroplane."

Tom's face was serious.

"Zepps?" Asked Edie.

"I reckon."

"What do we do?"

"Well, they say that you're better off bein' indoors don't they? We should tek cover. I'll go and open front door... just in case. You get Alice and babby down to the parlour. We'll get table out; you can hide under that."

Tom slipped on a pair of trousers before stumbling awkwardly down the stairs as quickly as his damaged legs could carry him, fastening up the fly buttons as he went. Edie roused Alice. Just as she did so there were six short blasts on the siren. She gathered up Walter, and they met Tom in the parlour, where he had already opened out the leaves on the table. Crouched underneath it, they squeezed tightly together. Edie wrapped herself around her nephew as closely as she dared. She noticed that there was something different about the darkness tonight, and only soft moonlight lightened the edges of the objects that were silhouetted within the room.

"They've turned the streetlights out," Tom observed, reading Edie's mind.

"'Appen they're not comin' for us and goin' on somewhere else instead," whispered Edie.

"Mebbe lass... mebbe."

As the parlour clock ticked, its volume was heightened by the enveloping silence. Tom began to recite a prayer. Edie turned towards him, wide-eyed and open-mouthed.

"I never thought I'd hear such words comin' from your blasphemous mouth, Thomas Morton. You an't been inside a church since our weddin' day."

There was fear and sadness in his watery eyes as he replied,

"It's not said for me, my love... not for me."

Between the two of them Alice shivered, oblivious to everything and saying nothing. Before their next breath, the ticking soundlessness was obliterated by a deafening roar. A blue-ish light flashed, momentarily brightening the room and Alice screamed. Edie pulled her and Walter tightly to her chest, whilst Tom carefully shielded them all. There was another thunderous blast and an even brighter flash, and then another. As the next one ripped through the street, the windows in the parlour shattered, imploding into the house and raining glass noisily across the room. The sound of breaking glass chimed melodically around the house as the whole building shook. They sensed, though, that the next few bombs were dropping increasingly further away, as the intensity of their explosions appeared to lessen with each one.

"Come on," said Tom, "It sounds like they're away to the north, let's bloody well get out of here."

Outside the street was carpeted with broken glass. Tom surveyed the scene. Not one window in any of the houses he could see remained intact,

"Bloody hell!"

Edie realised that she and Alice were still in their nightclothes, but then so were many of their neighbours who were starting to spill out into the street. Nobody seemed to mind their attire, and there was no panic amongst the dazed and relieved faces.

"Look... up there!" a raised voice instructed, alongside a finger waving towards the sky.

Heads turned in the direction in which they were pointing. High up in the darkness a tiny, finger-shaped, object twinkled silver in the sky like an alien moon. It was sailing serenely through the night air. An even tinier pinprick of light fell from it and another explosion soon followed, with an accompanying flash of blue light. This time, though, it appeared to be over on the northern edge of the city.

"That's Victoria Station I reckon," calculated Tom.

"You Hun bastards," a man cried out behind them, inducing other insults to be aimed towards the blackened heavens. A woman responded,

"Well, what do you expect from them animals? That's why our boys are fighting agin the buggers, in't it?"

There was muttered agreement and much nodding of heads.

A man appeared, breathlessly running around the corner of the street. He yelled over to the people milling about in between the houses,

"The Zepps hit a couple of houses in Newthorpe Street! We need all the help we can get!"

He ran back in the direction he'd come from and other people began to follow him, hesitantly at first, but then with shared urgency and purpose.

"I'm goin' to see if I can help," said Tom.

Edie grabbed his arm.

"No Tom," she implored, shaking her head.

"Look Edie, what am I doin' in this bloody war? Nothing, that's what... so this is summat I can do, in't it?"

He handed Walter over to his wife,

"Here you go, grab the lad... I'll fetch me coat."

He limped off back into the house.

Alice's face was a picture of fear. Suddenly sober, she grabbed hold of Edie's arm, her fingers digging into the flesh.

"No Edie, you can't let him go... what if something happens?"

Edie wrapped her free arm around her sister-in-law's still trembling body and pulled her close.

"Alice, duck... Tom's a grown man, he can mek his own choices. He's big enough to look after himself in't he? I've got to trust him to do what he needs to do."

Alice pressed her head into Edie's neck.

"Listen to me love. You've got to let Bert go you know... it's the only way."

"I'm on my own Edie."

"Just look around you, lovey. Look closely... can't you see? You're not on your bloody own."

***

The morning light revealed the full extent of the devastation in Newthorpe Street. Edie and Alice stood amongst the crowd of still disbelieving onlookers. Some of them watched the rescue efforts, shaking their heads, others were in tears. Where two houses had stood the previous evening, there was now nothing left but a smoking mountain of bricks and wood. The only indication that the rubble had once been somebody's home was the intricately patterned green wallpaper that still clung to one of the upper walls, adjoining a house that was still standing. Its fireplace remained with coal still in the hearth, a shattered mirror hung precariously above it, reflecting the image of a room that no longer existed. Where a bedroom once stood, a painting of a country landscape in a cracked frame hung at a gravity-defying angle. The acrid smell of sulphur still lingered in the air. As a horse-drawn fire pump was dampening down still-glowing embers, firemen, policemen and civilians who had worked through the night, including Tom, picked hopefully through the debris.

***

Alice removed the photographs of Bert from their frames and placed them inside the wooden box so that they rested on top of the telegram and letters. She slipped off her sweetheart brooch and her wedding ring too, dropping them into the box, closing the lid and locking it shut. She handed the box to Edie and then gave her its tiny key, which she placed in her apron pocket.

"Are you sure you want to do this?" asked Edie.

"You were right... this is the only way."

Tom had propped a ladder up against the trapdoor into the attic at the top of the stairs. Edie handed him the box, and he disappeared up the ladder and into the darkness of the roof-space, returning empty handed a few moments later. Alice lifted Walter from his pram and took him through to the parlour.

"There's just me and you now, Walter... my son. I'm so sorry. I don't know how it happened, but I forgot just how beautiful you were."

She kissed him softly on the top of his head. Her lips lingered there for an instant, delighting in the softness of his skin, and her eyes closed to savour the moment,

"Will you forgive me?"

After she'd opened them again she proudly studied the reflection of mother and son in the parlour mirror. She began to bounce Walter gently up and down in her arms and started to sing,

"Lavender's blue, dilly, dilly,
Lavender's green,
When you are King dilly, dilly,
I shall be..."

Her words trailed off, and an unexpected chill ran quickly through her body. Gripping Walter a little tighter, she moved smartly over to the open door which led into the hallway and pushed it firmly shut.

Chapter 17.

England: 1918.

Even before she had struggled to force open her eyelids, Alice sensed that the world was spinning around her. It did so at such great speed that it made her feel sick, like taking a turn on the Galloper at the Goose Fair with her eyes closed. Her head hurt too, pulsing with a terrible throbbing pain which seemed to radiate from the very core of her skull. Despite the pounding in her brain, and even as she fought to control the urge to retch, she thought she heard her name being spoken. It was a man's voice, distant and dreamlike.

"Alice, me duck... are you wi' us?" the voice asked, softly.

"She's out cowd Jimmy," another voice - a woman's this time - joined in.

Alice recognised its nicotine-roughened drawl well enough, but she sensed too that the mouth delivering the words was trembling badly.

"Maud?" Alice managed to mumble, afraid to open her mouth too wide, "Is that you?"

There was a strong taste of something sharp and acidic as her tongue licked grainy dust away from her dry lips.

"Oh, duckeh!"

Alice felt Maud kiss her face a couple of times, but this only served to intensify her confusion. Why was Maud, of all people, kissing *her*? After all, in their team of 'canary girls' in the south Press House, Maud was the dour one, emotionless, sullen... evidently hard-hearted. Alice strained hard in another attempt to force open her grit-filled eyes. The effort made her head scream even more. As her lids finally tore open and she blinked them clear, Maud's features came slowly into focus, her face looming large. Their heads were so close that their noses gently brushed against one another. Alice could see tears running down her colleagues yellowed cheeks which were dotted too with pinpricks of red. More of them welled up and trickled from her eyes, cutting tiny valleys through the mask of thick dust. Maud broke into a quivering smile that revealed her tobacco-stained teeth,

"Oh, duckeh... I'm so pleased that you're gunna be alright," she gushed.

Alice raised herself up to a sitting position. Maud leaned forward and wrapped her in a tight hug.

"My head aches," Alice said, rubbing her temples, which felt sore on the outside too, "and what the hell is that awful smell?"

The Amatol used to fill the shells had a distinct, pungent, chemical odour that had made Alice gag when she had first encountered it back in 1916. It had taken her months to get used to it, but now, combined with the smell of smoke and the bitter stench of burning oil, it made a heady cocktail. Her supervisor, Jimmy Moss, was standing behind Maud looking worried and sweating profusely. He was no longer the calm and wittily encouraging voice she was used to, guiding the girls through the monotony of their shift like a kindly schoolteacher. He seemed to be lost in a daze, hopping slowly from one leg to another and carefully supporting his right arm with his left hand. His wrist hung at an odd angle and blood dripped with a regular beat from the open cuff onto his burgundy-spattered overalls. Jimmy too was covered in yellow dust and there was glass in his hair.

The electric lights in the huge hangar-like building had gone out. Alice was used to them humming with life, giving the place its energy, but now they were deathly silent. A strange grey-yellow lustre had attached itself to the shapes of people and machinery in front of her. It made them looks like statues hewn from alien stone.

As her focus returned, she could see that a huge section of the inner part of the roof had fallen to the floor. A tiny shaft of light penetrated the hall from outside, but the thick swirling dust dulled much of the brightness it brought with it. It cast only the tentative shadow of a cross underneath the fallen girders.

A muted counterpoint of voices, moans and sobbing resounded from the greyness, accompanied by the sound of straining metal and the distant clatter of an alarm bell. Even so, the usually bustling Press House was as still and quiet as Alice had ever known it. As she scanned the carnage around her, a sudden, rumbling crash made her start. She turned her head towards the source of the sound and her heart quickened. The lights buzzed angrily and flickered back on and then, just as suddenly, died again.

In that moment, she thought she saw the familiar silhouette of a man. He was wearing the uniform of a sailor, arms still at his side, his face lost in shadow.

"No!", she protested resolutely, screwing up her eyes and turning her head away before opening them again. This time her eyes opened to see another shape. It was difficult to make it out at first, but the outline was distinctly softer than the contorted collapsed air duct and the roughly scattered munitions and overturned tram-trucks that lay strewn around it. Then it dawned on Alice that she was looking at the shape of a woman. It lay on the floor in amongst some unfilled shell cases, some of which lay across its torso. The figure lay still, its arm bent under its back, a rag covering its face. A damp patch of deep red defied the greyness and seeped brazenly through it. Nausea rose into Alice's throat and then pounded against the inside of her forehead. She fought against it with every ounce of her returning energy, her eyes then turned a sad, questioning, glance towards Maud.

"It's Elsie," Maud replied, her voice still trembling.

"What's happened here Maud?"

It was a demand rather than a question.

"We've bin bombed, duckeh."

Alice's eyes didn't flicker, and she pushed herself unsteadily to her feet.

"I've got to find Florrie," she said calmly, dusting down her overalls with stilted, painful, movements of her arm, whilst trying desperately to recover the missing shards of her broken memory.

That afternoon had begun like every other late shift at the National Shell Filling Factory, since the day, not long after the Zeppelin raid, that Edie had persuaded Alice to sign up.

"We need to pay summat back to the bloody Germans and them murderin' Turks," was Edie's way of justifying her decision.

Alice was simply happy to have something else that would give a focus to her thoughts. Florrie had joined them not long afterwards. They called themselves the 'Arkwright Street Pals' and, between them, they arranged shifts so that at least one of the women could look after Walter, and Florrie's son Arthur, whilst their mothers were at work in the factory.

That afternoon it was Edie's turn to babysit. She wasn't on shift until the following day, so it was only Alice and Florrie who made the short walk to the Midland Station to catch their train to the village of Attenborough. As they left home at half past four, the late-afternoon air was still muggy from one of the hottest days of the year, and it didn't take long for the sweat to break from their skin. It was stifling and airless on the train too, its carriages packed to the brim with factory workers, men and women, heading for the six o'clock shift.

The little oxygen that remained had been thickened by the heat, and it resisted the exertion of straining lungs. Alice sought out the cool breeze from the open window, staying silent as Florrie talked about her day taking 'little Arthur' into the town to do some shopping. She listened as her friend described in detail how, after shopping, she sat Arthur on her knee in slab square and counted the different types of uniform on show, before she had wheeled the pram to Calvert's Café on Long Row for tea and fruit cake. She was still in full flow as the train rattled and shuddered into its destination.

Sweat was pouring from their skin, even before they set off together for the mile-long walk from Attenborough railway station to the factory. The bright sun hung low in the sky in front of them, causing them to squint their eyes.

"There'll be packin' ice 'round the TNT to cool it down today I reckon," they heard a man say behind them.

"It won't tek long for it to go up like Mount Pee-lee if they don't," prophesised another.

"I could do wi' some of that ice meself, Alice... and I'd pour it all the way down me back if I 'ad some," laughed Florrie.

The Man Who Found Treasure

Carefree Florrie. Beautiful, carefree Florrie.

They joined forces with the battalions of other workers from Long Eaton and Beeston, merging together on the High Road as they marched into the factory complex together. As usual Alice and Florrie first made their way to the changing rooms, where they slipped into their khaki-coloured, all-in-one, cotton overalls. They put on their caps and soft shoes, before grabbing their cotton wool respirators. Then they went their separate ways, waving to each other as Alice set off in the direction of the Press House and Florrie to the TNT Mill. They had already agreed to meet up at the changing rooms after completing their shift, to take a bath before their return journey to Nottingham. They were compelled to do this every now again under the factory rules, but it was no chore and the shower baths, with hot and cold running water, were a luxurious perk of the job.

Her work at the factory had given Alice new purpose and new heart. Her grief, and the cause of it, was finally locked away in the attic, beyond reach. Now she could focus on the future and on winning the war which had so dramatically changed the course of her life. In the process she and Florrie had, to her surprise, become the firmest of friends. If Alice's new-found toughness was interpreted as cold-hearted by some, Florrie Atkins was the complete opposite. Outgoing, blonde and prettily fresh-faced with a raucous laugh that turned heads and rattled windows, she was easy and popular company. And whilst some of the attention she inadvertently attracted was unwanted, she was an unrepentant devoted mother to 'little Arthur' and wife to her husband Bill, who was serving over in France. Whilst never short of conversation, Florrie still knew better than to talk about the latest news from the western front in Alice's presence.

Whilst the Press Houses were not the largest buildings on the factory site, they were still vast; a thousand feet long and clanking, rumbling, concentrated hives of activity. Alice made her way to her bench. She looked around her and felt a comforting sense of her place, both in the enterprise at hand and in the fight against the enemy overseas. She understood that she was a tiny cog in an enormous machine, where, just like her, each part knew its place and was geared towards doing its bit to churn out the munitions that the lads needed at the front. She allowed herself, briefly, to imagine the cleansing, cooling bath at the end of the night, knowing that it would be a well-earned prize for an evening's hard labour.

The other women around her donned their facemasks, their eyes now fixed firmly on the task ahead. There was no small talk. Giggly Elsie, quietened for battle, and dour Maud stood in the ranks either side of her, whilst Jimmy Moss strode up and down like a sergeant-major behind them.

"Come on then gels, how many shells can we gerr' out tonight? I'll wager me missus's best trench cake that we can mek more than last time… let's see if we can. Remember, each one o' them shiny bastards will be a kiss on the cheek, from you to Fritz. Let's make it a real smacker!"

The empty shells rolled into the Press House on tiny railway trucks from the store, growling along the rails as they did so. The Amatol powder came from the other side of the house, packed into tins and carried on hooks by a rope conveyor running from the milling buildings and then back again. Elsie called it 'the monkey machine'. Munitions and explosives met at the benches where Alice worked, where she poured the dry pungent powder into its forged steel container, carefully pressing it into each of the cases. Once done and checked, they rolled the filled shells back onto the trucks for their return journey to the to the store.

All around them the yellow dust invaded the air. After a while it had the effect of turning the women's hair and skin a luminous yellow colour, earning them the nickname 'Canary Girls'. This was no insult though, and the 'Canary Girls' wore their new epithet with shared pride like a regimental badge.

The Press House was only one organ within the pulsing body of the factory. Whilst Alice toiled at her bench, all around the site thousands of other workers were doing their bit to keep the machinery rolling; enabling the finished shells to be packed and loaded into the waiting lorries that would drive them away to the war. At the heart of it all was the boiler house with its tall smoking chimney. Next to it was the power house. They fuelled the stores, laboratories, melting houses, mills and drying sheds that kept the production line rolling. Nearby, the canteen powered the workers with meals of 'meat and two veg'. At the edge of the complex were the administration offices and an officers' mess. Railway lines, conveyor belts and ropeways connected everything together like arteries.

Over in the mixing house the powdered explosive was suffering from the humidity, and it clogged the machinery in the powder gallery making it slow work. Even with the humidity, yellow dust still floated through air around the heads of the red-faced men working there. It wasn't only the workers who were overheating. The equipment had been running all day in the intense summer heat. Inside this cauldron, a huddle of men wearing frowns gathered around one of the mixers. They had been told that a nut was missing after it had broken off from one of the conveyor belts.

"What if it's dropped into the gubbins? There's a chance it might cause a spark... in't there?" one of them said nervously, scratching his head and articulating the fear displayed in the worried eyes of the other men.

Other workers were organising the packing of some of the Amatol powder into a truck. Its doors were open and its engine left running on the loading ramp, ready for ferrying its dangerous cargo over to the Press Houses. It was needed there urgently because of a shortfall in the delivery of powder via the ropeway. The women, it seemed, were too good at their jobs. They were filling the shells too quickly.

And then there *was* a spark.

Alice experienced a flash of memory. It was about an hour into her shift, the big clock was showing just after seven. She felt sticky and hot, her breathing was laboured and noisy through the respirator mask. Then the lights flickered and went out. There was an earthquake under her feet, and a deafening roar burst through her ears. And then she heard Jimmy Moss' voice.

"Alice, duck... are you wi' us?"

Resurrected, Alice's senses fell back into place. Her headache dimmed a little. She turned away from her companions and strode purposefully through the rubble towards the exit.

"Come on you two, we've got to gerr'out of here," she called back impatiently.

Maud shuffled, and Jimmy limped along, in her wake.

Alan Williams

A wall of heat momentarily stopped them in their tracks as they emerged from the gloom of the Press House. The sky was obscured by a thin veil of smoke which also smothered the air, causing Alice to cough as she breathed it in. The landscape she witnessed as she recovered her breath was shockingly different to the one that had existed in the same place earlier in the day. Back then she had barely registered the scene outside of the Press House, so familiar was she with it. Now that same view was a contorted and smoking alien world. Its reconstructed flatness was interrupted, here and there, by mountains of twisted metal. It was the diorama of a battlefield, its warring tribes having abandoned the arena, unable to wreak any further devastation. In their stead only the dead and dispossessed remained.

Alice knew that she couldn't stand still; she couldn't let shock overwhelm her. She was alive, and this was now part of her world. She had to do something. She headed towards the TNT mill where Florrie worked. She couldn't see the building, so she followed the line of the conveyor belt, giving herself over to instinct, and letting it power her numb body. Maud and Jimmy called out after her, but she didn't look back.

In places - underneath the broken concrete and in the spaces between the deformed girders and fallen crossbeams - fires still burned. There were corpses too; blackened and red raw, they were just as bent and misshapen as the rubble they were now part of.

As her stride quickened, Alice stumbled over something and fell to the ground. Beside her lay a woman's leg, neatly severed just above the knee and still wearing the soft factory shoes that had supported it only moments earlier. The fabric of her overalls had become snagged and she turned to pull it free, only to find that it was caught on what seemed to be the remains of a rose bush. She was shocked that she couldn't even remember that the factory had roses in its grounds. Even more oddly, trapped between its canes and trunk was a doll's head; dead-eyed and charred. She was drawn into its gaze until she felt her eyes watering.

Alice pushed herself to her feet. She reached down and took the doll's head from the bush, caressing it with her fingers. She felt detached from it all now and surveyed the scene which played out in a kaleidoscope around her. Despite the energetic bustle and raised voices, the realisation came upon her that there was no panic. Everyone, every action, seemed to have a purpose. An unexpected surge of pride in her species lifted her heart. There were people of all backgrounds, wearing every type of uniform; men and women, old and young, coming together, forming a new army with a single purpose, one without an enemy other than time. Some of the troops in this army were bloodied and blackened, others were pristine; but all rolled up their sleeves. Together they bellowed instructions, put out fires, directed traffic, pulled at the rubble, cleared the pathways, formed rescue parties and tended the wounded. Alice let the doll's head fall unnoticed to the ground.

Many of the soldiers recruited to these new battalions pushed trolleys. Some were empty, waiting to be occupied. From others lifeless limbs dangled under the cover of sheets and blankets, often threatening to fall back to the ground as they were raced along, twitching and shaking, over the bumpy ground towards the main road. A screaming fanfare of alarm bells and sirens accompanied their desperate procession.

A running fireman crashed into Alice as she rested on her haunches. His face was turned skyward. He offered no apology and pushed her roughly aside whilst bellowing words of encouragement up into the air. Alice followed his gaze until she saw a man climbing up onto the still moving conveyor belt where a bucket of burning TNT was juddering on its way towards the explosives store. Barely hanging on, he somehow managed to reach out and tip the fiery load to the ground where it fizzled out in a bellow of yellow smoke.

Energised by what she had seen, Alice arrived at the spot where the TNT mill had once stood. It stood no longer, its foundations ripped from the ground. There was no hope of finding survivors in its tangled skeleton. She felt her body buckling and she closed her eyes, her stubborn hope for her friend now obliterated in much the same way as much as the physical structures of the factory had been. A picture of Florrie flashed into her mind... *beautiful, carefree Florrie.*

Then a hand yanked at her collar. Alice turned to see a man who she recognised as one of the works managers from the shell store. He looked her up and down, then beckoned her to follow him.

"There's no time for sitting down, gel. We can't bring the poor souls back. If you're up to it... come wi' me... I've gorra job for you".

He led her over to a group of uniformed men gathered at the centre of what was left of the Fire Station.

"You tek hold of this for me. Hold it out the way".

The man strained to bend back a thick piece of the station's roof structure, adjusting his hands, pushing and then pulling until it was in the position he wanted. His face turned bright red as he grunted with the effort and perspiration poured from his brow. Alice grabbed it from him and bore its weight. It was still warm.

"You got it gel?" he panted.

She nodded, gripping it with all her strength and resisting its surprisingly dogged inclination to spring back to the ground. The metal dug into her skin, etching purple lines into her flesh. She felt the muscles of her arm tense at the uppermost limit of her ability to bear the load. It hurt, but it was a good pain, she thought. She saw now that the other men included soldiers, policemen and fireman. There was a lad in a striped apron… a milkman perhaps? Or did she recognise him as a chap who worked in the canteen? Carefully and silently they pulled at the bricks, wood and metal at her feet, removing them piece by piece. They worked assiduously, occasionally halting to take stock and work out a new tactic under the direction of the fireman. A woman appeared, miraculously given the desolation under her feet, with a tray of tea.

"Here you go my lovely."

She offered a mug of brown liquid to a soldier as prosaically as if she was serving a neighbour in her own kitchen, but the rescuers stopped only momentarily for sustenance.

Suddenly the mood changed. The rescuers voiced their joy and slapped each other's backs. Alice saw a blackened face revealed under the mess of tangled debris. The face smiled; her heart soared. Its few remaining teeth glinted like diamonds in the lamplight that had become discernible around the site as darkness began to descend. The rescuers worked quickly to free the rest of the trapped fireman's body. They poured water onto his face, and he slurped in some of it before gruffly spluttering his thanks.

"I think I'm in one-piece fellers."

"Well, thank 'eavens for that me lad. It's good to know that I haven't wasted me Monday afternoon," replied a policeman with a wink of his eye.

Alice helped them lift the man from the rubble. She wanted to hug him, but she could see him wince in agony at every touch. He could walk, albeit painfully, and so she supported him back to a motor ambulance which was waiting on the Chetwynd Road.

"Are you married?" she asked him.

"Am I married? Are you proposin'?"

She laughed. She couldn't remember the last time she had done that.

"Yes duck... sorry to disappoint you, but I'm already hitched."

"Kids?"

"Two."

"They'll be pleased to see their daddy tonight."

The man glanced mournfully back into the darkness behind them. "Nobody'll be more pleased than me, duck".

She handed him over to a nurse, before, with her final reserves of energy, she carried on walking in the direction of the station.

Her legs felt like they were hung with lead weights as she turned into her street. People were gathered on the corners and their voices fell silent as she passed them. One woman called out to her,

"You alright love? We've heard the news from Chilwell".

But Alice had no energy left to reply. She raised her head and saw Tom at the window of his house holding one of the children. Which one she wondered? The one with a mother, or the one now without? Edie opened the front door and stepped outside onto the pavement, her face grave at first, before a look of surprise swept across it.

As Alice staggered towards her, barely able to move her limbs, blackened and dishevelled, her overalls ripped and bloody, her cap missing and hair falling about her shoulders - Edie couldn't quite work out why her sister-in-law wore a broad smile across her face.

Chapter 18.

Burma: January 1945.

The *SS Landstephan Castle* was a ship that had seen it all before. An old salt told me that she'd first seen service at about the same time that my dad was going to war... but that was on another blue sea and in an altogether different far-off land.

Her grey body groaned and creaked constantly as she rode over the gentle swell, which was about the worst that the beautiful Bay of Bengal was able to throw at her. It was the most benign I'd ever seen this country. No tropical typhoons or monsoon rains, hardly any insects and no trees for Jap to hide behind. In their place the sea brought us a soft warm breeze and turtles that lazily flapped their paddles alongside us, before floating off into the distance and then on to... well, who knows where. There were schools of smiling dolphins too. They raced like torpedoes and performed twirling acrobatics in the white water churned up by the old boat. Soldiers are a breed apart though, and many of them disregarded these natural wonders and chose, instead, to complain about the basic rations of biscuits and Bully Beef. Others judged the sounds of straining metal to be a bad omen, as if the ship itself was wailing its own prophesy of doom.

Other men, like Errol and Coggins, were getting excited about the invasion. We were steaming towards the Burmese coast to play our part in a 'proper' assault, borne on landing craft, replicating what had taken place in Normandy during the previous summer. Maybe, I thought – although I didn't share this confidence with anyone else – it also echoed in some way the assault on the Gallipoli peninsula in April 1915 that my dad might have taken part in?

"They won't be calling us the 'forgotten army' after this!" Errol grinned.

But Soldier was, as ever, sceptical, and he quietly shook his head. It couldn't be argued that we weren't ready for it, that's for sure. We'd been practising the landing drill for the days on end, out at sea, until we could do it blindfolded. I might have gotten excited about it myself… that was if I hadn't had other things on my mind.

Back in Chittagong, just after the new year turned, I had received the promised parcel from Mam. I had waited until I was alone before I opened it, but it was worth the additional suspense, for it contained treasure indeed. It brought me two small photographs of my dad, one in his RND uniform and one standing with his boot on a football, looking every inch like he meant business. It was the first time I had been able to look into his eyes, and I liked what I saw. He was a handsome man, I thought, in a plain sort of way. The picture with the football, especially, gave a hint of the carefree sense of humour which I liked to imagine that he had. I studied my face in my tiny, hand-held, mirror and concluded that the resemblance was strong. I asked Eric for a second opinion and he confirmed my analysis. I suddenly felt a lot closer to this shadowy figure who had so shaped my life.

There were some papers in the parcel too. The fateful telegram was there, a benign and insignificant piece of paper by itself, faded and yellowed. It was inertly oblivious of the mighty blow it had struck to Mam, and ignorant of the way it had scarred both of our lives. It chilled my heart when I touched it. A letter from Dad's regiment contained plenty of well-worn words, but disappointingly it told me nothing about the circumstances of his death. Stuffed between the pages of the letter was a condolence card from the King. It was replete with an impressive red crest declaring that it was from Buckingham Palace, and a printed signature, announcing that the King wouldn't have even set eyes on it, let alone known who my dad was.

The last item in the parcel was a still-sealed envelope. It was dated 1919, and I wondered why Mam had never opened it. I surmised that the Winchester postmark must have been enough of an association with the Army for her to have chosen the path of least pain. I, however, had no such qualms, and so I carefully levered it open, which was easy enough, as the gum holding it together had deteriorated quite a bit. I unfolded the single sheet of paper that was contained within it:

Winchester Barracks
30th August 1919

Dearest Alice,
I hope this letter finds you in better spirits. I'm sorry that it has taken me so long to put pen to paper, but I could not find the right words at first and I'm still not sure that they will offer any comfort to you. All I can say is that I am sorry for your loss. I know how it feels to lose my best friends - but perhaps that's not so hard as you losing a husband and I know that my scribbles here on this page don't really help anybody.
I am planning to travel to Nottingham on my next leave in September. It might be the last time I come back because the memories there are now not so good. I want very much to pay you a visit and to talk to you about Bert and if you want – I can tell you everything that happened. If you do not reply to this letter, I will take it that you are happy with this arrangement and I will see you in a few weeks.
Yours in friendship
George Pike
PS: I think often think of the good old days at Old Oak Farm before the war and of Bert and you back then. I hope that those memories give you comfort where my useless words can't.

I didn't know who George Pike was; Mam had never mentioned him. He clearly knew my dad and there is a hint at the end that he was a friend of them both during those 'good old days' before the war. It seemed to be a time that he, for one, had cherished. It occurred to me that if Mam had never opened his letter, then she wouldn't have replied to it either and so George would have assumed that she had agreed to his visit. I wondered what might have become of their meeting. For now, I filed the letter away with my things and placed the photographs of Dad in my shirt pocket.

The Man Who Found Treasure

A part of me cursed George Pike for not writing about *'everything that happened'* in his letter. If he had done, then perhaps, I wouldn't have still needed to find that slippery old snake Johnson.

Indeed, Johnson was the other matter that was exercising my mind. Since my encounter with General Slim, every time we had moved into a new camp, I had immediately sought out the nearest company of Engineers and quizzed them about the Lieutenant's likely whereabouts. Whether they were suspicious of my motives or not, I'm not sure, but not one of them ever provided the slightest clue as to where he might be. Despite Slim's confidence that he was still in the Arakan, it felt as if he had simply slithered away, deep into the jungle, to join up with the other secret things that are hidden there amongst the trees, perhaps never to be found again.

The 'invasion', when it eventually happened, was a breeze… at first. We gathered in our assault craft and watched the Royal Navy fire a barrage of shells over to where they believed Jap to be hiding. It was an impressive sight and an equally impressive ear-numbing noise. Believe me, just knowing that you'd got that sort of firepower on your side made you feel invincible in that moment. That feeling got even better when the RAF sprang into action. Liberators, with their distinctive double tail… as if Mickey Mouse's ears had been stuck on to the back of the plane, dropped their bombs over the middle of the island. Just in front of us, a Spitfire shot up the beach for good measure, our eyes following the chain of machine-gun bursts along the sand as it swooped by. Some men cheered. Now, you might think that it was a despicable act, acclaiming someone else's probable violent death, but I knew what they were thinking, and could forgive them. Under each cloud of murderous smoke you knew there could be at least one less rifle pointed at your head, and each gut-wrenching puff of sand made you feel just a little bit safer, even as you winced at the thought of being on the end of it yourself.

The landing itself was an anti-climax. The beach was golden, and the sea a shimmering tropical blue, as we disembarked the landing craft and waded through the shallows. Small fish nibbled at our boots. Our footsteps were tentative, as we expected a retaliation that never came. So then we turned our heads towards the mass of scrubby vegetation that lined the beach and wondered to ourselves what lay within it, and beyond it; knowing that, whatever it was, it would do more than nibble at our boots.

Most of what immediately followed our landing is now a blur in my memory. I put that down to fatigue, for we were a weary bunch by the time we headed into the interior. I have a recollection that we encountered Jap for the first time soon after leaving the beach, and that there was a firefight to secure the airport. After that we did no more than tour the island, which was a relatively pleasant jaunt compared to trekking through the jungle back in the Arakan - a few hills and a hell of a lot of mangrove swamp excepted. The villagers we met seemed to quite like us, but Soldier told us not to trust them all the same. After that there were a few skirmishes that have just about lingered in my mind, some more intense than others. In one fierce battle, along the length of a large chaung, where you never quite knew what was around the next gully, another company had been ambushed and had taken a few casualties. Smitty went into overdrive, chasing away a Jap unit like a screaming Geordie whirling dervish. Afterwards he returned to start tending to our wounded. We didn't know what had come over him, but he won the Military Medal for that. Towards the end of February we entered the largest town, the one after which the island was named: Ramree. My memory of what followed is the only other part of our time on the island that is as clear as day.

Whilst the days were indeed clear on Ramree, the nights were as dark as I'd ever seen. In the sparse jungle the blackness crowded in on you, and I was grateful to see any stars twinkle brightly above me. The more stars I saw, the less tense I felt. Our section was detailed to go and mop up some of the remnants of the Jap army who had fallen back towards the mangrove swamps near to a place called Kalaban. We moved carefully forward through the increasingly dense vegetation, in the pitch black, step by increasingly nervous step.

We guessed, although we didn't know for sure, that the retreating enemy had left booby-traps behind. It was still just about dry underfoot, but we never knew for certain how close to the swamp or the water's edge we might be, although we could hear the occasional splash or ripple somewhere ahead of us. Sound just didn't behave normally at night in the jungle, so that water could have been inches in front of us, or it could have been miles away. It might not even have been water at all. I remember feeling unusually edgy. This place was so different to anywhere else I'd been to that I felt well and truly outside of my 'comfort zone', as they like to call it these days.

Those bloody great trees loomed menacingly above us, each one no more than that the width of my arm, but together they stood like an impenetrable army reinforcing the wall of blackness. If you dared look up they seemed to rise forever into the inky sky, their canopy lost somewhere on the way to the stars. If you looked down, you met their tangled roots rising above the earth, sometimes to head height, forming all sorts of grotesque, twisted shapes. Most of the time the earth could barely be seen beneath them. Each of us tripped over them more than once, as we picked our way through that maze of knotted wood. It was like hurdling snakes, for the roots seemed to be alive, teasing your eyes as they slithered in the gloom. Every crunching footfall we made on the forest floor, however carefully done, had the power to alert even the least attentive enemy.

As I'd done regularly during every patrol since we had landed on Ramree Island, I rested my hand on the sweat-soaked pocket which contained the photographs of my dad, and I tried to draw some comfort… and inspiration… from knowing that whatever I was feeling now, he must have felt it too, thirty years before. It usually worked. I'm not a religious man, but I liked to think of him standing there beside me, giving me the courage to go on. That was much easier to do now that I knew what he looked like.

I was thinking about him when I heard another sudden rustling sound out in the murk, followed by the sharp crack of breaking vegetation, somewhere at ground level, in amongst the trees. This sound was different to the others. It was in front of us. We dropped instantly to our knees and Smitty put a finger to his mouth. I noticed that we were kneeling in thick mud. The only other sounds we could hear penetrating the blackness were the hum of airborne insects, and the faintest purr of the navy motorboat engines patrolling the strait somewhere beyond the swamp. I could also hear my heart beating and hoped that nobody else could as I willed the tension to be relieved. Remembering the Peacock incident back in the Arakan, when I'd first met Johnson, it crossed my mind that even a Python or a Cobra slithering out from underneath the tangled nest of roots now would be enough to break the spell.

Then Soldier suddenly and silently leapt into the air and dived forward into the darkness. There was a muffled cry and a momentary scuffle followed by a strange whimpering sound that could have only been made by a human being. We crawled forward to find Soldier with his body pinning down a Jap against the spidery base of one of the trees. A couple of us pulled the man out from underneath him and tied up his wrists and ankles. He offered no resistance. More than that he was clearly not capable of offering resistance. So thin was he that his rib cage was prominent within his open shirt, his cheeks sunken, and the skin stretched thin over his skull. He continued to whimper and he seemed to be in a daze.

"What do you reckon?" whispered Smitty.

"It's starvation", said Soldier, "I've seen it enough times before in India".

"How come?" asked Errol.

"Jap's abandoned the island I reckon. These men have been left to fend for themselves. Been out here for a while by the look of it".

"Out here"?

I was taken aback by the thought of there being more of these 'living dead' roaming around the swamp.

"Plenty of hiding places," Soldier rose to his feet warily, "we'd better be careful".

There was a crack and a whoosh. We knew what that meant. Soldier dropped languidly and wordlessly to his knees, and then toppled forward onto his face. Eric rolled him over, but Soldier had taken the bullet full in the left eye; he was already gone. We looked at each other, Smitty, Eric, Podge, Errol, Slowcoach, Coggins and I, panic in our eyes.

"What do we bloody well do now?" gibbered Slowcoach, forgetting to whisper.

And then the firing started.

The bullets snapped into the trees and kicked up the dirt beneath the roots around us like the deadliest of monsoon showers, as they enfiladed our position. We threw ourselves to the ground and Podge and Eric quickly set up the Bren and began to loose it off in the direction of the ambush. We recovered our composure and put our rifles into action too. Meanwhile, Slowcoach grabbed the starving and still-whimpering Jap and dragged him out in front of us.

"Come 'ere you scrawny bugger… you can 'ave a front row seat."

The next volley of bullets ripped into our prisoner and the whimpering stopped. The fire from the Bren gun did its work, and the incoming fire died down.

Smitty bade us to move forward, and we edged tentatively along the ground, firing whenever we could. Gradually we picked up speed, as we did so we began to hear running footsteps, crashing through the vegetation ahead of us. A beam of light from one of navy patrol boats suddenly flooded our vision. We must have been closer to the water than we thought. We could see the fleeing shadows caught in the beam of the floodlights, about ten or twelve of them, now splashing into the open lagoon where the swamp met the strait. We picked our targets easily, but the illumination abetted our foe too. Errol cried out as he was spun around by a bullet to his head. Coggins went to his aid, but he took a shot to the neck and his body buckled, before collapsing on top of Errol. I was nearest to them, so I dived across to where they lay on a fibrous cushion of mangrove roots. I could see that Errol was still alive, the shot had left a deep graze in the side of his head and taken off most of his ear, but he would survive. I turned Coggins over, only to see the light fading from his eyes, and so I held his hand tightly as his life slipped pointlessly away.

I knew I had to look after Errol now, so I pulled Coggins gently away from his body and laid him down beside us. Errol dragged himself up into a sitting position against the root bed. He looked down in horror at the body of the boy, for he was, in truth, no more than that.

"Is he dead?"

He spoke rapidly and breathlessly, his body shivering in shock. Blood ran into his mouth from his torn face, and he spat it out again with his words. I nodded.

"Where's the fuckin' sense in it?" he roared, tears welling in his eyes. "Can you fuckin' tell me that?"

I Couldn't.

There was another shot. My shin exploded with a fleeting mist of red and white vapour and the most intense pain that I have ever felt to this day. As I screamed, Eric was at my side instantly unwrapping a field dressing. I watched him look at my leg and wince.

"Is it bad?" I asked, not daring to look and trying, and failing, to sound composed.

"If it means your war is over... then maybe it's not as bad as it looks kiddo." He glanced down at the body of Coggins. "In fact, I'd say your luck's in Wally."

Smitty and the others fell back to join us.

"Listen," said Podge.

We fell silent. The shooting had stopped and, instead, the sounds of desperate splashing and panicked screaming drifted over from somewhere out on the water.

Now, there are screams... and there are screams, and these were the type that made your blood run icy cold. The splashing had become even more frenzied. A single flashlight from a patrol boat angled, once more, across the water and then scanned back in our direction. A flare went up. It burst high and white above a watery stage where, under its brief spotlight, a savage drama was being played out. The water in the lagoon seemed to be boiling, such was its ferment. Occasionally a large scaly tail thrashed and then rolled, kicking up the water even more. I thought I saw an arm and maybe a head, but it was only a passing moment and whatever it was soon disappeared beneath the water. Then, as the last molten splinters of light dripped from the dying flare, the scene became calm again, the only sound to be heard was the murmur of the patrol boat engines sweeping along the strait.

"Crocs," said Eric.

"Fuck me," added Slowcoach.

"Is there anybody left?" asked Podge.

There was no need for an answer.

"Let's get out of this fuckin' place", ordered Smitty. Broken and bleeding though we were, we couldn't move quickly enough.

Chapter 19.

Burma: 1945.

The sleeping Lieutenant was the source of much amusement amongst the fifteen junior ranks who were sprawled in various positions around the carriage. They had taken to mimicking the billowing of his moustache by placing their hands up against their mouths and wiggling their fingers, whilst whistling in chorus, in time with his snoring. The increasing volume of mirth had so far failed to wake the slumbering officer, and so they began to sing 'Kiss Me Goodnight, Sergeant Major', quietly at first, their voices growing braver and louder. The title was soon transformed into 'Kiss Me Goodnight, Old Lieutenant' and the made-up lyrics became increasingly raucous.

The joviality was partly down to their being taken out of the line and partly because of a now deep-rooted sense that the war in Burma was coming to some sort of close. The train was more than large enough for the company and there was, unusually, plenty of room to spread out. The rare comfort the extra space afforded further loosened their reserve. And anyway, the Lieutenant was the only officer around, and he was in no state to hold them to account.

The incessant vibrations which shook the carriage, began to have a soporific effect and, in time, the joke – unlike the train - ran out of steam. One by one, the sappers began to doze. The occasional sudden jolt caused no alarm. Neither did it disturb dreams of warm baths, clean sheets or the girl left behind at home, for those who were still asleep. Until one of the soldiers woke with a start.

"What was that... it sounded like an explosion."

"Go back to sleep Harris... can't you get this bleedin' war out of your..."

Before the sapper could finish his sentence, the carriage lurched forward wildly and then seemed to bounce up and down, throwing some of the men from their wooden seats. There was a short screech of brakes and then a long, chilling, grating scream of metal upon metal.

It was only when the train seemed to be taking flight that the Lieutenant woke up. As his eyes opened, he saw that the carriage was travelling almost vertically, but still with the unmistakeable surge of forward movement. As it plunged back down to the ground, bodies filled the air around him like puppets on strings. And then it rolled. And rolled again. Over and over, as if it was never going to stop. His head was pummelled against the skin of the carriage like a pea in a whistle. He closed his eyes, but he couldn't block out the screams, which pierced through the sound of shattering glass, splintering wood and crunching metal and then merged together with the unavailing screeching of brakes.

Crashing over all of this like a wave was the terrifying, tumbling roar of the crashing locomotive. Pain ripped through his body. Then, with a juddering smack, he abruptly stopped moving. Wedged against something hard and cold, he became the still eye of the storm that rotated around him. Whatever it was that had captured him, he grabbed onto it as tightly as he could.

He must have lost consciousness, because when he opened his eyes again, all was still. There was no sound to be heard besides the strained creaking of settling wood and metal, and the whisper of a breeze through the window grilles. The carriage was upright once more. He saw that he was lying on the floor, jammed beneath one of the seats, his hands still gripping tightly onto its under-frame; his knuckles protruding white through his tanned skin. Pain coursed through every part of his body and, when he looked down towards his legs, where the pain was the worst, he could see that the lower halves of both were set almost at right angles to the upper parts. He could see lifeless bodies too. Some lay on the floor around him. Facing him, another corpse had been improbably forced through the bars of the window, its arm ripped from the socket and hanging limply behind a torso which had the demeanour of a ragdoll or a theatrical dummy. There was a wide smudge of red on the carriage wall beneath where it hung.

Buried beneath the searing, stabbing pain, the Lieutenant felt something else; something that, even on that blood-spattered mortuary of a stage, drew a smile on his face... it was the rhythmic, undimmed, pulse of life. The agony of broken bones and ripped flesh didn't matter. He'd known that before. He had survived it then, and he knew he would survive it again now. It was non-negotiable. He felt inside his shirt for what he knew to be there, and he rubbed his bloodied fingers against its cold circular form.

"Thank you..." he breathed, "Thank you."

As he touched it he experienced an unexpected jolt of panic – not at his current predicament, but at the thought that *it* might have so easily have been lost to him altogether. It was a realisation that made its golden form even more precious. Then he remembered the meeting in the makeshift church, and all was suddenly well again. There was no guilt. Why should there be at something so generously given? It hadn't been stolen, after all. It had been handed to him by providence alone. It was beyond dispute. *He* wouldn't understand that of course. Still, one must stick to the next phase of the plan if it was going to be discharged successfully: avoiding any contact with... *with you know who*. Surely that was easily done now in a country of this size and with the war coming to an end. He glanced at his smashed-up legs and chuckled at the notion that promise of home was now tantalisingly closer.

The lieutenant's wandering thoughts were interrupted by agitated voices which blew into the carriage, carried on the breeze. They became progressively louder as they neared the wreck. He waited for a few moments, composing himself so that he could sound suitably distressed.

"Here!" he shouted, hoarsely at first, before finding a second wind, "Over here!"

Chapter 20.

India: 1945.

As usual, Eric's assessment was spot on... my war was over. My shin had almost been snapped in two. After being half dragged and half carried out of the mangrove swamp, I was put on a boat, but I have little memory of the journey. Either I was suffering from some sort of fever, or they had given me something for the pain that did its job extremely well.

I woke up in 152 General Hospital, tucked away in the green outskirts of Chittagong. I felt cool, clean and safe, tightly wrapped up in the bedsheets. It brought back a reminiscence of being a child all over again. My first expectation was to see Mam standing by the bed administering a cold-compress or bending down to stoke my hair, whilst speaking soothing words. Instead I heard the pacifying voice of my Irish QA nurse, who told me that they had managed to save my leg, and I would be fine, eventually. It was only then that I felt the throbbing soreness in my shin. I knew there and then, and a I consider still, that a permanent limp is a small price to pay for getting through the war alive. I'm not one to gush about it, but I mean thousands of our boys never made it back home, Jap lost twenty times as many men than us, and hundreds of thousands of civilians never saw their homes again. Who really knows what the final toll was? Just calling what happened to me 'good luck' doesn't do justice to what I really felt, and so I was determined to make the most of the time I had left on this earth. Back then though, I still had some unfinished business.

After several weeks of immobility, my bones were considered well enough healed to allow me to be set free. While my return to Blighty was being arranged, I was given leave to hobble around the grounds on my crutches. The place was surrounded by jungle, so part of my me still expected to see Jap rushing out of the trees at any time, but it was a great feeling to get my freedom back. Without the threat of imminent death everywhere I went, it was the most relaxed I'd been since the war started. I was savouring exactly that feeling when, one morning whilst having a smoke after breakfast, I realised that the chap leaning on the hut wall next to me was a sapper.

"Are you gonna be here long?" I asked, nodding towards the sling around his arm.

"Aye, that's ma plan," he chuckled, "a sapper's nae use without an arm now, is he?"

"Scots? Where you from?"

"Peterhead, Aberdeenshire," he replied. "And you?"

"Nottingham".

He nodded and smiled, pulling back on an imaginary bow and arrow with his good arm,

"Where Robin Hood lives? I saw that flick with Errol Flynn… before we came out here."

"What company you with then mate?" I continued, matter-of-factly, but aware that my pulse was starting to race. He looked at me warily, as if my angst was showing a little too much.

"236th Field Company… City of Aberdeen. Why are you askin'?"

"I've got a mate in the 506th. I don't suppose you know if there's any of them here?"

Even as I asked the question I realised that the chances of him saying "aye" were almost zero, and I blushed with the absurdity of it. Instead his eyes widened, and he almost choked on his cigarette.

"Aye, I do… there were a bunch of 'em in that hut over the way there. We had a good old natter this morning. Whole bunch of 'em got caught in a train crash. They're movin' the buggers out today as a matter of fact."

I waited for a moment to make sure that it wasn't a wind-up, but he appeared to be sincere.

"Moving out? Do you know if there was Lieutenant with them... name of Johnson?"

"Fat old bugger... Colonel Blimp type?"

I nodded,

"That's him."

"Aye... he was there alright. He was the only survivor from his carriage... knocked about something bad he was, pretty much every bone broken. Bloody miracle he got out alive they say."

He grinned with astonishment.

"You're nae sayin' that he's that mate you were goin' on aboot?"

I didn't hang around to answer him. I threw my cigarette to the floor and lurched off in the direction of the hut as briskly as I could manage, swinging my body unsteadily between my crutches. The hut was empty. An Indian nurse was collecting the used sheets from the beds, so I pleaded breathlessly to know when the men had left.

"Just a minute ago... they're loading them into that truck just outside," she pointed a finger out of the window.

I flew out of the door, sticks flailing. As I stumbled outside the tailgates were being fastened on a couple of open backed Bedford trucks. I could see Johnson sitting at the rear of the group, his arm too was wrapped around a pair of crutches. He looked straight at me. I imagined I saw fear in his eyes, or maybe it was simple bemusement at the stumbling idiot rushing towards him. I'll never know for sure, but before I could catch up with the truck, my balance gave way and I crashed sprawling to the ground. The nurse ran out from the hut. As she did so, the truck engines fired up, and they trundled off towards the gatehouse. Johnson and I maintained eye-contact until, just before the trucks disappeared from my view, he signalled our parting with a gentle wave of the hand.

"What on earth were you doing?" the nurse railed, pulling me to my feet and batting the dust from my uniform. "You could have broken your leg all over again."

I shrugged my shoulders,

"My usual trick... chasing shadows."

She gave me a stern look and then marched back into the hut, exaggeratedly shaking her head.

***

I have little memory of the journey home either, other than I took a train to Bombay and then sailed on a ship called the *Capetown Castle*, bound for Liverpool. It was heaving with hundreds of returning troops, but I kept my own counsel; the future was weighing heavily on my thoughts. Upon our arrival, it took a while to process us. I was paid and provided with travel warrant, before being pushed down the ramp in a daze, towards a fleet of trucks waiting to ferry us to the station. As I reached the bottom of the ramp, weary from the journey and feeling the bitingly cold English air for the first time in years, I was jolted into life by somebody screaming my name.

I turned around to see Elizabeth sprinting down the quayside in her NAAFI uniform, a hand resting on her hat to keep it from flying away. After a moment of wondering whether my tired imagination was playing even more cruel tricks on me, she launched herself upon me, and we spun around for a moment with her feet off the ground as she planted a kiss on my cheek. The press of her body tight against mine and the warm touch of her skin on my face... well, I can tell you that I still cherish those feelings now. I don't mind admitting that it brought a tear to my eye.

"I'm so proud of you Walter," she said, flashing those heart-melting, beaming eyes. "Welcome home, duck."

Then she closed those eyes once more and kissed me again, this time firmly on the lips, and this time her pride flowed through the wetness of her lips and into my veins like osmosis. I felt ten feet tall at that moment and I could feel the sharp piercing envy of the men around me which added another couple of feet. When she faced me again, there were tears in her eyes too.

"It's all over now Walter... it's all finally over!"

"What are you doing here?" I asked incredulously, suddenly realising how bizarre this all was and feeling like I was stuck in the strangest of dreams.

She pointed down the quayside to a mobile NAAFI canteen.

"I couldn't believe it when I saw you dawdling down the ramp," she laughed as tears trickled into her mouth.

"Come on lad, there'll be plenty of time for canoodlin' when you get hom'. That train won't wait for you tha knows," growled a burly RASC Sergeant.

I reluctantly prised myself away from her and she blew me a lingering final kiss. As my truck drove away, Elizabeth waved me off energetically, and I watched her diminishing silhouette disappear into the distance. She didn't stop waving until I was out of sight.

There was nobody to meet me as I got off the train at Victoria Station in the early afternoon. It was just as grey and cold as it was when I left Nottingham for the first time, several lifetimes before.

I meandered through the busy City with my kitbag, all the time reflecting that these were streets I used to know so well, ones I had walked often. And yet there was no sense that I was back amongst old friends. The sombre stone faces of Gladstone, Cobden and Bright, which looked down upon me as I passed the old Express offices, were as welcoming as those belonging to the grey-faced people who brushed by me without heed. If you'd have told me then that I'd be settling down to a new job within its ornate walls within a few years, well... I'd have laughed in your face.

Although a few people stopped me to shake my hand along the way and others greeted me with a "Well done son" or a "Good to have you home, duck", there were just as many others who didn't even seem to register my presence. I suppose that they were going about their business as they'd done every day for years. Nothing had changed, apart from me. The place felt as foreign and alien to me as the first time I had landed at Bombay.

Finally, once I'd navigated my way through slab square, Exchange Walk and Lister Gate, I emerged onto Carrington Street. A few more steps over the canal bridge and I found myself standing in front of the pinky-orange stone arches of the Midland Station, staring across towards the austere facade of the Queens Hotel on the other side of the road. With its Doric columns and heavy emotionless front-door, it was the sentinel guarding the way to my old world, but there was no welcome here either... only reproof.

So, even here, on the streets where I grew up, there was no sensation of 'home'... not that I was sure what that meant any more. I did experience fear though. Perhaps it was exacerbated by my tiredness, but it was palpable all the same. It's funny when I look back now, I realise that it was the same feeling of fear that gripped me just before a battle.

As I dared to walk on past the Queens, I can remember a passing thought about Dinah popping in my mind. I realised that I hadn't even thought of her, not even in a guilty way, when I encountered Elizabeth on the quayside in Liverpool. Now my mind was briefly curious about whether she knew I was coming back, and whether she'd even care. Perhaps she was already seeing someone else? I tried to rehearse what I might say to her if we accidentally came across one another, but the effort required was too much and I gave up.

I knocked on Mam's door, but nobody answered. Whenever she was out, she always locked the door and left the key at Edie's, but there was no one at home there either. I was beyond the point of being simply tired by now and I'd drifted into a kind of hazy dream world, but I managed to drag myself through the echoing cobbled entry passage between the houses and into the back yard. I collapsed down on the outside toilet… we called it a 'privy'… and made a pillow, of sorts, with my kit bag stuffed between me and the wall. Then I curled myself up and fell asleep.

Chapter 21.

Turkey: 1998.

After Walter had finished his story, he sighed heavily. He took off his hat and wound down the window of the Land Rover, letting the cool air wash over his face.

"So, you married Elizabeth?" Barişfinally asked, after a moment of internal debate, his eyes flitting between the road and his client.

Walter allowed a few moments of suspense to elapse, before he answered with a chuckle, his voiced raised enough to be heard over the growl of the engine as the car negotiated a stretch of potholed road.

"Elizabeth? I should be so lucky! Believe me Barişs, I dreamed of walking down the aisle with her so bloomin' often back in Burma that there were times that I believed it might have really happened. She looked every inch a film star, you know. She even made her NAAFI uniform look glamourous. So much so that..."

Walter's words trailed off. For a moment his eyes turned their focus onto what might have been, and things that had long since passed. Then, just as abruptly, they returned sparkling to the moment.

"Actually, you know, *I was* the lucky one in the end. To answer your question... no, I didn't marry Elizabeth. You won't be surprised to hear that she married an actor. He was one of those blokes who seemed to have a bit part in every British film made during the 1950s. They moved down south somewhere... Surrey, I think... or was it to Kent?"

Bariş nodded sympathetically, making the briefest of eye contact with his passenger.

"Despite me sending Mam a telegram telling her when I would be arriving back, she'd got it into her head that I'd be on a later train. I don't know how... maybe I gave her the wrong information in the first place. Anyway, just as I arrived at the house, they were already on their way to the station to greet me... or so they believed."

"They?"

"Mam, Edie and Dinah... the full welcome party. You should have seen the look on their faces when they found me snoring away in the privy! Anyway, as soon as I saw Dinah, something odd clicked inside me. That distant ghost that had followed me around the jungle was suddenly gone. She'd been made flesh and blood again and I remembered, for a start, just how bloody pretty she was. Not like Elizabeth at all, but in a delicate sort of way; how I'd managed to forget that I don't know. Perhaps delicacy is the first thing to be erased by our memories. She seemed so genuinely pleased to see me... so full of emotion, you know... that I knew in my heart, there and then, that she was the girl for me. In a strange way, in that moment at least, I felt as though I had missed her terribly. You know they say that 'absence makes the heart grow fonder'? Well it did in my case... only just not during the time that I was absent! I bet you're thinking now that I didn't deserve her, aren't you? Anyhow, whether I deserved her or not, she stuck with me and I was grateful for that."

"You were married?"

"Yes, soon afterwards. Two kids and a dog, the usual trappings. We were very happy, all the way through to... well, to the end."

"I'm sorry..."

Bariş swerved the Land Rover off the tarmac road and onto a dusty track and announced,

"There's something I want to show you, before we go to the beaches".

Halfway down the track he pulled to a halt. He helped Walter down from the vehicle and led him over to a grave; one that stood alone. The grave consisted of a long wedge-shaped concrete slab. Upon it was a marble plaque affixed to a small plinth. Walter read the words upon it.

"Lieutenant Colonel CHM Doughty-Wylie, VC, CB, CMG, Royal Welch Fusiliers, 26th April 1915."

He scratched his head,

"That's the day after the landings."

Barış nodded.

"The lieutenant-colonel won his Victoria Cross right here, in this spot… the same spot where he breathed his last breath. He led the charge up the hill from the sea; the one that won the day for the British. He was a very tall man, and completely bald-headed, an impressive figure by all accounts. And he was also a friend of the Turkish people. When he led the charge here he carried no weapon."

Walter raised his eyebrows.

"He worked for the British Consulate in Turkey before the war. We awarded him our own medal, the 'Order of the Medjidie', for the good work he did on our behalf during the revolution. Look over there… you see that structure overlooking the water?"

Walter's eyes followed the direction of Barış' outstretched arm, across overgrown vegetation, Olive trees and Cypresses, down to the twinkling blue-grey Dardenelles Strait itself. Teetering on the edge of the water was a tall grey edifice that appeared, to him, as if a giant segment of Stonehenge had been transplanted between the trees.

"I see it."

"That's the Çanakkale Martyr's Memorial overlooking Morto Bay… a very special place for us. It's appropriate that Doughty-Wylie is buried here… within sight of the water and also the memorial, no?"

Walter nodded.

"I can think of many worse places than this to be laid to rest."

He closed his eyes and turned his head towards the sun, feeling its beneficent heat on his face. Only then did he register the chorus of birdsong being broadcast from the trees around him, and an overwhelming feeling of serene contentment washed over him.

"Do you know that you have something in common with Mr. Doughty-Wylie?" Barış asked, breaking the spell of the moment.

"Like you, he had two ladies fighting over him! His wife and the explorer Gertrude Lawrence."

"If only it were the case that Elizabeth and Dinah were fighting over me, Bariş. I would never have been so lucky. I think it's more appropriate to say that I was fighting with myself."

As they began to walk back to the car, Bariş probed Walter again.

"What about your comrades? What happened to them?"

"I didn't really have much to do with them if I'm honest, as much as it shames me to say it. I went to one of those big Burma Star bashes at the Royal Albert Hall, but only in a professional capacity… so that I could report on it. Old Slim was there, picking up his usual standing ovation, but none of my mates were there, to my knowledge at least."

Walter stumbled on the gravel causing Bariş to lurch forward and grab his arm. A cloud of dust rose between them and the old man brushed himself down with his hands.

"I did go to Slowcoach's funeral… in 1970 or 71, I think. Errol and Eric were there too. Errol had had a bad time of it. His looks were everything to him, and he was the most confident of us, but the facial disfigurement which that bullet had caused was hard for him to bear. I suppose they'd call it some sort of 'disorder' these days. He was working as a Bingo caller, of all things, and he had, at last, found a woman who wanted to settle down with him. After years in and out of 'madhouses' as he called them, he was finally looking forward to the future. As for Eric, well, he had stayed in the army for a few years after the war, and then he drove buses after he came out. We corresponded for a few years… sent each other Christmas cards, that sort of thing, but that somehow faded away too. Other than Slowcoach and myself, I can't say that I know what became of any of us who survived the war."

"Does that make you sad?"

Walter stopped at the car and turned to look Bariş in the eye.

"No, it doesn't. Because they are always with me anyway, don't you see? … Every moment of the day. You remember, I told you earlier about that memory of the section that keeps coming back to me, of all of us together in the Mayu valley? That was us at our best… in our prime, not the sad, useless, fucked up old men we became." Walter raised a hand and apologised for his language and grumpy tone. "I think often about Sergeant Dickinson and Fred Bailey, and in particular Soldier, who was a mentor to me… and young Coggins, of course. I feel sad for them, because they missed out on so much."

They climbed solemnly back into the Land Rover.

"It goes without saying that there is no joy in being a survivor. I'm sure that Mam... and even Johnson... would agree with me on that. On one level, it just means that the hell you've witnessed stays with you forever. But whatever good I've done with my life... and I'm grateful for the chance, don't get me wrong... then at least some of it has been done in their name."

"And what about Johnson?" asked Bariş, before turning the key in the ignition. "You said that he was the reason you remembered that day in Burma... and the reason for you being here now? But then you told me that you never saw him again?".

"I didn't say that exactly, now did I?"

"You found him?"

"Are you a football fan Bariş?"

"Yes, but what's that got do with it?"

"Do you know what happened in 1966?"

"I guess that you are meaning the World Cup. England won it in 1966, didn't they?"

"Yes, they won it alright. It was what happened in 1966 that eventually led me here. I don't mean that the football was responsible... but that year was full of many, many surprises".

Chapter 22.

Wales: Christmas 1965.

A nearly full glass of Sherry stood on a low table. It had long since been forgotten, but it wasn't alone. A flute of pale golden liquid beside it had lost its sparkle. So too had a pint of reddish-brown ale. Around and about them were vessels that *had* been drained, their dregs settled to the bottom, their odours filling the room. Stale potato crisps and peanuts decorated the table-top and littered the red carpet. In other corners of the barely lit room, their presence almost invisible, the three remaining survivors of the festivities slumbered. Each of them snuffled and wheezed in counterpoint with the others in an intricate, pulsing, fugue. Like the leftover booze, each of them was forgotten too, in their own way. Their heads were bent forward over their chests and their arms resting in their laps or dangling over the side of their armchairs. One of the men wore a green paper hat, cut like a crown. It was ripped at the seam and hung down at keen angle, falling just below his ear in a way that resembled a sash rather than a hat.

The old man who wore it was more restless than the others; his breathing more fitful. This was nothing new. The hours in which his body demanded sleep were full of all sorts of agonies, and he dreaded their coming. The punishing irony of old age was that the urge to sleep had become relentless, but the terrors it unleashed were increasingly vivid. Beneath the green paper hat a cratered purplish nose twitched above a sandy-grey moustache.

There were other odours now present in the heavy air of the room besides alcohol. One of these, the pungent smell of burning, fuelled an ancient reoccurring nightmare. The old man cried out, and his fear-laden eyes sprung open. Gritty soot abraded his throat causing him to gag and cough. It took a moment for him to realise that this was not another manifestation of his dream. He pushed himself out of the chair and turned to face the window behind him. Unmoving and saying nothing, he watched quivering red-orange flames as they danced and roared in the spot where the Christmas Tree had stood earlier that day. In their frenzy they had extended their glowing calamitous reach to the curtains, which were also now violently and noisily ablaze. He could feel their melting heat as they rapidly consumed the grey polyester drapes. The hot air sought out the spidery scars on his face and, for a moment, brought their damaged nerve endings back to life.

Nurse Jenkins crashed, screaming, into the room. She shook the nearest man to her awake and, despite his obvious confusion, guided him towards the door where he spectated on the scene from behind a glass panel. She made a grab for the other sleeping inmate, almost dragging him from his perch. Simultaneously she yelled out to the man in the green paper hat. He appeared not to hear her, or else he chose not to respond. Instead he shuffled even closer toward the flames, as if they were calling him home. When he did stop, he was so close that he could feel the inferno's long red fingers teasing his skin, making him sweat, waiting for their moment to curl around him and pull him into their embrace.

"What more can you do to me?" he remonstrated defiantly.

Ancient memories of former conflagrations and a rolling, tumbling, bone-snapping past were given life by the vaporous heat. Its energy was enough to bring back the dead, sucking them up from hell. They swirled about him, sneering, their faces green and contorted, envious of his immortality. Reaching inside the collar of his shirt, he pulled out the chain that hung around his neck and offered it to the fire. The chain was his protection and it steeled his doughty contempt for the flames and all that they stood for.

"Try and take me again then, you bastards! I know you… and I'm ready for you!"

He ripped away the remnants of the paper hat from his head and took a step forward.

Chapter 23.

England: 1966.

From the moment I stepped back into civvy street, my conversation with Slim in the jungle, and the mystery of what Johnson might still know about Dad, were both still fresh at the forefront of my mind. My last sight of Johnson, as he waved to me from the back of the truck in Chittagong, was an image that returned to me time and time again in the darkest moments of the night. The rage I felt at that moment still gnawed painfully at my insides, and the determination to track him down was renewed further with my new-found profession.

In my early days on the newspaper I had kept an eye out for details about regimental association gatherings, often getting in touch with colleagues who worked on papers in other towns, to see if they could share lists of attendees or at least arrange a conversation with any journos who might have reported on the event. I made a nuisance of myself with the army pensions people, often on the flimsy pretence of a story, until they began to sound suspicious of my intentions on the other end of the phone. I researched the history of the 506th Field Company, to see if that would reveal any clues - it didn't, and I tried to track down as many military Johnsons as I could find, in the desperate hope that they might lead me to my sweaty lieutenant. Frustratingly, none of this sleuthing led anywhere and, year by year, as work and family life became a more demanding priority, the whole thing slowly petered out... like a youthful hobby, the remnants of which you packed away in the attic years ago and never looked at again.

Then, one day, everything changed.

For a start, it wasn't every morning that I arrived at work at eight-thirty to be told by Majorie, our receptionist, that,

"There's a funny old Australian chap waiting for you upstairs Walter."

"I'm not expecting any funny old Australian chaps, are you sure?"

"Yes, quite sure, he asked for you personally. We've sat him down at your desk with a mug of tea."

"Did he give you a name?"

"I wrote it down somewhere, wait a minute... ah, yes, here it is... his name is Mr. Pike."

I must confess that the name didn't mean anything to me at that moment, and so I was extremely intrigued as I walked up the stairs to meet my mysterious visitor. As Majorie had promised, I found Mr. Pike sitting at my desk. I stopped and watched him for a second or two from a distance before I introduced myself. He looked uncomfortable and out of place, which was accentuated by the black suit and tie he wore that looked far too big for him. His shirt was open at the collar, even despite the tie. I judged that he was a short man, but stocky and probably a little overweight. Though I guessed that the paunch he carried covered up a fair amount of muscle too. He looked 'as tough as old boots', as Mam used to say. As for his age, I supposed that he was in his late sixties, or maybe early seventies. I might have described his hair, back then at least, as being 'Beatles' length, which was unusual for a chap of his years. It was very thin on the top and almost pure white in colour. This contrasted markedly with his skin which was lined, leathery and a sunburned reddish bronze. I walked over and offered my hand.

"Good morning, Walter Kingdom... very pleased to meet you."

He bounced excitedly to his feet and took my hand with a vice like grip, shaking it wildly. His free hand gripped my arm with equal force to exacerbate the shaking. All the time his blue eyes were radiant, and his walrus moustache was contorted to frame a wide grin.

"Walter, my boy! I can't believe it. You're the spit of your dad…"

His down-under accent was clear but gentle, and his zeal brought a smile to my face. The reference to my dad sharpened my interest even more. I pulled up another chair.

"I'm sorry Mr. Pike, but do I know you?"

"No, I don't suppose you do… but I know you right enough. Or rather I knew you when you were an ankle-biter, just before the first war kicked off. George Pike is the name."

I dropped down into the chair, at once recalling the name from the unopened letter that Mam had sent over to me in Burma. I ushered him to sit down beside me.

"You were with my dad in Gallipoli?"

His expression became serious.

"He was my best mate, your dad… we got each other through it, well, until… you know."

"You wrote a letter to my mam just after the war?"

He nodded his head without any indication of surprise at my question.

"That was all a bit queer. I suggested that we meet up, unless she wrote to me to say otherwise. She didn't write back, so I turned up on her doorstep on a freezing cold day in 1919. I knocked on that door forever, but she never opened it".

"She never did open your letter either… I did, but many years later."

"Oh," he said, his shoulders slumping.

"What are you doing here George?"

"I'm over here with the wife and kids… you know, looking up her rellies down south and checking out some of my old haunts… for the last time I'm guessing. Lo and behold I was reading the local rag, and I see an article written by somebody called Walter Kingdom. I thought to myself, that's got to be our Walter. What about old Alice… is she...?"

I shook my head and smiled at the thought of that long overdue meeting finally taking place.

"She's still with us. She lives in an old people's home, up on Mapperley top."

"Never married again?"

"No."

"Can I visit?"

"Of course you can, but be warned, she probably won't recognise you. She's kind of put my dad's death out of her mind too. I'll write down the address for you."

I scribbled the address on a sheet of paper and handed it over to him. My gaze remained in contact with his as I shuffled words around in my head, trying to find the right ones to form the next question I wanted to ask. His eyes widened in anticipation.

"Is there something you want to say to me, Walter?"

"It's been a long time, George… a hell of a long time… but I need to know exactly what happened on that day."

"You don't know?"

He looked a little distressed.

"If I'd have known that, I would have…"

"No matter. You're here now, that's the important thing. We can go somewhere for a cup of tea if you'd like, and you can tell me everything".

And so, we did, and he did.

George regaled me with stories about their time working at Old Oak Farm before the war. His was a different perspective to the memories that Mam had eventually drip-fed to me in her own, filtered, way. I got a sense of my dad as 'one of the lads' and not the great romantic hero that I had constructed for myself. In George's stories, the two of them 'mucked around' together with the best of 'em.

He told me about joining up and going to war and of their mate Stan, who was killed on that first day of battle.

"Stan's brother was our gaffer at Old Oak. He was conscripted in 1916… but the war got him too in the end."

I awaited further detail, but he replied with only one word,

"Passchendaele."

George told me that he wasn't present when my dad died, but that was only because he 'had the shits' at the time.

'I've never, ever complained about havin' the screaming trots since that day,' he confessed.

He recalled his final memory of seeing my dad, a speck in the distance with mules in tow, as he made his way down to the beach.

"Never a day passes," he said, "that I don't think about Bert Kingdom".

I asked him about Johnson, but he said he didn't know him. He had heard on the grapevine, though, that an officer of the Engineers was badly injured by the same shell that claimed Dad's life. That officer could only have been Johnson I concluded, and it reinforced my conviction that there was more to know.

George went on to tell me that he stayed in uniform after the war, joining the Marines. He got married in Plymouth, not long after he sent that letter to Mam. The family emigrated to Australia after he left the forces in the early 1930s.

"I scrubbed about for work for a bit, but eventually we made enough bucks to buy our own place, near a town called St. George in Queensland. We had to breed an army of kids to help us out… sheep take a lot of looking after. Things have dipped a bit with the drought of late, but I can't complain, we've done very well out there".

He was worried that the new Australian Prime Minister, Herbert Holt, was keen on getting the country involved in the war in Vietnam. The fear that his youngest son and grandchildren might have to go to war like he and Bert did was palpable.

"They never learn these politicos, do they? That's 'cos they never go to war themselves. Back in my day they all sent their kids instead… and half of them copped it."

We agreed to keep in contact, and George kept his promise to pop in and see Mam, before he travelled back home to Australia a few days later.

"She was quite a catch for old Bert was Alice, lucky bugger..."

Mam had no memory of his visit.

A week or so later, I was still digesting George's revelatory tales about my dad - to be honest I could think about little else for those few days - when Dickie Brownlow, my editor, tapped me on the shoulder.

"I hope I'm not interrupting a particularly exotic daydream Walter. You seemed to be miles away."

"No Dickie, I was just pondering this piece about the re-development of the Pearson's store."

I coughed and dragged myself upright in my seat.

"Good… good. I've got a couple of other ideas for pieces you might want to ponder on. As you're the only one in, you can take your pick of which one you want to run with. I'll get Ray onto the other. Does that sound fair?"

I nodded enthusiastically,

"Fair and democratic, Dickie".

"Well then… I want to do something about this new Hovership service across the channel".

"It's actually called a 'Hovercraft', Dickie," I corrected.

"Well, whatever it is. I also fancied it was about time that we did a *vox populi* piece about the nation's current feelings about our beloved Queen. It'll tie in nicely with her fortieth birthday celebrations and, I think too, with the State Opening of Parliament being televised for the first time in a few days. What do you think? Of course, you'd have to get down to Dover for the Hovership story. Perhaps we could raid the expenses for a trip down to Windsor for the Queen too. 'The view from her own doorstep'… so to speak. We could compare it with what they are saying in slab square."

"That's an easy choice then…it's got to be dry land for me, Dickie. I did my share of 'sailing the ocean wave' in my army days."

"Good… good."

And so it was that I found myself standing outside the grand red-bricked entrance to Windsor and Eton Central Station, looking across towards the castle. It had been a fallow day, it was lunchtime, and I was hungry. The Windsorians had clearly had enough of 'foreign' reporters descending up their little market town to interrogate them about their most famous semi-resident, and they were keeping their thoughts to themselves. I'd just about collected enough platitudes from passing tourists to put together Dickie's *vox pop* piece, and my boredom had been alleviated a little too by a colourful rant from an unrepentant republican Scotsman. I was half-conscious that I also had a meeting booked with a local council tourism representative that afternoon. However, by then, my mind was largely focused on where I might get something to eat.

As I looked around for a suitable watering hole I had to do a double take. A familiar figure was marching along the pavement opposite me; none other than 'Uncle Bill' Slim, dressed in a suit and a smart black over coat. There was no jauntily angled slouch hat this time, and his hair and moustache were a little whiter, but age aside, it was unmistakably him. I saluted instinctively.

He a had taken few strides further on, apparently without seeing me. A red double-decker bus passed between us. As it drove away, it revealed that the now 1st Viscount Slim had stopped in his tracks and was now looking directly at me. He smiled in that curious tight-lipped, lop-sided way of his and made a salute back. Then, to my surprise, he crossed the road in my direction. He extended an arm, and we shook hands.

"Burma?" he asked.

I nodded, "Yes, sir."

"Good to see you. In fact, I'm sensing that there is something familiar about you."

"We have met before, sir. In the Arakan."

"Well, I met a lot of soldiers, all over Burma. What's your name young man? I like to pride myself in remembering the names and faces of as many soldiers as I can."

"Walter Kingdom, sir."

A shadow crossed his face, and he nodded his head, gently.

"Ah, yes... Kingdom. We spoke about your father and the Dardanelles, didn't we?"

I nodded, a little amazed at his powers of recollection.

"Did you ever track down old whatshisname... Johnson?"

"No sir, he managed to elude me, despite my best efforts."

Slim fixed me with the same reconnoitring stare that I'd encountered twenty years ago. He jabbed a finger towards me.

"The old goat is still with us you know. Or at least he was last year."

My head began to spin, and I could feel the heat of long buried feelings oozing back towards the surface. My body shook, but all that erupted was a single word,

"Where?"

"A rest home for old soldiers, somewhere near to Monmouth... if I recall it correctly it was called 'Green Trees'. I couldn't forget it because the name reminded me of Burma. I opened a new building there seven or eight months ago. Rather surprised to find old Johnson of all people holding court in the lounge."

I must have appeared stunned for a moment. Slim rocked back on his heels and peered down at me expectantly, his face slightly upturned so that his eyes squinted over his nose and chin, framed by eyebrows that arched even more than usual.

"Thank you, sir," I stuttered.

"Not at all. Look, I've got to be off… they've made me Constable of the castle for my sins, and I have few things to attend to. I can see in your eyes that you'll be paying our engineer friend a visit. Go easy on him, won't you? Like all of us old soldiers he's a little on the delicate side these days."

We shook hands again, and he quickly resumed his march back towards the castle. I watched him merge in with the crowds of sightseers on Thames Street. Unlike me they indicated no recognition as he became camouflaged amongst them, his dark and distinctive frame occasionally visible as he charged around the corner into Castle Hill and out of sight.

***

It was almost as if 'Green Trees' didn't want to be found. I stopped the car several times in the leafy lanes north of the old town to consult my increasingly creased Ordnance Survey map, convinced that I was close. Several times I ended up retracing the same ground. The trees in Wales were every bit as disorienting as they were in the jungle. Eventually I threw the map to the floor and pulled up beside an elderly lady who was shuffling along the pavement in the company of an equally elderly, equally shuffling, Corgi. I wound down the window.

"Good afternoon."

She regarded me suspiciously and sort of nodded her blue-rinsed head. I smiled as reassuringly as I could.

"I'm looking for Green Trees."

"Green Trees? I'm afraid I don't know what you mean."

Her accent was school ma'am genteel with the merest shade of a border twang.

"It's a retirement home… for old Soldiers."

"Green Trees? Hmm… Oh yes, of course, you must mean Coed Gwyrdd! Well you're not far away, but…"

Her face darkened.

"Take a left and then a right, you'll see track on your left… there's a sign that's still there."

"Is there a problem?"

"Well, yes, there is. There's not much of it left you see. There is a caretaker, Mr. Jones I believe is his name. He still lives in the bungalow next door, so it might be worth having a conversation with him?"

"Thank you. I will."

"I hope you find what you're looking for."

She smiled, before shuffling on her way.

I discovered Coed Gwyrdd, as the old lady had foretold, hidden away at the end of a long and narrow track. The trees around it were doing their best to shield it from view. There wasn't much of it to shield though, exactly as she'd described. Only a few crumbling and charred walls remained. They were overgrown here and there with weeds and clumps of grass which sprouted amongst the blackened splinters and broken glass. What was left looked like it had been newish, or at least newly renovated, at the time that it met its end. I stood in front of the ruins and scratched my head hoping that I'd not driven a hundred and twenty miles on a wild goose chase. Then I noticed the bungalow.

"Mr. Jones."

"That's right. Who's askin'?"

He was younger than I expected. The accent, this time, was straight from the valleys.

"My name's Kingdom. I'd been told that an old army pal of mine lived here."

"Not any more he doesn't."

"What happened?"

"Just went up in flames one day. Some old boy havin' a nap with a fag still hangin' from his mouth I reckon. Hadn't been opened long. Nearly did me out of a job, it did."

"Nearly?"

"They moved 'em back into the old place around the corner... luckily it hadn't been sold. Border House it's called".

Border House consisted of three dour stories of charcoal grey-brick with a matching slate roof. The general impression it created was one of gloom, especially under the increasingly leaden skies that accompanied my visit. As I walked towards it, gravel crunching beneath my feet, I surmised that in its heyday, whenever that might have been, it had probably been the house of a doctor, or an esteemed Master at the boarding school in Monmouth. There was a large black door, surrounded by a growth of some type of creeping plant that was attempting to devour the entire lower half of the property. Fixed upon the door was a notice, red text upon white, which instructed me to 'Please use visitor's entrance'. A helpful arrow pointed me in the direction of a slightly more modern extension.

"Hello."

A pony-tailed, fresh-faced young nurse opened the door.

"How can I help?"

"I hope you can. I'm looking for an old comrade of mine… Johnson is his name?"

Her smile faded and she fixed me with a sceptical eye.

"You mean the Lieutenant?"

I nodded.

"He doesn't get many visitors. Actually… he doesn't get *any* visitors. Not in my time anyway. He's not been well of late… he suffered from the smoke you know."

"Yes, I'd heard he'd been unwell," I lied, so unconvincingly that I carried on talking to mask any hint of dishonesty.

"In fact, I've just come from the old place, Green Trees. It's a bit of a mess, isn't it?"

"The Lieutenant was closest to it. He was lucky to get out alive."

I decided that a bit of name dropping might help my cause.

"I was talking to Viscount Slim a few days ago, he suggested that I should pay him a visit."

"You know the Viscount?"

"We are acquainted."

Well, that wasn't *exactly* a lie.

"Then you'll know that he opened Coed Gwyrdd just last year? Seems a lifetime ago now."

"Yes."

Her smile returned.

"Follow me, I'll see if the Lieutenant is awake for you."

She led me through to a large conservatory at the back of the house. There were five residents in the room, four of them asleep. The fifth had turned his high-backed chair to face the window. He was bent forward, arms folded over his blanket, staring out at something over in the trees beyond the lawn. The nurse touched my shoulder, smiled and nodded her head towards him. I thanked her and dragged across a chair to sit down beside him.

"It's a pretty garden, Lieutenant," I observed.

"There's a bloody huge squirrel out there somewhere. One of those red buggers."

His gaze remained focused on the trees. The voice was thin and struggled out upon wheezing breath. Close up, I noticed that the scar on the left side of his face had become even more conspicuous than I remembered it back in Burma, ruddier and stretched by age. The yellow hued and almost translucent pallidity of his skin exacerbated the effect. His hair too had thinned to almost nothing and his moustache, which had been a spectacular bushy affair, was a limp shadow of its former self. There was no Colonel Blimp bluster left to see here, just an old man whose only focus now was catching a glimpse of a squirrel hidden amongst the greenery outside. For one fleeting moment I almost let myself feel sorry for him… or at least my conscience prickled enough for me to doubt the propriety of what I was doing. The urge for answers was far too strong though, and I'd come too far and was just too close.

"Do you remember me?" I asked.

He didn't reply at first and, just as I was about to repeat my question, he cast the swiftest of glances towards me. His pale blue eyes carried out a cursory inspection, before resuming his gaze through the glass.

"No," he said, sniffily.

"We met back in Burma, during the war."

"I met a lot of people in Burma. Horrid country."

"I remember you telling me that Burma was 'a walk in the park', compared to the Dardanelles."

He didn't reply, but I persisted anyway.

"Burma was a 'walk in the park' because the Dardenelles… Gallipoli… was the place where you got your scar and your limp, wasn't it? Did you get caught in an explosion? … An explosion on the Helles peninsula?"

He turned towards me again, this time with fear – an expression I knew so well – etched into his watery eyes and quivering lips.

"Yes… and it almost bloody well killed me."

A tear trickled hesitantly from his eye and apprehension now also infiltrated his voice, as he spoke again.

"Who are you and why are you here?"

"My name is Walter Kingdom. My dad was Albert Kingdom. I'm here because I want to know how Dad died. I believe that you know how he died, and I believe that you had the opportunity to tell me this at least three times in the past and…"

I succumbed to the pent-up emotions that my own words had released, and a choking sensation gripped my throat. However, I was determined to say what I had wanted to say to this man for the past twenty years. The words tumbled out in a fast-moving stream before they could be choked off again.

"And I need to know why you didn't tell me when you had the chance!"

The tears now started to roll from my own eyes. As I finished speaking, Johnson vented a muffled cry of the type you might imagine that someone who had been stabbed, or punched, might make. His head drooped, and I was concerned that he might have had a stroke or something. I was on my way to fetch the nurse, when he waved a hand in the air.

"Wait".

He nodded his head

"You're right of course, it's time. I know it's time. Time to do the right thing. I'm so sorry my boy… I'm so sorry. They do get harder to live with you know."

His already shaky voice trembled even more in tune with his dark lips. He seemed to be wrestling with what he should say next, his head shaking from side to side.

"You said 'they'?"

"The dead of course… the dead"

"Take me into the garden, will you?" he said finally, after a long pause, his eyes fixing upon mine. They seemed to be bursting with a sadness, or perhaps regret, that they could no longer conceal.

"I will tell you everything Walter Kingdom. It will be a burden relieved."

We walked out onto the lawn, my arm supporting him on one side, and his stick doing the same on the other. He could barely move under his own steam and it was painful to watch. The grass was badly in need of mowing and new daisies were just beginning to open their eyes. It was still wet from the morning rain and the dampness soaked into my shoes, staining their usual tan a darkish brown.

This time, finally, Johnson was true to his word. He told me about being new to the peninsula and meeting my dad and a Scots lad during the first few days he was there, whilst carrying out a recce for a new water supply system. He described their walk to W Beach, with mules as their companions, and how they negotiated the bare and sometimes precipitous paths which led to the supply depot. He shuddered as he spoke of the regular rumble of explosions that he could hear in the distance and which he sensed were getting louder. It made him nervous, but there was reassurance to be had from his companions, who went about their business calmly; fatefully inured by their long tenure on the peninsula to the sound of shelling.

"It was still new to me, well at least that amount of noise was", Johnson admitted. "I remember standing on the beach stroking the neck of one of the mules, trying hard to look as calm as everybody else, before it struck me with a start that, if the explosions *were* getting nearer to us and their trajectory put them on track to land straight on our heads".

The next thing he recalled was regaining consciousness, his face planted firmly in the sand, and feeling the most incredible pain he'd ever felt over every inch of his body. Neither was he able to hear anything but a deafening ringing in his ears. It was Slim who had come to his aid on the beach, and who had told him that the other men had not survived. He, himself, had seen nothing else of the aftermath of the explosion.

"I knew in my gut, though, as soon as I came to, that the others… that your father… had had no chance."

The squirrel that Johnson had been watching out for so intently chose that moment to make a dash from the trees, running across the lawn by our feet. The old soldier followed its journey with his eyes, until it scaled a fence at the edge of the garden and disappeared from our sight. I wondered how I'd managed to turn this sad figure of a man into some sort of nemesis in my head, it all seemed so silly now. I relaxed a little, feeling that my quest to find out the truth was, at last,

The Man Who Found Treasure

nearing its end; but I still wasn't completely satisfied, and something still nagged at the back of my mind.

"I know that it's hard for you to dredge up these old memories again Lieutenant... I can see as much in your eyes. I'm not sure that I would want to either, if I was in your shoes. But, if it makes it easier, I can tell you that it's been a great help to me... thank you."

Johnson acknowledged my words by turning his head away and then looking up into the grey sky. His silence suddenly provoked the realisation that there *was* something else I had to know the answer to.

"Tell me Lieutenant, would it have been any less hard to tell me these things back in that church in Dakshin in '43, rather than letting me sweat on it for these past twenty odd years?"

Johnson didn't flinch at my question. He seemed ready for it. He addressed the sky, to which his gaze was still fixed.

"You will think me foolish, and you would be right to. Sometimes when a chap does something foolish, he can't admit it to himself for fear of embarrassment. For fear of embarrassing himself. Then he compounds it by doing other foolish things over, and over, again... until he gets himself into a bloody mess with it. The truth is that I found myself creating a fantasy world that I wasn't in control of."

He turned to face me again.

"I'm so bloody tired now... so bloody tired. I can't keep running from you, can I? There's no point anyway, you'll keep on coming back, I suppose. I think, all things considered, it might be best to finally lay that particular ghost to rest".

"I'm not sure that I know what you mean?"

He stepped towards me and rested a hand on my shoulder.

"Back on that beach, after the explosion and when consciousness had returned to me... well, I was feeling wretched, as you might imagine. It got even worse when I began to understand what had happened to me. This other Lieutenant... Slim, as it turned out to be... was down on his knees cajoling me to realise that my luck was in because I was still alive. I didn't feel 'lucky' at all and, instead, the most horrible thoughts were rushing around my head. I could only see a tormented future ahead of me. Perhaps I would be horribly disfigured, or I would lose a limb... or two?"

Johnson stopped talking as his breathing became unsettled and difficult. His chest heaved to get it back into some sort of rhythm.

"Are you OK?" I asked.

He nodded.

"This happens sometimes... when I get excited, you know?"

"You were telling me about how you were feeling... after the explosion."

"Dark thoughts. Dark thoughts indeed. And then Slim told me that the others were all gone. Even the mules were dead. It was he who put the last one out of its misery. Believe you me, the sound of that gunshot was like a wake-up call. It had the effect of clearing my head completely. What had I been thinking? Of course, I was lucky to be alive... to be the only survivor".

He lifted his hand from my shoulder and stood a little more upright.

"Then Slim found something on the beach and I realised that it had survived the explosion too. Before I knew it, I was reaching out for it. I wanted it so badly you couldn't imagine... you needed to experience what I was feeling in that moment if you want to understand what I was thinking. I was convinced that if we two survivors pooled our powers of invincibility, then I couldn't die... even if the bastards threw me back into the blasted war".

My eyes pleaded with him to reveal all.

"I wasn't mistaken, was I... in the end? It did make me invincible in a way... after all, I made it through two wars. There was another time in Burma. I was in a train accident... the damn thing came off the rails and my carriage fell into a ravine. Every other soldier in it was killed. I got myself a pair of shattered legs, but it proved my belief once and for all... against the odds we had survived again. Together we were immortal."

He surveyed the garden and his eyes lingered on the grey bricks of the house.

"If you can call this survival! At the end of the day there is no getting away from the fact that we are all tightly bound to the inevitable, is there?"

Johnson flashed a rueful smile. He loosened his collar and his tie. He reached his hand inside his shirt, pulling out the chain which hung around his neck. He lifted it over his head and offered it to me.

"It can only have belonged to your father."

My body ran ice cold as I reached out towards him. He didn't give up his prize easily and, for a moment, we both held it in our hands, bound together by the unfathomable enchantment of that unprepossessing trinket. He resisted for a second or two longer, before at last letting it slip - link by link - through his fingers, until it was finally and wholly in my possession. Attached to the chain was a ring: a wedding ring. I rubbed my index finger along its golden and worn-smooth surface before, as my eyes adjusted their focus, I spotted the engraving inside the shank.

"I can't quite make it out", I said.

"*Your heart is my Kingdom*", replied Johnson.

The words tripped absent-mindedly from his tongue, like an oft-proclaimed personal credo. Without resuming eye-contact with me, he turned to shuffle back into the house, his stick tapping out the rhythm of retreat as he went. I watched him go inside and pull the conservatory door shut behind him with only the most cursory of glances in my direction. I lowered my eyes back to the ring, unable to settle on what to think or say. Whilst my head throbbed with every kind of emotion, my legs felt like lead weights had been strapped to them. I dropped to my haunches, as I might have done whilst on patrol in the Burmese jungle when my senses were pricked by a snapping twig or an unfamiliar bird call. I was drained of any will to set eyes on Johnson ever again.

***

Spring House was not built of grey bricks. Nor did it have vegetation, of any sort, creeping about its frontage. Its outer shell, at least, was young, clean and vibrant; orange bricks held together with sandy-coloured mortar and gleaming white-framed windows. There was no garden to speak of, and no squirrels, only a couple of pigeons strutting around in an aimless circle on the fresh tarmac outside. Its larger-than-life matron, Rosetta, buzzed me in through the wide red front door.

"Ah... it's Walter... good to see you my darling. *My Kingdom has come* at last!" she chortled with enough volume to wake any of the inmates who might have been taking an afternoon nap, even though she practised the same greeting every time I visited.

"Good afternoon Rosetta. How is she?"

"No need for the serious face, Alice is doing fine. She's no trouble to us… apart from when she's shutting doors. She still can't bear to see them left open… but we get used to it! Oh, and she still has a good chatter to herself when she's walking down the corridors."

"I don't think it's herself that she's chatting to," I corrected.

"Don't you get all 'supernatural' on me now! Come on my darling, let's go and find your mum."

Rosetta took my hand, leading me along like I was a naughty kid being dragged off to see the headmaster. My feet barely kept up past the clattering kitchen and the staffroom with its aroma of cigarette smoke, a surprisingly sweet antidote to the other smells that perfumed the corridor. In the spacious lounge Mam had secured her favourite chair in the corner of the room, her walking stick at rest against it.

At first, she appeared to be lost somewhere in the maze of her private thoughts, but as soon as Rosetta announced my presence her eyes brightened.

"Hello love. It's good of you to come."

I bent down to kiss her on the cheek.

"How are they treating you?"

"I don't suppose I can complain."

She leaned forward and whispered,

"But the rest of 'em here aren't exactly very lively, are they?"

I looked around the room. It was so quiet that I hadn't noticed that every other seat in the lounge was occupied. Most of the occupants were asleep, others stared out of the window at the car park, some studied newspapers or books.

"Look, I've brought you a copy of the newspaper. It's got that article in it that I wrote… you know the one I told you about, about the Queen's fortieth birthday."

"Thanks love. I'll cut it out and put it in my box with the others."

Her eyes studied me for a moment.

"What's wrong Walter?"

"What do you mean?"

"You've got that look in your eye. The one you had when you told me about… about… you know, that old lady."

"You mean Edie? That was a year ago, Mam."

Shock shot across Mam's face, as if the news of Edie's death was registering for the first time and, in a way, it was.

"Was it really? Poor Edie. You're here to tell me bad news though, aren't you? Well you must be, that's the only type of news you ever get at my age."

"Bad news? No, not really... but I think I've reached the end of a journey Mam. One that I began a long, long time ago."

"Now you're worrying me... are you quoting Shakespeare or summat?"

"There's something I need to see."

I reached down and gently took hold of her left hand. I began to ease off her wedding ring. She flinched, pulling her hand back, but I held firm and maintained eye contact and she relaxed. Her bemused gaze stayed in contact with mine as I twisted and rolled the ring, until it finally dropped into my palm. I glanced at the inscription inside with a quickening pulse.

"*My heart is your Kingdom,*" she said, beating me to it.

"You never told me about that. I can't believe that I never knew what was written inside your wedding ring!"

"Because that is between me and your dad... nobody else."

There was an edge of irritation in her voice.

"I understand."

"Why did you take it off?"

I pulled the ring that Johnson had given me from my pocket. After peeling away the tissue paper I'd wrapped it in, I placed the two rings together in the palm of my hand and offered them to Mam. She frowned, the creases on her forehead flattening out as her eyes narrowed. Eventually, with a shaking hand, she summoned up the courage she needed to lift them from the unwrapped tissue. Like a jeweller examining diamonds, she inspected them closely for a second or two, until tears began to spill across her face, her body heaving silently.

"How did you get it? Why did Bert take it off?" she eventually forced out the words between faltering sobs... and then again,

"How did you get it"?

Her escaping voice opened the door to a roar of unsuppressed emotion. She pushed both rings against her chest. Again,

"How?"

The word became so distorted as she repeated it, over, and over again, that it was no longer just a word, or a meaningful question.

"How?"

As she relinquished any control over the convulsions that wracked her frail body, her cry of *'how?'* took on the sound of something elemental and primitive, raw and scarred. It was propelled from the deepest atoms of her soul; the manifestation of more than fifty years of imprisoned pain, let loose.

The room began to awaken as the discord shattered the sleeping spell that had been cast upon its residents. Rosetta appeared at the doorway, her joviality quelled, her eyes honed to a patient in distress. I wrapped my arms around Mam, and she fell into them, my body absorbing the agitations of her tiny, almost weightless, frame and my jacket soaking up her tears. She looked over pleadingly towards the open door.

"How?"

Chapter 24.

Turkey: 1998.

A small group of giggling children chased each other along the sand of V Beach screeching with the elation of being unleashed. Their parents sat on deckchairs formed into a defensive circle in the centre of the beach, their heads either reclined, eyes closed, or buried in a book or a newspaper. A small black dog tried to keep up with the children, its tongue eagerly flapping from a grinning mouth, unperturbed by the constant changes of direction it was forced to make. Another small boy crouched over a red plastic bucket by the wave-less shoreline, scooping damp sand into it with his hands. He paused to admire his handiwork after each load deposited, before moving onto the next. Nearby a man stood in the clear water on a carpet of dark seaweed, hands in pockets, his jeans rolled up to just under his knees. He looked out across an Aegean Sea which wavered through every shade of blue between teal and a deep azure. None of the beachgoers realised that they were under observation. Nor did they notice the old man and his companion who stood on the crumbling bank which edged the thin strip of beach.

"It's not what I expected," said Walter, his voice edged with disappointment. "Somehow I thought it would be bigger than this... and perhaps a little more untamed."

"The world moves on my friend," replied Bariş, holding up an arm and waving it over to his left.

"Do you see that line of flat greyish rocks sticking out into the sea over there?"

"Yes... I see it."

"That was the place where the *River Clyde* was run aground, and where your father arrived in this place. The Turks fired at them continuously from the fort we just passed over there and from up on the high ground behind us. Excuse the pun... but our American friends might today call it a 'Turkey shoot'!"

Walter closed his eyes. He forced himself to imagine the bewildering barrage of sights, sounds, smells and emotions that his dad would have been subjected to as he disembarked the beached steamer, but he could only conjure up his own images and sensations from Burma. A sudden flashback of Coggins' dying eyes brought him back to reality with a start.

"Would you like to go down onto the beach?"

"No... no thank you." Walter turned to his right. "But there is something I would like to do in there."

His eyes flashed across to a wooden gate at the end of the path. The gate intersected the words 'V Beach' and 'Cemetery' which were carved into the limestone wall either side of it.

Walter carried a battered old khaki knapsack hung over his right shoulder. He lowered it to the ground and sifted through the contents of its outer pockets. He pulled out his spectacles case, along with a folded piece of tatty paper. Putting on his glasses, he unfolded the fraying page. After a moment of orientation, he set off along the neat rows of graves, hands clasped together behind his back. Each of the tiny blocks of limestone bore an inscription etched into a metal plaque affixed to the top. He stopped and bent his head to study a number of the graves, moving on several times, before arriving at a final standstill. Stooping lower, he read aloud the words inscribed on the plaque at his feet:

"K.P. 617 Able Seaman S. Cooper, RNVR. Royal Naval Division. 25 April 1915. Aged 20. Thy Will be done." Then, turning towards

Barış, he added with a sad smile, "Stan Cooper… a mate of my Dad. I made a deathbed promise to George Pike that I would look him up."

"He died on the first day," Barış observed.

Walter nodded.

"So, you met George again… after he came to see you at the newspaper office?"

The old man slipped a hand into an open pocket on the side of his knapsack, and this time he pulled out a small wooden cross. He studied it for a moment and stroked a finger across the word 'Remembered', which was scored upon it. He knelt on the ground and gently leaned it against the gravestone.

"Yes, I did."

Walter groaned as he levered himself painfully to his feet.

"It's a funny thing, but both of my daughters emigrated to Australia in 1969 with their families. I put them in touch with George, as he was the only other person I knew out there. My eldest, Debbie… well, she split with her husband few years later, and she ended up marrying George's youngest son."

"There is a certain… how do you say it? Symmetry?"

"Yes, there is. I like to think that Dad would have been pleased. I know it brought a smile to old George's face. I was out there for a few weeks around Christmas in 1978, with Dinah. We took in The Ashes Test Match in Brisbane while we were there. A compatriot of mine… Derek Randall… was doing rather well with the bat at the time. Anyway, George was in his eighties and not at all well. He told me that his one regret was never going back to Gallipoli. He knew it was too late for him by then. I told him that I'd like to come here one day and that's when he extracted the promise from me… a promise to make sure that Stan wasn't forgotten. The old boy died a few weeks after we'd returned home."

At the end of a short drive along the dusty track from V Beach stood the Helles Memorial, a beacon-like stone column which dominated the cliff top and which could be seen for miles around. Barış pulled the Land Rover into the empty parking area and helped Walter down from it.

"Impressive. It fair takes your breath away close up."

"I brought a party of ex-soldiers here from Yorkshire a couple of years ago. One of them joked that it reminded him of a factory chimney back home in England, only that it must have been bleached."

Bariş stayed by the vehicle, lit a cigarette and watched his current party-of-one shuffle uncomfortably across the dusty ground towards the monument. Today the brick-patterned obelisk itself was almost greyish in hue, although the clean white edges of the panelled wall which surrounded it almost glowed in contrast to the cloudless royal blue sky.

As Bariş looked on, Walter consulted his scrap of paper once again before inspecting each stone panel in turn. Then the old man stopped, suddenly rigid, took off his sunglasses and removed his hat. It slipped from his hands and floated down onto the patchy grass at his feet. He reached out a hand towards the panel in front of him and traced a finger along the names listed upon it. Then his arm recoiled, and his face fell into his hands. Even from the distance that he was observing, Bariş could make out that Walter's shoulders were shaking. He immediately felt uncomfortable, a voyeur, and so he turned his eyes away to look out over the sea, which he knew would welcome his attention and absorb his gaze for hours if necessary.

Bariş didn't know how long had passed when a hand tapped him lightly on the shoulder.

"I'm done here, I think," Walter said matter-of-factly, with no trace of emotion, his eyes now obscured by his Polaroids. His reddening face was not turned towards his guide, however. It too had been attracted by what lay upon the cerulean sea. He took a few steps beyond the car, coming to a halt at the edge of a newly planted field of wheat which ran all the way to the cliff top.

"What is that?" he asked.

"What?"

"That island out there".

Bariş looked out towards a shimmering, elongated, hazy land mass which appeared to hover just above the water on the horizon, its flatness broken only by the shape of a pyramid about halfway along its length.

"That's Bozcaada. In the old days, when your father was here, it was called Tenedos. The legends say that the Spartan's hid their ships in the bay behind it to fool the Trojans into thinking they had gone home."

"It looks like Heaven," Walter said distractedly after a thoughtful pause.

"They wouldn't have believed that Heaven existed here back in 1915. I'm sure that there was only room for Hell in those times."

"No, I don't suppose they would... not back then."

Walter retraced his steps to the car and then lifted his hat to ruffle his sweat dampened hair.

"Now then Barış. There is only one thing left to do."

After re-joining the main track Barış took a left fork in the road and, a short distance later, turned abruptly onto a narrower trackway which seemed to be made up mostly of potholes. They bumped and rocked as the car descended through trees and scrub until they met the sea. Barış pulled up hard, lifting a cloud of sand into the air around them.

"Here we are... W Beach. You're lucky, it used to be forbidden to come here, the military used it for training."

There was a nervousness in his voice born from long experience and his eyes shifted edgily as he surveyed the space around them. He opened the door warily.

Walter crunched across the rough white sand until he reached the rocky water's edge. The wind had picked up again and the murmuring of the sea had grown louder, like disembodied voices whispering into his ears. He walked along the edge of the surf, treading carefully in order to retain his balance on the uneven surface, until he came to a rusting frame. He had first noticed it from the edge of the beach although, at first, it was unclear what it might be. With his curiosity piqued by the hope of lost treasure, he had made a beeline for it. Jabbing a finger excitedly in the direction of his discovery, he yelled over to Barış, who was lazily walking parallel to him across the top edge of the shoreline, hands in pockets.

"Is this what I think it is? Does it date from..."

Barış had anticipated the question and was already answering it before Walter could finish.

"Yes, it's an old British lighter, I think. Maybe they used it as part of a pier here... you know, for landing supplies."

Satisfied, Walter made a final, careful, assessment of his surroundings and then purposefully and ungracefully strode back up the beach to where his guide stood. He looked thoughtful.

"You know I wrote a poem about this place once - when I was still trying to get my head around things. It's a place that has had a big impact on my life one way or another. Funny, considering I'd never even set foot here."

"And now, here you are."

"Yes... and what a strange feeling it is."

The two men allowed themselves a moment without words. Each of them closed their eyes to the sun and the quickening breeze. Barış sensed that only he could break into the tranquillity that had enveloped them.

"I'd like to read it... your poem."

Walter, increasingly solemn faced, only nodded his head in reply before kicking at the sand.

"I think this is as good a place as any," he announced, catching his breath, before feeling the need to qualify his certainty, "although I don't suppose I can ever be one-hundred per cent sure."

Barış returned a blank look.

"I'll need your help of course Barış. Come on... we'll do it here."

Walter dropped to his knees, wincing in pain and grabbing for his guide's arm for support as he did so. Barış took this as a cue to lower himself down beside the old man.

"What are we doing Walter?" he cast another nervous glance around them.

Walter dropped his knapsack onto the sand and unbuckled the cover. He rifled around amongst the contents contained within its deep pocket, before lifting out an object wrapped in brown paper. He carefully unwrapped it and dropped the paper back into the bag, before placing the newly revealed object on to the palm of his hand and offering it towards his companion. Barış looked at an old tin, tarnished almost to the point of rustiness, but not quite. It was covered with red and yellow paper which, although a little dirty and ripped and scratched in places, was remarkably intact. The top of the tin had been neatly removed. As soon as he had seen it, Barış knew what would be written on it in white lettering. As he read the words aloud, he also beamed at the thrill of being in its presence.

"Fray Bentos! It's a Bully Beef tin!"

Walter's eyes twinkled and grinned back.

"I searched around junk shops for years looking for one of these. It's from the period, I found it in a little shop in Ypres."

Then, without further delay, he began to dig energetically into the gritty surface using the tin as his shovel. A quick glance towards Bariş encouraged him to do the same and the guide joined in, scooping large handfuls of sand into a pile at the side of their excavation. As the hole became deeper, and the sand wetter, their pace slowed. Walter's reddening face poured with sweat until, with the crater about a foot deep, he pulled himself away and recovered his breath. He wiped his forehead with a handkerchief.

"That should do it."

He tapped the upturned tin on his thigh to loosen the dirt stuck inside it and used his fingers to clear out any remnants. Then he scooped up some sand from the newly dug hole with cupped hands and raised it to his nose and then his lips. Closing his eyes, he pushed his face into it, before gently sifting it through his fingers so that it fell back to where it came from. When his eyes reopened his gaze was fixed on Bariş. Without diverting it, he wiped his hands and unbuttoned the top pocket of his shirt, pulling out an object that glinted brightly in the sunlight.

"Your father's wedding ring!"

Walter opened out his palm to reveal that there were two gold rings lying upon it.

"She made me promise two things in her last days. One, that her ashes would be scattered in the churchyard at Attenborough, where the victims of the Chilwell munitions factory explosion lay. Two, that both of their rings are reunited at the place where he fell. This promise has taken a bit longer to get around to I must admit."

He closed his eyes and folded his hand back around the rings. It was more difficult than he'd imagined. He thought of Johnson and, in that moment, he knew exactly how the old Lieutenant had felt. Giving the rings up - *giving them back* - was a final act. Once they were gone... then what was left?

To put an end to his dilemma, he unfurled his palm and, with a jerk of the wrist, dropped them into the tin in one brisk movement. He took a relieved breath and then covered the tin with his handkerchief. In cupped hands he carefully lowered the tin, under its pall, into its burial chamber. With Bariş's eager help, the hole was refilled with the sand piled up around its rim. When it was full, they patted the surface until it was smooth and tightly packed.

After a moment the tour guide jumped to his feet and brushed the sand from his jeans. As he did so he heard Walter whisper something so quietly that it seemed to be in chorus with the breeze.

"…but on another shore and in a greater light, that multitude which no man can number, whose hope was in the Word made flesh, and with whom we for evermore are one."

"Your poem?" asked Bariş.

"No, they're not my words… it's a kind of prayer."

"But I thought you told me that you didn't believe in that sort of thing?"

"I didn't say it for me," replied Walter, with a gentle smile.

Bariş helped his charge to his feet. They shook hands.

"Thank you," said Walter, a quiet sadness edging his words. Then he turned and walked towards the sea.

"Do you want me to mark the spot in some way?" Bariş called after him.

Walter stopped in his tracks and swivelled round.

"No. There's no need for that. I won't be coming back."

"But who will know?"

Walter looked heavenward and shrugged his shoulders.

"Well… *you* know Bariş, don't you? *You* know".

"What about your family?"

"I'll leave them your card… maybe one day they'll wake-up wanting to know about these things. If they do, then they can call you, and you can tell them."

"But you can tell them yourself."

"Perhaps."

The old man resumed his journey across the beach, his feet crunching through the gritty sand between the rocks. At the surf-line he knelt and rinsed the sand from his hands in the cool clear water. Then his gaze was transfixed once more by the shimmering island of Bozcaada, which floated, still, in a haze above the blue sea. A tune popped into his head from long ago, and he sang out the words absent-mindedly to himself, in a whisper that was drowned out by the sound of the sea and the breeze.

"Lavender's blue, dilly, dilly,
Lavender's green,
When you are King dilly, dilly,
I shall be…"

The Scarlet Rain.

A poem by Walter Kingdom (1967).

The flash becomes the devil's roar.
A hammer blow of silence rings.
My head pulsates a moment more;
A postlude as the scythe it swings.

Time slips away through wraith-like claws,
Like ticking sand which bears my pain;
A dust that tells of dreams no more,
All drowned beneath the scarlet rain.

From high above the tented hordes,
I spy a man draw up a list
Of names for sad songs sung abroad,
By torn lips that are long since kissed.

Through wailing wires their voices soar;
Eternal chorus of the slain!
They sing in search of other shores
And shelter from the scarlet rain.

Death swings a cloaked-hand 'gainst a door.
A hammer blow of black on white!
Pulsating, sad and soundless words,
They scream me into darkest night.

And there revealed a heart's deceit,
False air we breathed; a life we feigned.
Which borrowed time allowed accrete,
Entombed in pools of scarlet rain.

Acknowledgements.

Even though they exist only in fiction, it would have been impossible to write anything close to a truthful tale about Bert, Alice and Walter – the three Kingdoms – without immersing myself in the histories of the Gallipoli and Burma campaigns and the lives of those left behind at home. Some of this was territory that I had already explored when researching the life of my Great Great Grandmother's brother – Jack Oscroft – who met his demise at Helles in 1915. A visit I made to the Gallipoli peninsula in 2013 was essential to properly understanding the landscape upon which that tragedy was played out. Unfortunately, I was unable to visit the places in Burma that I write about in this book, so I hope you forgive me for that. Nottingham – the third theatre of this drama, is in my blood and on my doorstep.

As the ideas in this novel took shape, I read – and listened to - as much material as I could before I felt able to commit my own interpretation of these forgotten worlds to paper. I say 'forgotten' advisedly. The men who fought in Burma had already been labelled as the forgotten army even before that conflict had ended. I came to realise that this was – to some extent – also the case for the British (and French – not forgetting that country's dominions) who went to battle in Turkey. Their role in that conflict has subsequently been overshadowed, at least in popular media, by the unarguable heroics of the Anzacs. The fact remains, however, that most of the dead of that campaign were British, French and, of course (overwhelmingly so), Turkish. The third forgotten 'army'– represented by Alice in this story – are those amazing women who suffered and battled. as much as the men, but on the home front, during both world wars. Part of my motivation in writing *The Man Who Found Treasure* was to shed a little more light on these disregarded battalions, and the unbelievably brave men and women who made up their number.

Before I acknowledge my textual inspirations, I must give a mention to Alan Smith for his meticulous help with the German translation and to Kara and Özer for their assistance with the Turkish text. Proof reading is always a bit of a slog, so I owe a debt of thanks to James for lessening that burden, and to Ali for her clear-headed judgement and wise advice. I am also grateful to Peter Robins' research which enabled me to confirm the identity of the statues adorning the Guildhall in Nottingham, courtesy of the Nottingham Post.

Whilst it would be impossible to list everything that have I read in preparation for writing my novel, some things are worthy of specific acknowledgement. First and foremost, the words of the original combatants themselves – military and civilian (for it wasn't just those wearing a uniform who fought in these wars) - is akin to gold dust for anyone writing about historical events. Whilst many of their recollections have been woven into a multitude of written histories, many of which are available in cyberspace, the treasure trove of recordings held by the Imperial War Museum has been invaluable. The fantastic work done by the IWM to preserve the first-hand memories of those who sacrificed so much is something that we should all be thankful for. Just as enlightening has been the film archive of Pathé, also now available online. Reading or listening to the words of those who acted upon these stages is one thing, but to see them in the flesh brings a completely different perspective to those words.

As for specific texts worthy of mention, it is difficult to pick out individual stars from an impressive galaxy of thoroughly researched material, but I'll give it a go:

The Man Who Found Treasure

Field-Marshal Viscount Bill Slim's analysis of the Burma campaign, *Defeat into Victory,* is an incredible roller-coaster ride, indelibly stamped by its author's personality. It is a must for anyone wanting to understand how the Burma campaign was conducted from a British General's perspective. Russell Miller's excellent *Authorised Biography* gave me an insight into Slim's story pre and post Burma and it enabled me to feel confident about weaving him into the narrative as a character in his own right. I long-ago read George MacDonald Fraser's *Quartered Safe Out Here* and deliberately kept it in mind, but at armslength, whilst writing this story – Fraser's world is indelibly imprinted on my mind when thinking about the Burma campaign. As an antidote to Slim's volume, anyone wanting to read the soldiers eye-view of the campaign, written by a great storyteller, should look no further than Fraser's book.

Gallipoli-wise, Leonard Sellers' superb history of *The Hood Battalion* was extremely useful in understanding the timeline of movements of the Anson Battalion. I must also mention the excellent work being done by The Gallipoli Association in preserving the memory of the campaign, through some excellent and enlightening published works, covering detail not otherwise written about elsewhere.

I could not have delved into the world of the home front in both wars without the archive of newspapers – local and national – now available on the internet. This is an indispensable resource for adding colour to a story and, while researching it, I read stories from the past that touched upon and coloured my thinking on all the elements of my novel. As well as the contemporaneous newspaper reports, it would have been impossible for me to write the chapter concerning the Chilwell explosion without first reading *The Chilwell Story* by M.J. Haslam – which is the definitive history of the Chilwell VC Factory and Ordnance Depot.

Finally, I mentioned at the start of this page my previous research into the life and death of Jack Oscroft (1881-1915) which, amongst other things, introduced me to what happened in Gallipoli (or "the Dardanelles" as my Grandmother called it). His was a tragic life to match his tragic end. It is safe to say that this novel wouldn't exist without the sacrifice he made. In acknowledging him, I must also mention his son Wilfred (1910 – 1984) who served in the Burma campaign, and I thank his children, Pauline and Michael, for making me aware of their father's story. Although Jack served and died in Gallipoli (and like Bert he served with the Anson Battalion) and Wilfred lived through the deprivations of Burma – and as such both, in part, inspired what I have written here – I must make it very clear that that is where the similarities with the Bert and Walter Kingdom of my story, and their families, end.

Alan Williams,
Nottingham. 2019

Printed in Poland
by Amazon Fulfillment
Poland Sp. z o.o., Wrocław